The storm had Krysty in its thrall, whirling her up and over

Ryan was after her, feet skidding on the wet planks, blinded by the spray. One hand reached for the slippery rail, while the other grabbed helplessly at the torn canvas shroud that held his lover.

His fingers brushed it, and he saw it snag for a moment on the stanchion on the end of the stern. The one-eyed man snatched the moment to lock his hand in the rough, soaked material, steadying it for a couple of seconds on the brink of the drop, feeling Krysty's weight tugging against him.

Agonizingly it was shifting him as well, lifting him, pulling him up and over the rail, following her toward the thrashing, whirling paddle.

He was over, managing to twist like an acrobat and grab the iron stanchion, hanging on to the suspended canvas with his other hand. Ryan clung there, poised between life and death, aware that nothing could save them. In a few seconds his grip would go, and they would be doomed.

He had closed his eye, then opened it once more—to find that he was staring, inches away, into the blankly incurious steel eyes of the Magus.

Also available in the Deathlands saga:

JAMES AXLER

DEATH LANDS®

Eclipse at Noon

A GOLD EAGLE BOOK FROM
WORLDWIDE®

TORONTO • NEW YORK • LONDON
AMSTERDAM • PARIS • SYDNEY • HAMBURG
STOCKHOLM • ATHENS • TOKYO • MILAN
MADRID • WARSAW • BUDAPEST • AUCKLAND

This, like so many others, is for Liz.
But this one is with all my thanks for the happiest
and finest life together that anyone could ever have.
Whatever happens, a part of me will
always be with you.

First edition September 1996

ISBN 0-373-62533-2

ECLIPSE AT NOON

Copyright © 1996 by Worldwide Library.

One should head eventually for the place where the land becomes mainly sea and the sea becomes mainly sky.

—From *Midnight Rambler, the Collected Thoughts of Chairman Mark*, published by Islander Press of Key West, 1995

Prologue

The paths across the side of the tree-lined valley seemed endless to the terrified woman. If only she'd thought to bring a blaster, she could have gunned down the madman who pursued her with such relentless ferocity. But she'd trusted Straub.

As she ran and dodged, water showering off overhanging branches, Countess Katya Beausoleil swore a dreadful oath to herself to slaughter Straub, slowly and in the utmost agony, for what he had done to her.

Ryan Cawdor was about thirty yards behind, clumsy with his wounded leg, unable to run flat out. His arms were stretched in front of him, fingers aching to grasp the slender white neck and tear and mangle and throttle it, to force the life from the protruding eyes and smile at the purpled tongue.

At least there would be that.

But the woman kept ahead, arms pumping, racing toward the end of the path. The observation platform over the gorge was at the dead end of the path a hundred yards away.

SHE WAS BACKED against the raw face of the cliff, trembling, mewing like a kitten, fingers knotted into the flimsy wire fence, her weight against it, making it sway back and forth. Ryan faced her, blocking the exit back toward the ville, his spine touching the rusting supports. Behind him was the drop of hundreds of feet, the last hundred or so sheer down to the thread of foaming water racing below.

"You didn't have to butcher them all," he yelled, voice torn from his throat in a scream. "It was just you and me."

The countess made a move toward him, her mouth working. "Listen to me," she began. "Straub played—"

Ryan swung a roundhouse, feeling the satisfying force of the impact as the woman's cheekbone splintered, the force of the punch knocking her down against the rocks, the back of her head cut and bleeding, her hair soaked and matted. Her bright eyes half closed for a moment.

"Get up, bitch," he whispered, inaudible above the thunderous roaring. "I'm going to beat you to a bloody pulp and then drop you over the fucking edge. One way all the way down. Pay a fraction the price. Then Straub."

Her eyes blinked open, and he stooped and swung her up, gripping the torn material of her dress, holding her balanced while he measured the next punch.

Krysty Wroth was in sight, stopping and cupping her hands. "Ryan! Hey, Ryan!" she shouted in a voice that would have shattered crystal at a hundred paces.

Ryan started to turn, disbelief stark on his face, his mouth sagging open. He blinked through the driving rain, seeing a blurred vision of a tall woman with a shock of bright, fiery hair. Another figure, hair like snow, was at her side, as were three others, farther back, staring at him.

"Krysty..." he whispered, a rush of knowledge paralyzing him for a moment.

Katya Beausoleil pushed against him with all her failing strength, catching him off balance, propelling him hard into the frail fencing. He heard rusting iron creak and snap.

And he was staggering backward, feet brushing air, falling away.

Krysty screamed once.

Ryan was over the edge, pushing the limp body from him, rolling onto a steep slope of treacherous mud. His fingers scrabbled to find purchase, but failed to find a grip. He spread himself, his arms and legs wide, somersaulting over and over, the gray sky and the dark, shining dirt whirling around him.

He glimpsed the white dress below him, vanishing over the last sheer brink and tumbling into the water, disappearing from his sight.

He quickly reached the final frontier himself, skidding over it, hopelessly out of control.

Flying.

Flying, falling, spinning.

He hit the surface of the flooded river with a crushing, fearsome impact, trying to keep his body straight, blacking out. The shock of the icy, raging torrent brought him around for a snatched moment.

The force of the current was unimaginable, filled with sucking maelstroms and murderous smooth boulders. Ryan was sucked under and spit out into the air, then drawn deep under once more, into the welcoming darkness.

His eye closed.

Chapter One

Krysty Wroth stood and stared blankly into the singing space, spray pasting her fiery hair across her forehead, her bright emerald eyes dulled and lifeless. Her fingers gripped the rusting remains of the security fence that ringed the crumbling viewing platform above the abyss.

Her lips moved, and she whispered Ryan's name as she peered into the gorge. The two tiny figures were spinning, vanishing and rising again in the turbulent water of the racing river, moving at incredible speed between the sheer walls of wet rock.

"Mebbe he can stay up," said John Barrymore Dix, the Armorer, as he stood by her elbow, pushing back his fedora.

Jak Lauren shook his head, his red eyes glowing in the gloomy half light like burning rubies. His torrent of snowy hair dripped in dreadlocks across his scrawny shoulders, his face, pale beyond belief, staring out over the steep ravine.

"No," he whispered, responding to J. B. Dix's comment. "No way could make it there. Not after fall."

Mildred Wyeth, the stocky black woman doctor of the group, had one arm resting lightly around Krysty's waist, comforting her. Her right hand was on the butt of her Czech target revolver, but there was nobody left to shoot.

The last member of the group, panting heavily, arrived late as ever. Doc Tanner had witnessed the last scene of the dreadful drama from farther away, blinking through his watery blue eyes at the fight and the fall. Now he stood stricken, his hands clasped in mute prayer in front of him, the ebony swordstick glistening with water, its ferrule resting on the soaking concrete.

"I wonder whether we should not be trying to convey ourselves down the stream, following it along, until we can do something to recover the body of our dear, dear friend."

Krysty turned slowly to face the old man, seeing the tears that clung to his lined cheeks, and felt the first numbing awareness that Ryan was possibly dead.

Probably dead.

"He's gone, Doc," she said quietly. "Never be able to find the body."

Jak coughed. "Look far along. Seems cliffs get lower. Not right leave Ryan to vultures and coyotes. Rest of you stay if want. Going to try find him." He looked at the other four companions. "He'd have done it for me."

THEY LEFT the huge mansion behind them and set off along the windswept, barren rocks, moving westward, following the line of the river.

A watery sun peeked through ragged strips of dark purple clouds, barely bright enough to cast a weak shadow behind the friends. They picked their way, slowly climbing lower toward the river, though its foaming surface still seemed to be several hundred feet below them.

Ryan's body had long vanished.

The woman's corpse had been caught within their sight for a few minutes in a vicious backwash under a jagged fall of twenty or thirty feet, where the water stripped away the tattered remnants of the clothes, leaving the corpse pink and dappled with blood, then as white as a wind-washed bone.

Finally, perversely, the river let the body go, washing it farther away at dashing speed until it, too, vanished as the gorge curved toward the north.

Evening was closing in.

J.B. eased the Smith & Wesson M-4000 scattergun on his shoulder. "Take five, people." With Ryan gone he had automatically assumed control of the friends.

Jak was carrying Ryan's rifle on his back, the Steyr SSG-70 bolt-action, 10-round, 7.62 mm hunting weapon. Though their exit from the ville had been close to the edge of panic, everyone had their clothes and weapons.

Krysty sat and leaned against a stunted piñon a few paces from the edge of the drop. Her face was drawn and tense, her hair matted close to her nape in a tight ball. She closed her eyes and spoke a brief prayer to Gaia, the Earth Mother, that a miracle might have happened and that Ryan might be spared from the pounding, grinding doom.

But her heart told her the inalienable truth—that nobody could have survived that drop.

Not even Ryan.

THEY FOUND WHAT REMAINED of the corpse of
Countess Katya Beausoleil just as the sun was finally
sinking in a copper glow behind a range of low hills
toward the west. The river was widening and becoming a little more gentle, flowing between wooded banks
of thick gray mud.

The head was missing from the body, sunk in some
deep pool, ripped away in ragged tendrils of sinew and
gristle, the flesh a dirty white color. One arm was
gone, torn off at the shoulder, and the other had disappeared. The legs had both been broken a dozen
times, splintered stumps of bone showing through the
wrinkled, pallid skin.

There was no way of recognizing the elegant, powerful woman who had been their hostess and had
brought murder and disaster to them. What remained
of the corpse lay sprawled in the mud at the edge of the
river, water lapping at it, making it rock gently back
and forth.

"Should get it?" Jak asked hesitantly.

As they looked across, a pair of mutie fish-falcons
swooped in from the north, out of the pines. They had
wingspans approaching twenty feet and huge bronze
hooked beaks. Golden eyes looked incuriously at the
five invaders of their territory as they sliced through
the dusk, settling on the raggedy flesh of the dead
woman.

"Let it lie, Jak," Mildred said. "Bitch got something like she deserved."

Doc nodded his agreement. "I have encountered
divine vengeance many times in Deathlands. To be
ripped apart and then be food for the fowls of the air

in a river of vile, stinking mud is an apposite ending for that ghastly, murderous person.''

"No sign of Ryan. Not even a rag of his clothes,'' J.B. commented. "Nothing.''

Krysty sighed and stretched, standing to stare around in the dying light. "Nothing more we can do tonight,'' she said. "We might miss something.''

"Camp a little way inland from the river,'' the Armorer suggested. "No sign of any pursuit from the ville. Must be a good ten miles away by now.''

For a few moments they watched the rapacious scavengers as they ate, peeling away a long strip of intestines, squabbling noisily as they tugged it between them.

Krysty shook her head. "Just hope that what's left of Ryan isn't..." She let the sentence fade into the darkness.

"We'll make an early start in the morning,'' Krysty announced, heading away from the quiet river.

Behind her, Jak and J.B. exchanged a meaningful, hopeless glance, but neither of them spoke.

Chapter Two

Ryan had lived within the silent shadow of death for all of his adult life. Indeed, as a child his constant companion was the tall man in the hooded cloak, with the scythe across his shoulder.

As the river dragged him under, already barely conscious from the steepling fall, he slipped in and out of blackness, his fading mind dragging up images of some of his other close calls with mortality: an ax, wielded by a man dressed as a monk, in a brown habit and shaved head, the huge blade slicing a crescent-shaped cicatrix of flesh from Ryan's arm, hissing by to strike golden sparks from the stone-flagged floor of the chancel; a ball from a nineteenth-century dueling pistol, plucking at his sleeve, barely drawing a bead of blood; a cell in the Everglades, where tidal water swilled in and out, rising within inches of the packed mud ceiling, forcing him against it, struggling for life for the long, cold hours until the salt waves receded once more, kicking away at the deadly snakes that swam around him; pinned to a giant sequoia with a hunting arrow through the sinews of his shoulder, holding him helpless while he struggled to reload his musket, watching the black-masked warrior moving toward him through the pools of bright sun and dappled shadow, another shaft already notched and ready.

The waters carried him along at a terrifying pace, faster than a man could run, bouncing him off boulders, rattling the teeth in his head. An undertow tugged him down into icy deeps, holding him there for eternities, blacking him out again. His mind plucked memories from his past.

He lay on a truckle bed in a shotgun shack in rural Georgia, as weak as a kitten from an amoebic fever, helpless while a little girl of eight years climbed onto his chest holding a filthy pillow in both hands. She leaned over his face, smiling gap-toothed into his eye, and began to suffocate him.

He ran along the corridors of an old mansion in the hills above the Cific Ocean, a hundred miles inland from where the coast had been before skydark, fleeing the flames. He had iron shackles around his ankles, the flesh suppurating beneath the rusted and bloodied metal. The ceiling burned as the bright golden flames flashed overhead, scorching Ryan's long hair. He could smell his flesh roasting.

Ryan saw the jabbing tusks of a rampaging elephant in the private zoo outside the ghostly ruins of old Sacramento. The animal had trapped the Trader in a corner of its enclosure, trying to knock him down and kneel on him. Ryan and the young John Dix had gone in unarmed against the massive beast, and he felt the pain of broken ribs set against the exultation of winning the combat.

Ryan drew in a screaming gasp of air, filling his tortured lungs as the racing current threw him momentarily to the surface. His right leg was numb, and he guessed it might have been broken. The original gunshot wound was painless against all the other injuries and bruises and cuts. His whole body was solid pain, and he was so weak that he couldn't even kick to stay on the surface. Once more he was drawn under into the world of singing blackness and desperate memories of hard times gone.

He tried to retain his hold on sanity in the pit filled with cockroaches. He was bound hand and foot, helpless on the slimy floor, in total darkness. And the mutie insects, some of them nine and ten inches long, covered him, countless thousands, scurrying, rustling as their long tendrils brushed Ryan's naked skin. He kept his eye and mouth closed, but was unable to check them from investigating his nostrils, probing into his ears. He had rolled back and forth ceaselessly, crushing hundreds of the vile insects, feeling their bodies crunch and squirt, mingling with his own blood and sweat.

A baron had tried to put pressure on the Trader by capturing his young one-eyed lieutenant and burying him alive in a mahogany casket with silver handles, the lid screwed tight. Ryan had been drugged, wrapped in a silken shroud, his head placed on a satin pillow. He could hear the earth thudding on the top of the heavy coffin and tried to take shallow, slow breaths to make the small amount of trapped air last that few vital minutes longer, fighting blind panic.

He had still been conscious when the Trader broke in the lid with the butt of his Armalite and dragged him out from the premature burial.

The baron's death had been long, slow and infinitely, exquisitely painful.

He remembered the twin sisters, each gripping a straight-edged razor. Both of them giggled, slack mouthed, wide-eyed, edging him between them around the huge bedroom. Ryan had been naked and intensely vulnerable, already bleeding from a number of deep gashes across his forearm, with one low across his stomach, the crimson stream matting in his pubic hair, covering his genitals.

He had managed to reach a set of heavy brass fire irons, finally battering them both to death with a long poker.

The memories were fading.

Even Ryan's great reserves of strength had their limits. He could hardly resist any longer; his head was thrown back, gulping in mouthfuls of water. He hardly felt the buffeting as the river raced over a series of short, savage falls, each of them between ten and twenty feet in height.

Now the remembrances of the bad times past were slipping away along with his mind and his life, blurring, the lines blurring between fact and fiction.

Between dream and memory and nightmare.

Some small part of Ryan was still functioning, and that small part realized with a faint shock that he was dying.

He'd taken a ferocious blow to the back of the head, just behind the ear, and final blackness was folding him gently into itself.

Everything stopped and his eye closed.

Chapter Three

The next morning Krysty was first awake.

She'd also been last to sleep, dropping finally into a restless, disturbed slumber, filled with confused alarms and dark threats. At one point she had tossed and turned, wondering whether the loss of Ryan had actually tipped her brain over the edge. She was racked with a mental puzzle. If she could solve it, then she could sleep and it might mean that all would be well with Ryan. He would be miraculously saved from certain death, and they would be reunited once again.

But the trouble was, she didn't even know what the mystery was that she had to try to work out. The clues made no sense and kept changing.

Once she woke, sweating, to find Mildred kneeling at her side, squeezing her hand.

"Bad thoughts?"

Krysty had nodded slowly, wiping her forehead. "Could say that. Was I making a noise?"

"Sort of quiet muttering, on the side of weeping. I'd got up for a piss, so I heard you. Don't think you disturbed the others. Doc's still snoring away like an old steam engine taking a steep grade."

Krysty had smiled, though she hadn't believed her friend. She knew from long experience that even a very slight noise in the night would be enough to wake Jak and J.B., light sleepers both.

Now she was up, her Western boots pulled on, washing her face in an icy stream that trickled among mossy rocks into a kind of grotto at the side of the narrow hunting trail.

"Good morrow, dear child of nature," boomed Doc, who'd been sitting silently on the rotting trunk of a fallen larch. "A new day. Mayhap a new hope."

"Mayhap not, Doc." She stood, then walked to sit beside him, feeling the need for a human touch of comfort. She leaned against his shoulder. "I know that Ryan's gone. Nobody could have survived the fall, then the river and the canyons. My brain tells me that the best I can do is find his… Find what's left and lay it properly to rest." She swallowed hard. "Just hard to close the book on all your hopes."

He didn't reply for a while, and they shared the dawn stillness. A red-breasted jay, with its plume of turquoise feathers and bright yellow beak, settled on the end of the tree, oblivious to their presence, pecking busily at some tiny translucent grubs that lived in the soft fungoid wood.

"We shall all miss him most dreadfully," he said finally. "He was the finest friend I ever had. He saved my life…so many times. Inspired me to carry on when all my senses wished only to give up and succumb to my own heartbroke weakness."

J.B. appeared with Mildred, passing Krysty and Doc on their way to the stream, followed a half minute later by Jak, his white hair blazing in the dawn sunlight like a magnesium flare.

"We still looking," he said in what was an irrevo-
cable statement and not a question. It carried no doubt
that the search would go on.

THE SUN ROSE HIGHER, and they plodded on, following the course of the river. It widened, then narrowed
again, taking in a couple of tributaries on its far bank.
There was no sign of life, apart from a scattering of
wild pigs drinking on their side, the animals fleeing
nervously when they spotted the human intruders.

There was no sign of Ryan's body.

"Smoke," Jak said, pointing ahead of them to the
north, where a thin gray column was spiraling into the
air above a stand of aspens.

"Looks like a sodbuster's shack," J.B. commented, shading his eyes with the brim of his fedora.
"Mebbe they've seen something on the water."

But the river was too wide for them to get across to
ask. They all shouted, and the Armorer fired a volley
of 9 mm rounds from the Uzi, tearing the quivering
leaves off the trees. Nobody came, the half-open door
of the hut seeming to tease them. It gave the illusion
that someone was standing just inside it, lingering in
the deep shadows, mocking them, waiting for them to
leave.

"Wasting time," Mildred said. "Probably out
hunting or something."

J.B. finally nodded, replacing his hat. "If Ryan...if
he was still a floater and came this way, odds are that
he'd have passed this way in the dark."

They moved on, Krysty giving a last glance behind
at the tumbledown shack.

INSIDE THE SHACK Ryan lay deeply unconscious on a filthy mattress on the dirt floor, his head bandaged with bloodstained rags, his leg splinted.

The man who sat in the darkness, peering through the doorway, cackled to himself as he saw the group of travelers moving away along the far bank.

"All that shoutin' and shootin' and tarry-hootin'," he mumbled. "Guess it must be you they's lookin' for, friend. So near and so far."

IT WAS LATE that afternoon when Krysty saw a trio of ragged men walking slowly toward them from a side trail that wound down from a low, heavily wooded hill. Two of them were carrying the carcass of a large boar, slung onto a pole.

All had long muskets across their shoulders, and they lowered their burden and readied their blasters when they saw the five strangers.

"No trouble," J.B. called, holding out both hands in the universal Deathlands gesture of peace.

"We had enough bastard trouble for one day, mister," grunted the leader, a broad-shouldered man in a fur jacket, bunch-backed and squat.

"How come?"

The man who had been struggling with the other end of the wild pig straightened, wiping sweat from his face. Krysty's breath froze in her throat for a moment when she saw the dark patch over the socket of the left eye, giving a brief resemblance to Ryan. But the man was inches shorter and many years older.

He caught her stare. "Seen a ghost, lady?"

"Yeah. No, not really. Just that you look like someone I know real well."

The third of the hunters laughed harshly. "Your friend looks like Jake here, then he sure must be no painting."

"You said you'd had trouble," J.B. said. "See blood on the pig's tusks."

The bunch-back sniffed. "Gutted my brother. Spear broke just when he had it hooked. Came all the way down the shaft after him, before we could get a shot at it. Spilled his tripes all over the forest."

The Armorer nodded. "Seen it happen. Sorry to hear it. You come from near here?"

"Don't live nowhere," Jake replied. "Aim to butcher this and sell it as meat. Hardly any pestholes round this godforsaken place. You seen any life?"

"No. Shack some miles back. Nobody around." J.B. looked at the board. "Be glad to share a meal with you. Haven't had good meat for a while."

"What'll you pay? Cost a handful of jack."

"Pay you in ammo."

"We use ball and powder, stranger—"

Jake interrupted the disabled man. "Listen, Harve, we might as well be neighborly. This bastard's breakin' my back. Let's make a camp and share a portion with these outlanders. Just don't feel like tryin' to carry old man pig any farther. Not with only the three of us. We'll never sell it in this rad-blasted wilderness."

Harve hesitated, then nodded. "Hell, why not?"

JAKE, HARVEY AND GUS. Harve's brother, Little Johnny, was buried in a shallow grave a few miles back in the trees. Jake and Gus were cousins, and they had all traveled south and west from the hollers of the Apps, working their way cross-country, scratching a living by hunting and trapping.

Now they sat together around a bright fire, with Krysty and the other friends, relishing the scent of a haunch of pig roasting on a spit. The meat was crackling, the skin charring, fat dribbling into the flames.

Krysty hadn't wasted any time asking them whether they might have seen anything of Ryan, dead or alive.

"He went in the river upstream, with them currents and whirlypools, then I have to figure your man's chilled, lady," Jake said softly.

She nodded slowly, controlling her emotions. "Sense tells me you're right. Just that there's still that spark of hope. Until I see him . . ."

"What happens to river farther west?" Jak asked, breaking a long silence.

"Runs across into the Sippi. Way along. Still the biggest and busiest river in all Deathlands." Gus was busily picking wax out of his ears as he spoke, flicking it into the fire, where it hissed and bubbled along with the pork fat.

"Any villes on way?"

The three hunters shook their heads like a trio of synchronized dolls, with Harve answering the albino teenager. "Not that we seen."

"Exceptin' that ruined place. Burned out. Day back from here." Jake shook his head. "Some kinda raid. Happened coupla weeks ago, by the look of it. No trails left. Rained out. No bullet marks. Just a lotta fire. Half-dozen shacks. No bodies."

"Is that not a sign of those treacherous mutations known as stickies?" Doc asked.

Mildred looked at J.B. "They like fires and explosions, don't they, John?"

The Armorer was busily polishing his glasses, peering shortsightedly at her. "Could be. Haven't had a run-in with stickies for a while. Glad to say."

Harve grinned and spit in the fire. "Some barons pay bounty on stickies. Handful of jack for a handful of hands. Reckon we might go hunt them on the morrow. We be a match for a gang of white-bellied muties. Pay better than dead pig."

"Don't taste so good as pig," Jak said with a grin, poking at the cooking meat with the point of one of his throwing knives. "Soon be ready eat. Hungry."

The aftermath of the devastating nuking of the United States, during the brief and final world war nearly a hundred years earlier, had resulted in enormous geophysical and climatic alterations to the country. It had also induced profound biological changes in all living creatures, with no species spared the bizarre and extreme mutations.

Stickies were one of the most common and vicious of the humanoid muties.

Their faces were often badly disfigured with running sores, diseased noses and lipless mouths with rows of filed teeth. They usually had thin, straggling hair and scrawny but muscular bodies. Their name came from their very specific mutation: their fingers and palms, and sometimes feet, would be covered with a number of tiny, powerful, toothed suckers, like miniature mouths, capable of sucking strips of skin and flesh from anything they touched. In extreme cases some stickies might have these hideous suckers distributed all over their bodies.

They were generally of extremely low intelligence, though possessed of a brutish cunning. Stickies often roamed in small packs of a dozen or more and rarely used weapons, except for clubs and rough spears. Their particular love was for explosions and fires, the bigger and brighter the better.

Stickies loathed norms.

Talk of the possibility of the vile creatures being in the region killed all conversation for a while.

TIME HAD NO MEANING for Ryan. There was only a total dull blackness with no sense and no sight and no sound. His pulse was slow and irregular, his breathing even slower.

The old man had carefully washed him and re-dressed him. Amazingly his clothes had more or less survived the dreadful fall and the torrent, though the SIG-Sauer had been removed from its holster and hung on a hook behind the rickety door of the shack, cleaned and oiled.

During the first twenty-four hours, after dragging the apparently lifeless body from the muddy fringe of the river, where it had snagged on a fallen live oak, the man had tried to feed him warm potato soup, but Ryan's mouth remained limp, letting the liquid trickle back out again. Even a spoonful of clear spring water was ignored, barely touching the dry, cracked lips.

"Live or fuckin' die. Not much to me," his savior had muttered crossly.

The spark of life was tiny and remote, gradually flickering toward extinction.

THE PORK WAS DELICIOUS. Though the boar had obviously been a tough old animal, the flesh was rich and tender, flavored delicately by the herbs that grew wild among the tall trees. Even with no bread or vegetables to accompany the meal, they all ate their fill. In the case of Jak Lauren, more than his fill.

"Smell of this must be drifting for a good twenty miles," J.B. said, lying back and picking at his teeth with a splinter of bone.

"Would've been good for bringin' some customers," Gus said. "Kind of free advert."

"Long as it doesn't bring in the bears and wolves and all the vermin." Harve looked thoughtfully at the carcass, which was missing one gigantic hind leg. "Wonder whether anyone could manage a mite more if we was to slice some more."

Nobody answered for a while, considering the possibility. Jak licked his thin, pale lips. Krysty stood, shaking her head. "Should be moving on before it gets dark," she said. "Search goes on, friends."

The three hunters all shuffled to their feet, wiping hands on greasy trousers, shaking with the five companions.

"Best of luck," Gus said. "We find your friend, and there's a burying . . . we'll do it right."

Doc cleared his throat, flushing in embarrassment. "I feel a call of nature coming on. A sudden spasm of intestinal pressure. So much rich meat after a relative dearth of sustenance. Would you all mind waiting a moment or two while I retire to...to do the necessary?''

"Means he's taking a dump," Mildred explained, seeing bewilderment on the faces of the three hunters.

Doc pointed his swordstick at her in a mock-threatening gesture. "Duty calls and I must away," he chanted in a nasal, folky voice. "Over the hills and far away.''

He wandered off from the camp, the wondrous odor of the roasting pork gradually fading behind him as he picked a path through the thick forest. He brushed against the moss-covered trunks of ancient pines, stumbling through deep leaf mold, which made his Victorian frock coat even more stained.

"Perdition! Confusion as I wander alone upon this winding path through a tortuous wilderness. All I have need of now is a dark tower to come to." He smiled to himself, pausing a moment as he saw a clearing ahead of him. "Perhaps it will be a pretty rest room made of gingerbread and sugar icing. Or a grim place. Grim. How clever.''

It was silent, the sounds of voices having vanished behind him. There was just the rustle of the rising wind soughing through the topmost branches of the trees. Very little direct sunlight penetrated to the forest floor, and there was a dank, alien smell hanging in the air.

Doc sniffed. "Like the cave of a hibernating grizzly? Or the home of a family of incontinent felines. Unpleasant. Best do what I have to and be on my way.''

He dropped his pants, making sure that he had plucked a handful of broad green dock leaves to clean himself. Then he looked around with a sudden attack of nerves, fancying himself no longer alone. But he could see no one near.

The old man had propped his cane against a handy spruce, and when he had finished and readjusted his clothing, he reached for it, fumbling in space.

Doc turned and found that the swordstick was no longer where he'd placed it.

Now it was held in the suckered fingers of a tall stickie, one of a band of half a dozen, all leering at him. They'd sprung from the shadows like infernal spirits of the woods, watching him in total silence.

"By the Three Kennedys!"

Chapter Four

At times of sudden shock or tension, Doc had an unfortunate tendency to freeze. All the time-trawling experiences that had blighted his life, plucking him from his happy family in 1896 to the late 1990s, then shunting him forward to the corroded heart of Deathlands, had shifted his mind several points off center.

Now he stood and stared at the half circle of grinning stickies, looking around at their pale, glittering eyes, the drooling mouths, soft lips barely concealing the needled teeth, their eager hands, the suckers opening and closing with a malignant life of their own.

"Shitting norm," hissed the mutie holding his beloved swordstick.

Doc casually allowed his right hand to fall to the butt of the cannon-sized Le Mat blaster on his hip, feeling the reassuring chill of the etched walnut.

"You got other shitters? Eating pig?"

The stickie's voice was harsh and distorted, difficult to understand, sounding like bubbles of stinking gas bubbling through boiling tar.

"Limited vocabulary, my dear fellow," Doc replied, his own voice feeling as frail as a dry leaf.

The eyes didn't alter their blank, hating expression. In the stillness Doc could actually hear the tiny suckers opening and closing against the polished ebony of his swordstick. The obscenely threatening sound turned his stomach, as he imagined what those rending suckers could do to his own flesh.

"How many you shitters?"

"An infinite number. Alpha to epsilon. Many a memorable zeugma out yonder."

"Stop talk shit!" The voice was raised, sibilant, angry. "You get chilled."

Doc considered the oldest trick in the book, deciding that it was just about the only trick available to him with the muties clustered so close around him. Warning the others was the main requirement.

"I won't get chilled, my raggedy friends," he said, admiring his own calm. Suddenly he pointed behind them with his left hand, and at the top of his voice shouted, "Shoot them, friends!"

To his delight and amazement, it worked on the stickies' stupid brains like a magic charm. Every one of them swung around to stare suspiciously into the pitchy shadows beneath the trees.

Doc drew the Le Mat with the liquid speed of a great shootist and thumbed back the scattergun hammer, squeezing the trigger on the gold-plated, black weapon.

The 18-gauge shotgun round exploded from the wide barrel, starring out at close range, hitting the bunched muties with devastating effect.

The one holding the cane was almost blown in two. The shot ripped into his stomach, splintering his spine, sending him staggering backward, his own blue-pink guts tangling around his ankles.

The two to his left were also hit, one in the groin, the other in both thighs.

The remaining three stickies were totally shocked by the thunderous roar of the handblaster, bemused by the great cloud of powder smoke that enveloped them. They heard their companions' screams of shock and agony, watching them thrash on the ground, blood spouting across the clearing.

The frail old man who they'd been about to butcher had produced a weapon of the gods.

The only problem with the Le Mat was that it took a few fumbling seconds to change the hammer from the scattergun to the chamber holding the nine rounds of .44s. Doc recalled J.B.'s warning words, repeated many times. "Fire it and run!"

He paused only a moment to snatch up the fallen swordstick, wincing at the stickiness of the warm blood that streaked its smooth, polished wood, then turned and ran back in what he hoped was the right direction.

JAK WAS QUICKEST to respond to the distant boom of the Let Mat, jumping to his feet. "Doc!" he said.

J.B. was a nanosecond behind him, his head turning as he tried to locate the precise direction of the distant shot.

The three hunters froze, gripping their own muskets. "What kinda blaster's that?" Harve asked. "Like a fuckin' cannon."

"That way," Krysty said, pointing.

Jak was already moving, light-footed, like a wraith through the black shadows under the trees, his own Colt Python .357 blaster in his right hand, looking disproportionately large in his skinny fingers.

"To me, friends!" Doc roared, blundering along, his skin crawling at the expectation of feeling the hungry suckers tugging at his clothes and skin.

He was aware of noise behind him, a thin screaming, like a bullock at the gelding block, running feet, barely audible in the soft leaf mold of the forest's ferny floor, panting and a high-pitched cursing.

"Stickies!" he shouted, twisting, dodging and ducking the low-jagged branches.

"Coming, Doc!" J.B. replied. Generally he wouldn't have wanted to give their unseen enemies any warning of reinforcements, but the old man sounded as though he needed encouragement, as well as a voice to aim at in the woods.

A few paces ahead of the Armorer, Jak dropped to his knees and leveled the big blaster. "Go left, Doc!" he yelled, his voice cracking.

Doc immediately dodged right.

Cursing under his breath, the teenager adjusted his aim and fired three spaced rounds at the trio of stickies that was pursuing the old-timer through the trees.

Guns weren't Jak's strong point, but he managed to put one of the muties down with two full-metal-jacket rounds through shoulder and chest, the third bullet missing high and left.

Behind him there was the ripple of tearing silk, and J.B. fired a short burst from the Uzi, stopping the other two stickies dead in their tracks, the 9 mm rounds kicking them over in a welter of sprayed blood and splintered bone.

Doc was still running when he reached Krysty, who reached out and grabbed him by the arm. "Whoa back," she said loudly and firmly. "Safe now, Doc."

"Walked straight into them," he panted, steadying himself on her shoulder, waving the swordstick in a vaguely threatening manner. "Are they done for?"

"All dead, Doc. How many did you take out?" J.B. was already reloading the Uzi.

"Certainly one, and I think two others."

"Best take a look. Keep together."

The three hunters had caught up with them, lumbering through the forest, staring down at the three corpses, one of them still twitching as the neural lines finally closed down.

"There more?" Harve asked, breathing hard.

"Three," Doc said. "I most certainly sent one off to the vale of tears, and I believe I wounded the other two rather severely."

There was a corpse, its guts spilled all around it. The one hit in the groin was close to death. Its feeble attempts to stem the arterial blood from the shotgun pellets weren't enough. Its watery eyes turned up at the sight of the norms, and it clamped its teeth together.

"Don't waste a bullet on it," J.B. warned. "You said another one, Doc?"

"Yes. I believe I hit it in the legs."

"Lotta blood this way," Jak said, stooping over the muddied, trampled dirt to the east of the small clearing. "Dragged itself away."

"Best chill it," Krysty said. "Stop it reaching any camp, if there's more of them around."

The albino nodded and ran into the shadows, while the others waited in silence.

The shot came less than a minute later, a single booming round that echoed through the wood.

IN THE EXCITEMENT it was Mildred who noticed that all of the dead muties wore the remains of shackles and chains. Ankle locks had worn a deep weal in the stickies' flesh, while two had rusting iron links hammered around their throats.

"Someone's been working them," Gus said. "Heard of slavers owning plantations farther west on the Sippi. All kindsa stories about it."

"Like what?" J.B. asked curiously.

The hunter looked at his friends for confirmation. "Heard a coupla names. Been hearing them around Deathlands most of my life. Swift and evil."

"Gert Wolfram and the Magus," the Armorer guessed, firing the shot at random. He saw from the expressions on the faces of the three hunters that he'd hit the center of the target.

"Right," Jake said. "You crossed their paths before, mister?"

"Some. Used to ride with a man called Trader. He knew them years ago. Gert Wolfram is supposed to be the fattest person in all Deathlands. Gross. He's known as the person who first discovered stickies could be caught and slaved. Man he sold them to was called the Magus."

"They call him the Warlock," Gus said.

"And the Sorcerer," Harve added. "They say he's only part human."

J.B. nodded. "I heard that also. Then again, I heard plenty of stories about them both. You reckon they might be involved with these stickies?"

"Too late to ask them now," Mildred said.

"Couple got whip marks on their backs," Jake told them, stooping over the stickie who'd been groin shot and had just died. "This one and the bastard the old man chilled."

Doc had recovered his breath, looking at the two corpses. "Perhaps we should move on from this region, in case there are more of these inhuman fiends concealed among the trees."

"Sounds good," Krysty agreed. "Cut back to the river and keep moving and heading west."

"End up at the Sippi," Harve said. "Might hear news there of your *compadre*." He looked up at the darkening sky. "Not far off for a chem storm. Time we was moving on. Get back and pick up the carcass of old boss pig."

Farewells were brief, clasped hands and a nod and a word, and promises to look out for the others farther down the line.

Then J.B. led the five friends toward the west, cutting through the fringe of the trees, aiming for the slow-flowing river. Harve and his cousins went back east, toward where they'd left the hacked remnants of the wild boar.

THEY'D BEEN MOVING only about fifteen minutes when Krysty held up a hand. "Listen," she said.

It was a thin, ragged sound, torn apart by the rising wind, like the dismal piping of a lone bird, far away across a bleak moorland.

They all stood still, listening, straining for the noise above the whispering of the swelling river on their right-hand side. The breeze through the high branches rose and fell, covering up the strange sound.

"It's a loon," Doc said doubtfully. "I think . . ."

Jak's right hand was on the butt of his blaster, his head turned to look behind them in the direction taken by the three hunters. His eyes seemed to glow with a buried fire in the shadows of the trees. "Not bird," he said.

Krysty agreed with him, shaking her head slowly. "No. Reckon you're right, Jak. Not birds. It sounds more . . ."

The noise was repeated, clearer, surging and then fading away like a whisper.

"There's smoke," Mildred said, pointing back to a patch of smudged gray above the topmost peaks of the forest.

"Bad news." J.B. pushed back the brim of his fedora. "We going to take a look?"

Krysty had slipped into the role of second-in-command of the friends, and she nodded slowly. "I guess so. Got a bad gut feeling about what we'll find."

IT WAS OVER by the time they worked their way back and tracked down the source of the fire.

There had been no more noise, though they had disturbed a raucous flock of mutie birds, like large crows but with yellow-and-white plumage, who rose screaming into the smoky air, giving a warning that their territory was being invaded.

The small clearing was only a couple of hundred yards to the east of where they had eaten the haunch of boar. The ragged bones of the animal lay stripped in the center of a pile of glowing white ash, the wind brightening an occasional ruby ember.

The bodies of Harve, Gus and Jake were raggled together among the silent trees.

J.B. held up his hand, and everyone stopped, looking at the grim scene. "Think they've all gone."

"One of them has remained behind," Doc said, pointing at the corpse of a stickie that was hunched over by a frost-shattered boulder, a dark powder burn in its chest showing where it had been shot at close quarters by one of the hunters.

Before they'd been overwhelmed.

"Mutie's got a neck collar on," Mildred said. "Another of them escaped slaves?"

Nobody answered her.

J.B. walked over and looked down at the trio of corpses. "Sure took them quick," he said. "Must've been a lot of stickies to do this so fast."

The bodies had been stripped, and their muskets taken. All of them showed the undeniable mutilations so typical of stickies' work.

Strips and patches of skin had been torn away from living flesh by the voracious suckers, eyes sucked from sockets, faces reduced to weeping masks of raw meat and white bones. Teeth gleamed like small pink pearls among the ruin of the men's features.

All three had been emasculated, but not neatly with keen flensing knives. The genitals had been brutally ripped and torn from their bodies, the thighs and groins showing the marks of the toothed suckers. The extremities had also been burned in the fire, fingers and toes blackened and charred like the stumps of small branches. A sharp spear, its point flame hardened, had been thrust through Harve's humped back, as though he were a hooked whale.

Krysty sighed. "Sick, sick bastards."

"All they know," Mildred countered. "Didn't ask to be nuke-altered mutations. Blame the warmongers and whitecoats back in the 1980s and '90s. It's their long-dead hands that marked what happened here."

"Guess so. Hadn't thought about... We going to stay and bury them?"

"No, Krysty," J.B. replied. "Tracks show as many as twenty stickies in the gang. Must still be within a quarter mile or so of us. We leave now and carry on west. Fast and quiet. What's happened here's over."

As they left the clearing, they were watched from the undergrowth by a host of bloodshot, watery eyes.

It was beginning to rain heavily from the leaden sky.

Chapter Five

The storm forced them to seek shelter.

It was a triple-chem tempest, whirling in with roiling clouds that changed shape every second, tumble topped, filled with the stench of ozone and leaking the purple lace of lightning. The thunder was constant, buffeting the senses, making Doc cover his ears, his face showing his anguish.

"I am stricken like Lear himself," he raged, shaking his head back and forth, the streaming rain pasting his silver hair against his lined cheeks. "Can we not seek a place for us, somewhere, a place for us...?"

It was J.B., leading the way, who spotted the squat shape of the ruined building, standing alone at the edge of a deserted highway. The flank of the side wall was toward them, the stucco peeling and weathered. But the lettering still showed through, in an ornate Gothic script: Faust's R&R Metal Heaven.

They huddled together, peering at it through the driving rain. "What in the name of all perdition can that have been?" Doc asked.

"Heavy-metal rock and roll," Mildred replied. "Past your bedtime music, Doc."

"But does the store still have a roof to it?"

"Yeah. Looks like."

"Then that is most certainly the place for me." He led the way at an ungainly gallop, his long legs angling out like a demented stork, waving his swordstick and yelling as if he were leading a forlorn hope into the breach at Badajoz or attacking the cannon at Chickamauga.

The rest followed, splashing through the deep puddles scattered over what had presumably once been the parking lot for the store and was now a blank expanse of weed-strewed tarmac, cracked and rippled by earth movements across the years.

A steel-framed door swung open, clattering in the strong wind, leading into a single stripped concrete box of a room, some twenty feet square. The store's main window had probably caved in at skydark, but it had been skillfully boarded up, and kept out the worst of the storm.

Now they were out of the elements, it seemed shockingly silent. The companions shook themselves, removing soaked coats, rubbing hands against the chill.

"Looks like someone's been living rough here," Mildred commented, pointing to a charred section of wall in the corner, where a pile of half-burned wood lay. A stained mattress was on the floor next to it, along with a few rusted self-heat cans and some empty bottles of cheap red gut-rot wine.

"Let's get that fire going again," J.B. said, kneeling by it and igniting a self-light from one of his pockets. "Get dried off."

"Might as well stay the night here," Krysty suggested. "Storm's in for hours."

"How about our stickie brethren?" Doc asked worriedly, brushing water from the shoulders of his antique frock coat. "Might they not come a'calling?"

"Stickies hate rain," Jak said. "Won't be out in it. Find some place hole up."

"A place like this, do you mean, my snowcapped young companion?"

Jak grinned, his teeth peeling back off his lips like a young wolf. "Don't worry, Doc. Can bolt door. Side window's too small. Any trouble can hold off army from here." He glanced at the Armorer. "True?"

J.B. sniffed and nodded. "True. Walls and roof are solid, Doc. Take more than a few muties to give us worries. Good, solid little fortress for us."

"Well, I trust implicitly your judgment in matters of military logistics, my dear John Barrymore. I offer my profound hope that you will not disappoint me." He sat by the crackling fire and made himself comfortable.

"Wish we'd taken a few slices of that pig," Mildred said, joining him. "Going to be a long, hungry stay."

THE RAIN WAS STILL falling when Krysty jerked awake sometime after midnight.

Not knowing what had awakened her, she lay still, eyes open in the blackness, every sense straining. But she could see and hear nothing in the empty store. The only sound was a faint rustling of paper from high in one corner that she knew was the torn half of a frail predark advertising poster that had somehow clung to the wall. It advertised a bulky, long-haired singer

whose name, oddly, appeared to have been "Loaf."
At least, that was all that remained under the menacing black-and-white photograph of the looming figure. The remnants of a slogan suggested that the rock singer had come from Hell.

"Ryan?" she breathed, somehow feeling his presence.

She could hear J.B. on her left, breathing as soft and gentle as a fox. Doc was across the room, alongside the crumbling ashes of the fire, snoring surprisingly quietly, the breath rasping at the back of his throat.

Krysty closed her eyes, overwhelmed by a sense of loss. An emptiness filled her heart, the desolation of knowing that from now on she would walk alone through life.

And yet . . .

The feather-light flickering of the Gaia power taught to her by Mother Sonja was whispering at the very back of her mind, in a locked room at the end of a deserted and dusty corridor where memories lived.

"Ryan," she said again.

THE SODBUSTER'S SMALL, filthy shack was around fifteen miles away from where Krysty lay wakeful.

Rain pounded against its mud-slick walls, streaming off the crudely thatched roof. Under the torrential downpour, the whole structure seemed about to collapse, and rain trickled through the sheaves of long straw in a dozen places, pattering on the packed earth of the uneven floor.

The old man, muttering and cursing under his breath, had been hobbling busily around like a malevolent gnome, pushing the iron pot of rancid rabbit stew from under one of the leaks, dragging Ryan's unconscious figure and his worn mattress from out of the way of another. He moved his own bed nearer the rattling window to avoid a third steady flood.

"Bastard rain. Should've left fucker out in the mud. Why bother? Dyin'. Only, though, if he had lived, I could've..."

He stopped, his red-rimmed eyes darting to the door, where he thought he'd heard something scratching at the wood. He picked up Ryan's blaster, handling it with an innate clumsiness, thumbing back the hammer. He sidled to the entrance and applied an eye to a long split in the planking.

"Jesus on the Cross!" He took a step back as he saw a large black panther, its coat sleek with rain, pawing hesitantly at the makeshift door. The animal's eyes gleamed a golden green in the frequent flashes of chem lightning that tore at the darkness.

He pointed the heavy automatic and tugged on the trigger. He made no effort to brace himself against the recoil and yelped at the explosion and the kick that nearly sprained his wrist. The 9 mm bullet tore a chunk of wood from the door, going high above the head of the snarling predator and scything out across the river.

The animal jumped away from the cabin in an amazing four-legged, stiff-backed leap, its head turning from side to side, tail whisking angrily.

"Git fuck away," the old man yelled, "or you get another one through the head."

Ryan twitched at the familiar sound of the SIG-Sauer being fired, then lay motionless again.

The huge panther turned around and moved silently inland, not once looking back at the cabin.

"Teach yer fuckin' lesson, big shitter!" He flourished the blaster in triumph.

The storm hung around for hours, dumping a ceaseless flood of water, raising the level of the river by a couple of feet. But the old man had lived there long enough to know the tributary of the mighty Sippi in all its moods and had built his raggedy home high enough above flood level to avoid all but a freakish breaking of the banks.

Now he sat by the window and peered out past the flap of sacking, waiting for the storm to pass as all storms eventually did.

And Ryan lay still, locked into the heart of his own personal darkness.

If he dreamed, he dreamed only of black pools in deep-buried caverns where no shred of moonlight ever penetrated. No light of star, no glimmer of the noon sun. Occasionally, if you'd watched him very closely, you might have seen a small movement of a finger, closing and opening, a twitch of the great scar that coursed across his face.

But the heartbeat and respiration continued slow and regular. The old man had already come to realize that his guest was someone very different. Any ordinary man would have died some time ago. The dreadful bruising of his body showed the extent of a great fall, and he appeared to have come through the worst part of the gorge, where the torrent raged and the fanged rocks waited.

Yet his body showed all manner of old scars, cuts and bullet holes. It was the body of a fighting man.

A killer.

IT WAS NO MORE than a breath of wind on the cheek, the touch of a down feather as it settled on the mirrored surface of a woodland pool, the brush of a moth's wing, a whispered sentence in the dark corridor of a long-abandoned mansion.

Ryan.

If he had been linked to the gleaming banks of sophisticated preskydark medical monitoring equipment, then there would have been a fractional change in the beeping and in the peaks and troughs of the printout of his life functions. It would have been marginal but readable.

Ryan.

Krysty concentrated with every ounce of her powers to mindlink with him. Her thoughts reached out through the dark and stormy night like the frail beam of a lighthouse, searching through the storm-racked skies.

On the other side of the hut, oblivious to anything else, the old man slept restlessly, his dreams filled with voracious creatures that scurried blood-eyed through moist, dark places and tore at living flesh.

Ryan's fingers opened and closed again. His lips moved, his dry tongue pressing at his teeth. Beneath the closed lid, his good eye flicked from side to side as though it were scanning a document, and his pulse quickened.

Ryan.

The rain flurried against the wall, bringing a scattering of fallen leaves to brush at the door.

The old man turned over, disturbed by the sound, his dream changing from dark to light, to driving a rocking Conestoga wag across endless, sunlit prairie, heading toward the jagged silhouette of Ship Rock.

Ryan, I'm here, my dearest love. Are you there, Ryan? Krysty bit her lip so hard with the effort of trying to send the soundless message across time and space that a worm of blood inched over her chin.

He stirred again, his mind groping toward the surface like a drowning man clawing his way upward from the great mysteries that inhabit the abyss of the deeps.

In the abandoned store Krysty was disturbed for a few moments by Doc rolling over, coughing, mumbling to himself. "A man would as lief travel from Dan to Beersheba and then find himself without horse."

Krysty smiled to herself, then forced herself back into the trancelike state, trying to send her thoughts to Ryan, if he still lived. She hoped against hope that she might receive some sort of signal back from him.

Ryan, lover. Speak to me, lover, please.

He was breathing faster, hands both clenching, nails biting into his palms.

Krysty was rigid with tension, every muscle and sinew strained taut. The worm of blood had become a steady trickle, and her face was screwed up into a rigid mask.

Come on, Ryan, hear me. Come on, lover.

Outside the hut, driven up from the rising waters, a mutie cottonmouth—full thirty feet long—came crawling slowly along the path outside the hut. Pausing, its tongue tasted the air, sensing life close by. But the door was closed and it passed by, vanishing into the trees beyond the hut.

Ryan.

He was lying on his back, his head turning from side to side as though he was disagreeing with something someone had just said. But he could hear the words.

Feel the words.

Ryan opened his eye.

Chapter Six

"Eight days ago I figured you was ready for bone-yard."

Ryan sat on the porch of the little hut, enjoying an afternoon of watery sunshine, whittling away at a short piece of broken beechwood, trying with little skill to turn it into a whistle. He shifted sideways, the SIG-Sauer clunking in its holster against the leg of a broken chair.

"Careful there, Ryan," Paddy Maxwell mumbled. He was sipping from a chipped jug of rot-gut hooch that he'd traded for the previous morning. He'd dealt it for a skein of fresh-gutted catfish that he and Ryan had caught the day before, with an inbred family of moonshiners who lived in squalid poverty a few miles up a side creek.

The old man had warned Ryan to sit inside the cabin and keep the SIG-Sauer drawn while the trading went on with the family of a mean-eyed father, three sons with barely a single brain between them and a pretty, vacant-eyed daughter.

"Turn your back on them scum, and you end up pickin' steel out your fuckin' spine," he said.

Ryan finally tired of his clumsy attempts at carving and heaved the piece of wood toward the muddy edge of the water, now back at something close to its normal level. What had been a nameless stretch of river he now knew was known locally as the Big White.

"Wasn't no river here before the Russkie nukes fucked the land. So they say. Land jumped and rolled, and water flowed up the hill and down the hill. Lakes turned dry and mountains sprung up. Now the Big White runs clear through to the Sippi."

"There a ville down there?" Ryan asked. "Generally is where big rivers meet."

"Yeah. Riverboat crossing there. Fancy ville. Get fucked every which way but clean. Gamblin' and whorin' and a contract killer for a handful of small jack. Place is called Twin Forks." He cackled and rubbed at his permanently sore eyes. "'Course, the trash calls it 'Twin Fucks.'"

Ryan stretched. "Reckon that's where I'll make for. Soon as I got a mite more strength back."

Paddy stood up from his chair, shaking his head in a nervous tic that got worse when he'd been drinking. "You ain't fit to shovel goose shit out the pen, Ryan."

The one-eyed man laughed. "Can't stay here forever. Got friends I should be going after. Be worried sick about me. Likely think I've gone west on that last train."

Over the week since he'd finally recovered full consciousness, Ryan had come to be oddly fond of his rescuer. Paddy Maxwell was physically filthy, foulmouthed, violent, short-tempered, racist, murderous, parblind, most parts drunk.

And cripplingly lonely.

He hawked a sort of living from fishing and some trapping, trading for liquor and for other supplies with infrequent passagers down the Big White.

After three days Ryan was able to stand unaided and was beginning to think about moving on as soon as he could. Paddy had been vehemently opposed to that, arguing, shouting and spitting to try to stop him. He'd even threatened Ryan with a smoothbore musket, forcing him to lift the little man by the throat and pin him to the wall of his hut with one hand. He held the SIG-Sauer in his other hand, pressing the four-and-a-half-inch barrel into Paddy's throat until the cartilage creaked and his red eyes watered with impotent terror.

Now it was eight days, and Ryan reckoned that he'd probably recovered about seventy percent of his strength.

And Paddy was drinking himself into a despondent stupor at the thought of being left alone once more.

"We could go a make of it here, Ryan," he insisted, tangling his words. "Could clean the place up. Mebbe build another cabin. Take in travelers. Get a coupla women to cook and whore."

Ryan shook his head. "Said the answer was no, Paddy."

After another deep slug at the jar of liquor, Paddy changed tack again. "Mebbe I'll come to Twin Forks with you, Ryan. Hold your fuckin' hand, like."

Ryan shrugged. "Hell, why not?"

"When you goin'? Next week? Week after that?"

"Sooner." Ryan got up off the porch and stared toward the setting sun. "Day after tomorrow. Start at dawn. Welcome to come along."

"Really?" A note of total disbelief was in his quavering voice. "Why the fuck's that?"

"Why what?"

"Why you want a wore-out old shitter like me along with you, Ryan?"

"You saved my life, Paddy. Not for you, I'd have drowned or just rotted away out on that very mud bank. I owe you that. So come along to the ville."

The little man clicked his heels together. "Never been to Twin Forks, 'cept on my own. Be a real fuckin' treat, Ryan. Yeah, it will that."

KRYSTY WAS ALSO WATCHING the sunset, sitting out on the balcony of her bedroom of the Grits and Greetings boardinghouse, a once-white frame house that now squatted drunkenly close to the edge of the junction of the Big White and the mighty Sippi. The landlady had told them when they booked the rooms that it had been the flood of 1989 that had washed away some of the underpinnings and made the whole place lean like a Saturday-night drunk on a friend's shoulder.

The house dated back to predark times, when Twin Forks had been a small, nameless settlement, twenty miles or more from the Sippi. Then the earth had moved, and now it was perched right on the edge of the great waterway. In another year or so, the way it looked, it would be floating off toward Norleans.

They'd been in Twin Forks for four days.

The trip down, searching the banks of the Big White for some trace of Ryan or his corpse, had taken a total of four days, and ended in utter failure.

But Krysty insisted that her lover still lived, that she had felt a message from him over a week ago, felt him respond to her sending out the Gaia-powered words.

The rest of the party was more than happy to humor her by staying in the sprawling ville, questioning travelers, particularly those who came in from the east. Since the big river wound away north and south, this was the principal direction of trade. Not many had come from the hinterland of old Tennessee. But none had any news of a one-eyed man, alive or dead.

To pay for the three rooms that they'd booked, J.B. and Jak had taken on part-time jobs as sec bouncers at one of the biggest of several saloons and gaudies. The Montana Queen was run by a tough, silver-haired woman named Dolores Stanwyck. She had hired J.B. on the strength of his superior armory of the Uzi and the fléchette-firing scattergun.

She had been less easily convinced about taking on young Jak Lauren.

"Might frighten away clients, lovely lad. You look like a cheesy fart'll blow you off the boardwalk." She laughed throatily. "Wouldn't want to be responsible for you getting trodden into the street, kid."

"Don't call me 'kid,' please," Jak said quietly as he looked around the ornate, gold-painted interior of the building. It was only a little after nine in the morning when they called, and Miss Stanwyck was finishing her breakfast, counting up the night's take. Some of her whores drifted down to eat, looking curiously at the ill-matched pair of strangers, particularly at the skinny boy with the dazzling mane of white hair.

"What're you looking for, son?" Dolores asked.

"Show you can look after self." He pointed at a fat-faced golden cherub that decorated the staircase. "Nose."

She dropped her knife and fork. "Don't you dare go shooting at that. Cost me a fortune from a greaser in Phoenix who... Holy Madonna!"

Jak had reached casually around to the small of his back, under his jacket, as though he had a twinge of discomfort. Then his hand came forward with a crack like a Concord whip. There was a blur of shimmering silver light across the dusty shadows of the saloon and a dull thunk.

A leaf-bladed throwing knife, with a taped hilt, was quivering in the center of the cherub's gleaming nose.

Dolores stood slowly, peering a little shortsightedly at Jak's demonstration. "That is something, boy," she said. "Be glad to take you on along with J.B., here. Just don't be too fast in drawing your blade. Don't want to lose all the customers of the Montana Queen."

So they had steady work, and they brought home enough jack-in-hand to pay the landlady at the Grits and Greetings.

And Krysty, Doc and Mildred passed the days asking the same question again and again around the ville, getting the same shake of the head.

"HOW DO I LOOK, Ryan?" The question was asked with a touch of nervousness, the little man primed up, ready to snap at Ryan if he criticized his ensemble.

"Look a deal smarter than me, Paddy."

The coat had the same slightly phosphorescent green glint as Doc's frock coat, a somewhat sinister sheen that meant you could almost see your face in it from age and wear. The pants were hoicked up in a bunch around Paddy's midriff, seeming to belong to a much taller and bulkier man. The vest was torn and neatly mended, though no more than two of the buttons matched. To crown things, Paddy was wearing a sporting derby, perched on the side of his head.

"You sure I look all right?"

Ryan nodded. His private opinion was that the little man looked like a badly made-up corpse, but he wasn't going to hurt Paddy's feelings by telling him that.

"Fine. You going to shave?"

"Have done."

"You have?" He peered at the scabrous, silver stubble that lined the cheeks and jawline. "Mebbe you missed a few places, then, Paddy."

"You reckon? Could go and do it again. Stand a mite closer to the shittin' razor."

"Let it lie," Ryan said. "Time we was hitting the road into town."

THEY STOPPED the first night at a dismal rooming house set back off the trail along an unmarked side road. Ryan would have easily walked past it if Paddy hadn't grabbed at his arm. "Up here," he said.

It looked as if it had once been the biggest of a complex of vacation cottages, perched on the side of a small lake. Ryan guessed the water might once have been crystal clear, filled with leaping rainbow trout. Now a thick layer of green algae covered it like a winter blanket, and there was little sign of any life—except for a sullen, coiling movement near the center that looked like a large reptile of some kind.

The rooming house was run by a couple of deaf-mutes, in their middle twenties. The wife took the greasy handful of coins that Paddy laboriously counted out from a tattered wallet and indicated room 5, at the top of the stairs.

There were two narrow beds there, each with an undersheet and three threadbare blankets. The chamber itself was fairly clean, with scrubbed pine flooring.

The window looked across the contaminated lake, and there were two pictures on the walls. One was a pallid watercolor of a small church set against the background of what Ryan recognized as the Tetons. The other picture was much older, in dark oils, showing a Spanish duenna riding a high-spirited stallion in front of a Moorish mansion. The caption said it was the Doña Maria Elena Cantrell riding Firestart in front of the ranch of her father.

"Mighty pretty slut," Paddy said, seeing Ryan admiring the painting.

"Not sure that *slut*'s the right word for someone like that, Paddy. Little more classy."

The old man shrugged. "You say so. See them three shitters at the table down the stairs?"

"Sure." Ryan hadn't just seen them. He'd weighed them up and checked out what weapons they were carrying. Sheer habit. He put them down as hired hands, the kind that wouldn't argue too much about what kind of work they got paid for.

"Playin' cards."

Ryan nodded. The journey had tired him more than he'd expected, and the bed looked amazingly inviting.

The old man grinned, showing the mix of rotten and missing teeth, like peering into a long-lost graveyard. "Figure go and show the hick fuckers how to play some serious poker."

"Take it easy, Paddy," Ryan warned. "Three of them and one of you. Didn't look like good losers to me."

The old man cackled and slapped him on the shoulder. Reaching inside his shirt, he showed Ryan a slim-bladed cutthroat razor. "Slice them shitters thin and raw if they fuck with me," he said boastfully. "Young blood spills easy, Ryan. Anyways, I get trouble, I'll call and you can come runnin'."

Ryan nodded. "Sure. Just take it careful."

The door closed behind the eager Paddy Maxwell, and Ryan lowered himself onto the bed, sighing at the sensation of ease, resting his head on his hands, closing his eye.

Sleeping.

HE WASN'T TOTALLY SURE what had awakened him. It seemed as though there'd been a shout or a disturbance from somewhere else in the rooming house, down the stairs in the room beneath him. But now there was only late-afternoon stillness.

He swung his legs over the side of the bed, ready to get up, when he caught the sound of feet moving slowly along the corridor toward him.

One man, alone.

"Paddy!" he called, but there was no answer. Ryan felt the familiar prickling at his nape. There was something wrong, but he couldn't quite turn his mind to what it was. There hadn't been any shooting. He was certain of that.

The steps were much closer, slurring and scuffing, as if it were too much trouble for the man to walk properly.

Ryan stood, glancing sideways out the window, seeing from the light and the shadows that he'd been sleeping for something between half and three-quarters of an hour.

The doorknob started to turn slowly, rattling as if the person were having trouble gripping it properly.

Ryan's hand was on the butt of the SIG-Sauer, ready to draw it. "That you, Paddy?"

"Yeah," the voice said, like a ragged whisper from the far side of eternity.

The door swung open slowly and the little man stood there, his face like parchment, left hand clasped tight across his belly, the other still holding the door-knob. For several long heartbeats he didn't move.

"Trouble?" Ryan said quietly.

There was a slight, almost imperceptible nod of the head. The room was in shadow, but Ryan thought he could see something glinting stickily on the old man's fingers.

"Won't be...to the ville with you.... Sorry...never had much of fuckin' friend.... Sorry..."

Then he knelt down very carefully as though he were on a precious Oriental carpet and slid forward on his face. His body jerked, and blood flowed from his stomach across the floor. He sighed, then lay still.

Ryan looked down at the body for a moment, then straightened as he heard boots clattering on the stairs.

Chapter Seven

"Find yourself in a hole, get out of it" was one of the Trader's many thoughts on living and staying alive in Deathlands. It came to Ryan as he stood by the body of the little old man who'd saved his life.

It didn't matter much what had happened downstairs at the poker table. Perhaps Paddy had cheated or tried to cheat, or the three men had combined to cheat him. The only hard fact was that Paddy Maxwell was very dead, his stomach sliced apart with a long blade. And his killers were at the top of the stairs, coming for Ryan. Nothing else mattered.

Ryan glanced around the room, considering the possibility of using the window to escape. He who didn't fight but ran away, lived to run away another day. That was another of the self-evident truths that the Trader had held to.

But the layers of cream paint looked solid and cracked all around the frame, as though the window hadn't actually been opened in years.

Which turned the bedroom into a trap.

All of that took less than half a second, as Ryan's combat-honed brain weighed the possibilities, coming up with the answer that had occurred to him first.

Get out shooting.

The door still stood open, and he didn't hesitate a moment longer.

He dived through it, out into the passage, rolling agilely on his shoulder, coming up in the classic gunman's crouch on the far side. He sighted down the barrel of the SIG-Sauer P-226 and opened fire instantly on the three men advancing toward him from the top of the stairs.

The leader was stout, with long hair tied back with a length of green ribbon. He held a Civil War bayonet in his right hand, its narrow shaft slick with blood. In his left hand was what Ryan had spotted downstairs—a Heckler & Koch automatic, looking like the P-9 S 45, the model that had been rechambered to take the .45 round.

At his shoulder was the youngest of the three, peach fuzz on his pale cheeks. He had a Smith & Wesson double-action revolver, the 64 model.

The third of the trio was holding an ESFAC Pocket Pony, a rare, single-action, 6-shot, .22-caliber revolver.

One of the things that had rung small alarm bells for Ryan when he'd passed the trio downstairs was their weaponry. The blasters were good ones, in top condition, not the kind of guns you associated with drifters.

His sudden appearance at floor level, rolling in a tangle of arms and legs and coming up shooting, totally threw the three killers.

The first one went down to a head shot, the side of his skull exploding as the full-metal-jacket round angled to the right after penetrating an inch below the eye and fragmenting inside the cranium.

As he fell, the man was in the act of hurling the bayonet, but it flopped weakly from his fingers, penetrating the toe of his boot as it dropped.

The next round sliced between the second and third of the men, hitting an imitation chandelier at the head of the stairs, shattering it into shards of glass and clear plastic.

The double-action Smith & Wesson barked once, but the youth was partly blinded by a faceful of puddled brains and splintered bone, already staggering backward. His bullet went wide and high of Ryan, eventually hitting the ceiling at the farther end of the corridor.

Ryan shot him twice through the throat and upper chest, one of the bullets going clear through and hitting the man behind him in the shoulder.

"Bastard!" The cry of anger and anguish came from the last of the trio as he dropped his .22, fumbling for it with his free hand as it fell, but missing it. He saw it clunk into a puddle of splattered blood on the carpet in the middle of the corridor and started to stoop to reach for it.

Ryan had a moment to aim, and shot him precisely through the top of the head.

The bullet slanted downward, forcing the right eye from the socket, where it dangled onto the cheek, held by the sinews of the optic nerve. The bullet, distorting as it rolled, plucked out three teeth from the upper jaw, smashing it as it passed by. Crimson flooded over the man's check shirt.

All three bodies were flopping around in a tangle of limbs, blood splashing high up the walls.

Ryan stood watching them, in case another bullet was needed, seeing that the residual twitching was slowing as the lines all went down. He reloaded the warm gun.

"Stupes," he said to himself. "Cold-heart stupes." He noticed now that the youngest of the corpses had a deep, fresh cut across the inside of his right arm, where the sliced material of his shirt flapped, blood-stained. It looked very much like the cut you might get from an enraged old man wielding a cutthroat razor.

Maybe Paddy Maxwell had it coming after all.

Either way, it didn't matter.

You can't breathe life back into a corpse.

Ryan went into the bedroom, picked up his coat and walked past the butchered trio, wincing slightly as the soles of his combat boots stuck for a moment in the crusting blood.

He went cautiously down the stairs, expecting the gunfire to have brought some eager, and possibly murderous, spectators. But the lobby was deserted.

Then he noticed that the young wife was on the far side, near the half-open front door, polishing the top of a player piano, her back to him.

For a moment Ryan was totally confused at her seeming indifference to the butchery that had been carried out upstairs in her house. Then he remembered that she and her husband were both deaf.

Ryan considered creeping past her and sneaking out of the building into the darkness of evening. Then he stopped, not wanting any sort of alarm. If he'd known that her husband was safely out of the way, he might have succumbed to the temptation to quiet her while he escaped.

At that moment she had to have sensed his presence or the movement of his shadow, and she turned with a startled expression on her face. Ryan managed to paste a smile in place, holding out both hands to show that he hadn't meant her any harm. He spoke slowly, watching her eyes.

"Sorry to make you jump."

She shrugged, then walked quickly to the desk and started thumbing through a box filled with rectangles of white card, picking one out to show him.

"Supper in a half hour."

He nodded. "That'll be fine."

Another card read, "Would you like a bath?"

He was desperately conscious of the blood that splattered all over his boots, but they were out of sight behind the registry desk. He shook his head. "No, thanks."

She mouthed, "Your friend?"

Again Ryan shook his head. "No. He's . . . he's taking a rest in the room."

The woman smiled and nodded, looking intently at Ryan and rubbing her stomach.

"What? Oh, am I hungry? Yeah. Guess I am." He could smell the delicious aromas of roasting meat filtering along into the lobby from the kitchen. Paddy Maxwell hadn't been too strong on cooking, and it was tempting to take a chance on the four corpses remaining undiscovered in the quiet upstairs corridor while he snatched a quick meal.

"Going for a short walk," he said. "Get me some fresh air. Be back in time for supper." The risk was too great, and the last thing he needed was to get hauled up in a small pesthole, involved in a multiple murder. In places like this, it wasn't that hard for a penniless stranger to finish up dancing on the end of a length of hemp.

The woman nodded again and smiled. Ryan walked onto the porch and turned left, heading westward, in the general direction of the township of Twin Forks.

RYAN STEPPED OUT along the rutted trail, keeping to his path by the stars that were already glittering coldly from the dark velvet sky. All his senses were alert for some indication that the bodies had been found, and he was ready to slip into the brush if he heard any sign of pursuit.

But time passed, and he had put four or five miles between himself and the small ville. Far enough to be reasonably safe that they weren't going to come after him.

HE HAD JUST DECIDED that it was probably safe to look for an abandoned building to sleep the night, when he caught the sound of dogs, echoing from some distance behind him.

"Fireblast!"

Nobody would be just exercising tracking hounds in the middle of the evening. The corpses had been found, and someone had decided that the murderer should be hunted down. Maybe they figured that a man responsible for a pile of bloody dead might well be carrying some kind of a price on his head.

The river glinted to his right through a thin screen of willows.

Above him the moon was glittering like a new-minted coin, giving plenty of light to pursuers.

At his best, given such a good start, Ryan would have backed himself to simply run away from whoever was trailing him. But he was still far from peak fitness, plagued by the repeated injuries to his wounded thigh.

He was already limping, ready to rest.

The ground was low and the track was winding between swampy meadows, with pools of brackish water seeping between the tussocks of coarse grass. It looked like the only thing to do was keep going on the country road and hope to find some way of cutting off it and throwing the dogs off his scent. Right now Ryan wasn't keen on blundering into the muddy waste that stretched both sides, to the river on his right, or toward the indistinct shape of a lake on the left.

Trees closed in on him on both flanks, and the trail snaked sharply left and right, making it impossible to see far ahead. Behind him the baying of the dogs was closer. Ryan knew how difficult it was to judge sound at night, but his best guess had to put the pursuit around two miles back. Call if fifteen minutes if they were moving fast.

He moved on at a sort of shambling, limping jog, wincing at the strain on his injured leg.

The bends opened out, and he was finally able to see for a good mile ahead of him, the road now running arrow straight. It was built up higher on a levee, with the swamp pressing on both sides, the river bending away a quarter mile or more to the north. There was absolutely no sign of any cover.

Ryan stopped, biting his lip, considering the possibility of plowing through the bayous to his right and then risking swimming the river. But it was the best part of a half-mile wide, and there was a fair risk that the swamps would be home to all manner of murderous creatures.

He ran on.

Ryan was within a hundred yards of the far end of the straight section of the trail when he heard a gleeful yell from behind him and the crack of a rifle. There was no sign of where the bullet went, but he was confident he was safely out of range of anything except a fluke shot with a spent round.

Feeling the sharpness of a stitch biting under his ribs, Ryan turned, doubled over, fighting for breath. He made out the dark smudge of his pursuers, the noise of the dogs flatter now, out in the open.

At best they were less than twelve hundred yards behind and closing fast. He wasn't sure, but it looked as if there were horsemen among them. Now that they had him made, there was no need to wait for the hounds. They would simply spur on and hope to ride him down within minutes.

In less than five minutes they'd be on top of him.

He turned again and stared ahead, spotting the golden glimmer of a collection of oil lamps off to the right, down a narrow spur track toward the north.

Toward the river.

There was no way of concealing his route. The few clouds that decorated the starry night were nowhere near the moon. Ryan had simply to choose between the inevitability of being caught on the main trail or chancing the side track with the strong possibility that it would finish in a dead end, offering him only the dubious hope of trying to swim the big river.

THERE WERE four or five small huts, gathered close together at the end of the narrow road, with a tumbledown jetty and some nets hanging over poles.

Ryan realized with a frisson of something close to fear that he was nearly at the end of his tether. The battering in the gorge and his time in the coma had caught up with him, and he was on the brink of exhaustion. He stared blankly across the endless expanse of the river and knew deep in his heart that he had no chance of swimming it. No chance at all.

A mongrel dog came snarling out of the nearest cabin, tail stiff, teeth bared, sidling toward him.

Behind him, no more than two or three hundred yards, there was the pounding of hooves. There'd been no more shooting, no more wasted ammunition. He figured that they knew the area better than him and were confident of being able to ride him down without any trouble.

At least he could make sure that the bastards paid a high blood price.

The dog came in so fast, low and silent, that it took Ryan by surprise, all of his attention diverted to the pursuers. He turned around to face it just as it was powering up at him, out of its attacking crouch, jaws gaping, a thread of slaver hanging silver in the moonlight.

"Fuck!" He swung a fist and caught the animal a glancing blow at the side of the muzzle, knocking it off balance, where it landed on its side in the dirt. It scrabbled to regain its feet and come in at him again.

The dog was still silent, a deep snarl muted in its throat. Ryan didn't want to disturb everyone, though the thundering hooves would rouse them quickly enough.

There was just time to draw his panga. It had suffered from the immersion in the river, and he had worked on it for hours in Paddy Maxwell's shotgun shack, polishing and wiping away the flowers of rust that marred the oily sheen of the eighteen-inch steel blade.

The brindled dog was going for his ankles this time. The honed cleaver thudded home at the base of the animal's stubby, muscular neck. There was the brief grating of the bones of the spine parting, then the blade was clear out the other side, and the dog's skull was rolling in the trampled dirt, jaws still clicking ferociously together on empty air.

The headless body hit Ryan hard below the knee, making him stagger, but he easily pushed it away, where it ran just a few hesitant, macabre, lopsided steps, then collapsed on its flank and lay still.

"You done for me dog, you outland bastard!" The man was very tall, looming out of the door of the same hut. "Come to steal our buggerin' boats, have you?"

"Boats?" Ryan suddenly saw them, pulled in tight in the shadows of the jetty, three small fishing craft with masts and sails stowed away.

The man held a long billhook and stepped out into the moonlight, waving it menacingly at the intruder. "Cut your bastard lights out for doin' that to good old Jerrylee." He suddenly was aware of horsemen, only a short distance away, shouting. "They after you... Yeah, that's it."

Ryan didn't hesitate. He drew the SIG-Sauer and shot him carefully through the exact center of the neck, the crack of the blaster almost drowned by the noise of the approaching pursuers.

He turned and fired eight spaced shots toward them, hearing at least two horses clattering to the ground. Someone screamed in shock and pain. Ryan waited a moment, hearing the rest of the riders reining in, fighting their galloping animals, cursing and yelling in total confusion.

He hobbled toward the jetty, gritting his teeth against the tiredness and pain, shooting a yelping woman through the face as she appeared around the corner of another of the huts, waving a long-handled ax at him.

"Five left," he reminded himself.

One of the boats was being repaired, its ribs stripped bare. Ryan fired three more of his precious 9 mm rounds through the bottom of the second boat, smashing holes bigger than a man's fist, seeing water bubbling in.

Now there were shots coming his way, one of them peeling off a long splinter from the jetty, inches from where he knelt. They were mainly muskets, from the sound, though there was also a more modern hunting rifle in among them.

The bloodied panga was still in his left hand, and Ryan swung it at the painter of the third of the boats, hacking clear through it in a single blow. The strong current of the river immediately began to tug the boat away from the jetty, bringing the bow toward the northern bank so fast that Ryan was taken by surprise and barely managed to throw himself clumsily aboard, jarring his shoulder and cracking the side of his head against one of the thwarts.

He fired one of his last two rounds into the darkness, where he could just see men rushing between the huts, toward the landing stage.

The boat was moving faster now, and Ryan flattened himself in the couple of inches of stinking water that swilled around the bottom boards. He could hear spasmodic shooting, and several balls thudded into the stout wooden sides of the boat. But he was floating faster now, away from the shore.

Eventually the shooting stopped, and the boat drifted on south and west.

Ryan slept.

Chapter Eight

The first pale light of the false dawn, fingering from the east, awakened him.

Ryan blinked and sat up, moaning at his stiffness. His head ached and his legs felt as though he'd run fifty miles across plowed fields with hot irons drilled through the muscles. As he moved his arm, he winced at a painful swelling in his shoulder, which he vaguely remembered had come as he'd sprawled desperately into the drifting boat.

He felt for the SIG-Sauer, drawing it from the holster, mentally reproaching himself for leaving it with only a single round left under the hammer. "Good job J.B. isn't here to see me getting so rad-blasted careless," he said to himself, carefully replacing the fourteen spent bullets.

When he reached down to the other hip for the panga, it wasn't there, and for a moment he figured he had to have left it out on the jetty. Then he found that the blade, with dark brown smears on it, was lying underneath him in the bottom of the boat. He quickly wiped it clean and resheathed it.

Only then did Ryan sit up on the seat and take note of his surroundings.

The river was even wider, its color changed, dirtier, carrying a lot of brownish mud. The land on either side was flatter, with a scattering of trees. Ryan spotted a couple of farmers, one walking behind an ox-drawn plow, the other working at laying a hedge on the flank of a large field.

Farther to the north he could see a trim farmhouse, with smoke curling from the chimney and a neat orchard to its side.

But it was what lay ahead of the boat that drew Ryan's attention.

Less than a quarter mile downstream were the beginnings of a large ville that he guessed had to be Twin Forks, where the Big White ran into the Sippi, forming one of the largest river meetings in the whole of Deathlands.

Ryan was sure that Trader had called there with the war wags several times over the years he'd ridden with him. But he could remember surprisingly little of the place. It was centered on the trade that came from the big river. The docks ran north to south, ready to cater to the endless stream of freighters and carriers. There had been a countless number of saloons and gaudies, as you'd expect for a busy ville like Twin Forks, making itself open and available, like a warm-hearted whore, to all of the travelers and merchants.

And there had been the big stern-wheelers, the paddle steamers, huge as a city block, brightly painted, going all the way down to Norleans, offering every kind of gambling and vice that a man—or a woman—could want. There had been all sorts of accommodation on board the splendid vessels, at all prices. Several of them had steam-powered calliopes built into their upper decking that would play all the popular old tunes as the great stern-wheels thrashed the river into white foam.

Ryan recalled that a couple of gunners from War Wag Two had deserted to work as sec men on one of the boats. *Delta Princess,* it had been called. The memory came back as Ryan drifted toward the edges of the ville.

Trader had trailed the boat all the way north, days out of his route, until it made a landing at Cairo, where he'd picked the two men off the boats, giving them both a good flogging and then abandoning them.

A young J. B. Dix had asked why the Trader had gone to all that trouble if he didn't want the men back.

"They go when I say, not when they say" had been the typically firm reply.

Something rattled under his feet, and Ryan realized for the first time that there was a pair of oars lying in the bottom of the vessel. He picked them up and slid them into the iron oarlocks, turning the boat around from its stern-first direction and aiming it toward the nearest of a long row of drab docks.

It was a fine morning, with the sun peering over the eastern horizon behind him. Ahead there was a three-masted schooner casting off, and a black-painted ketch was tacking away toward the west.

Despite the early hour, Twin Forks was bustling with commercial life.

KRYSTY HAD SLEPT badly that night, long dreams of slow confusion had kept her trapped in that uneasy world of half waking, unable to plunge deeper into sleep, equally unable to pull herself free from the nightmares into the real world.

Ryan had featured in some of the dreams, but he had been a stranger, walking among a crowd of other strangers. At one point Krysty had woken, dripping with a chill sweat, aware of the connotations of what she'd seen in the dream.

Her lover had been wearing a long gray raincoat, walking barefoot over cobblestones beneath a drizzling sky. He was part of a slow-moving column that trudged along, heads down, silent, some carrying bags and cases that held their few poor possessions. About a quarter of them were children. Hard-faced guards in slate gray helmets pushed them along with the muzzles of long rifles.

They walked down paths between countless huts. Beyond the buildings were the tall watchtowers, linked by high strands of coiled razor wire. Now the head of the column had reached double steel doors that opened into an underground bunker. Krysty was standing at the side, near the blank-faced Ryan, and she could see inside, see the rows of chrome showerheads and the sluices and drains.

Flakes of something that resembled black snow were falling all over the camp, landing on the thin covering of snow. Krysty had rubbed at them as they brushed her clothes, and they had smudged and smeared, leaving a filthy trail on the material.

She had tried to stop Ryan going in, but it hadn't been like a conventional nightmare. No screaming and shouting. It had been very quiet. Ryan kept vanishing into the crowd, then reappearing, but he kept his eye turned away from her entreaties, ignoring her whispered warning.

Finally she had seen only the back of his head as he vanished between the heavy double doors that closed behind him. It began to snow, white and black flakes mingling together.

Now she stood by the window of her room, forehead pressed against the cold glass.

There had been a mist on the river, wrapping itself around the shadowy buildings of the docks, shrouding the upper spars of the big sailing ships that waited to load or unload their cargoes.

It was barely dawn, and Krysty watched a black-painted ketch as it tacked across from east to west.

There was a quiet knock on the door of her room.

"Yeah? Come in."

"Greetings and salutations, my dear child," Doc said, walking to embrace her. "Mayhap this is to be the day when we shall receive some news of our lost companion."

"Be good to hear," she agreed. "Looks like it's going to be a fine day."

Doc stared out of the window, watching as a large three-master was warped away from the bustling quay, its crew scurrying around the deck to raise the sails and bring her out into the main current. The rising sun caught the gilt around the figurehead of a well-endowed blond woman in a blue helmet, gripping a yellow trident. The captain stood foursquare on the quarterdeck, shouting instructions through a brass trumpet.

"Wonder where she's going and what she's carrying?" Krysty said.

"Perhaps outward-bound across the bar... for Nineveh or for distant Ophir. Sandalwood, or a cargo of cheap tin trays. Who can say?"

Krysty eased the window open a few inches, and they could hear the flapping of the canvas and the shrill cries of the men as they scampered up the ratlines and out along the yards. From the decks there was the thin whistling of a bosun's pipe and the hoarse yell of officers on the bridge by the wheel and up on the beaked fo'c'sle.

"One day I'd like to sail away from Deathlands," Krysty said. "I know so little about what's happened in the rest of the world over the last hundred years."

Doc sniffed and wiped his nose with his swallow's-eye kerchief. "I suspect that I might have caught myself a small cold," he muttered. "Rest of the world, child? When I was an unwilling guest of the whitecoats, I learned something of the rest of the planet. Simply put, it suffered more or less equally all around the Earth. Europe and Asia and Russia and even far-off Terra Australis Incognito... nuclear destruction followed by the long winters. Followed by anarchy and mutations and a gradual return to a society similar to that of the Middle Ages." He shook his head sadly. "I fear that the entire world has become Deathlands, my dear. The grass is most certainly no greener on the far side of the hill. Regrettably not."

"Everywhere the same, Doc?"

He nodded. "Yes. I believe so."

"Still like to sail away one day. Ryan and me talked about it quite a few—" she stopped as her voice choked, and a single tear glistened on her cheek.

Doc put his arm around her. "Be of good cheer, my dear, and play the brave-heart. Hope dies only after the last breath has been breathed . . . the final chapter written . . . the end credits rolled . . . and the fat lady has sung. I have never met a man of the ilk of Ryan Cawdor and probably never will again. He is a titan among giants. If any man can survive, then it is Ryan. Let your hope still spring, Krysty Wroth."

"Thanks, Doc." She looked down again at the river and the growing activity on the dockside. "Love watching it all going on," she said.

"Have you noticed that magnificent building over yonder?" Doc pointed with his swordstick a little way downstream, virtually on the spit of land that jutted out between the White and the Sippi. "A baron of some wealth must have built it. That round tower . . . the view must be truly marvelous."

"Guess you can see the whole ville from there." Krysty shaded her eyes with her hand. "Caught a glint of the rising sun off glass. Think there's someone there with a telescope or binoculars. Great place to spy from."

Doc nodded, looking the other way upstream on the White. "There is a sturdy soul taking some early exercise in that small rowing boat. I wonder how far he has traveled this morning. The fellow looks a little fatigued."

Krysty looked casually down.

She looked away, not much interested in the dawn oarsman, who was splashing his way wearily toward the docks almost immediately below the rooming house.

Then she looked back at him.

"Doc..."

The old man had noticed flecks of mud on his worn knee boots and had knelt to wipe them clean. "What is it, my dear?"

He glanced up and found to his considerable surprise that he was alone in the room. The door was still swinging open, and he could hear feet running down the passage outside.

THE REUNION WAS WATCHED with great eagerness by two men in the round tower that Doc and Krysty had noticed a few minutes earlier. One held the focusing knob on a large and costly telescope, his eye pressed to the cold metal. The other stared intently through a large pair of German predark binoculars, fixed on a tripod for easier viewing.

They had been waiting hopefully for this moment for several days, since their spies brought them news of the arrival in Twin Forks of Krysty Wroth, J. B. Dix and the others. They'd been waiting for news of Ryan Cawdor.

They had an interest in Ryan from way back.

The immensely fat man using the telescope was Gert Wolfram. His colleague, skeletally thin, was known by many names, the most common being "the Magus."

Chapter Nine

Krysty almost exploded through the front door of the Grits and Greetings, turning left, her boots slipping on the dew-wet flags of the sidewalk. She recovered her balance and cut through a narrow alley and onto the dockside.

The oarsman had moored his little boat and climbed up the flight of stone stairs onto the quay, his head emerging into sight just as Krysty appeared.

He saw her immediately, standing still, hands at his sides, a broad grin slowly spreading across his face.

She ran at him, slowing at the last moment, and threw herself into his arms. Ryan was still some way from being his old self, and he staggered backward, fighting for balance, narrowly avoiding going over and taking them both into the water.

Aware that everyone on the docks was watching them, Krysty contented herself with a single slow, lingering kiss, her tongue darting between his lips. She hugged him, feeling the loss of muscle tone as her arms clasped him tight.

She eased herself down, feet back on the cobbles. "Hello, lover."

They stood a yard apart, smiling and nodding at each other, neither able to believe the wonder of the moment.

"So..." Krysty bit her lip to hold back the tears. "You made it."

"Looks like I did. Yeah. Times I didn't think I was going to come through."

"You look tired. All right, but tired."

"Just rowed half the White to get here. This is Twin Forks, isn't it?"

"Sure is. Prettiest little pesthole on the frontier. You name it, and they got it. Or if they haven't got it, then they'll sure get it."

Ryan nodded. "Been here years ago. Is everyone here? All of them all right?"

Krysty reached out and squeezed his hand. "All here. J.B. and Jak have jobs as sec men at a gaudy saloon called the Montana Queen. Had to get some jack to pay for our rooms at the rooming house. Been here close on a week."

"You saw me go over?"

"Yeah. Taking the bitch with you."

"More like her taking me with her. Railing broke, and over we went."

Krysty held up a hand. "Look, don't tell me now. Only have to go through it again when we're with everyone else. Let's go get the others, and we can eat."

"You mean food?"

"Sure."

He smiled. "Real food. Real, real food?"

"Promise. Hash joint around the corner called Toby's does the best all-day breakfast in the ville."

At that moment Doc appeared around the corner of the alley. His sight was notoriously poor, but he'd watched through the window of the bedroom and eventually been rewarded by seeing Krysty's mane of fiery hair, had seen her throw herself into the arms of the tall stranger who'd been rowing the boat, and realized. He awakened the others, then made his best speed down to join the couple.

"My dear, dear fellow," he kept repeating, wiping away tears. "So good. We all prayed and we never lost hope. Always said that you would rise again like the phoenix from the flames, though, of course, it was a river and not fire that engulfed you. Oh, my dear, dear fellow!"

The three friends linked arms and made their way back to the Grits and Greetings, and from there to Toby's eatery, where they stayed for all of the morning.

RYAN HADN'T REALIZED just how hungry he was until he saw the steaming platters of food brought in from the kitchens by the stout owner of Toby's.

The menu was chalked on a board on the wall, and he'd read it, feeling his mouth filling with saliva at the thought of eating properly again.

"Decided?" Toby had asked him. The others had already picked out what they wanted.

Ryan had nodded. "Sure. The lot."

"Everything?"

"Everything. Then after that I might just go through the menu again."

There was a goblet of orange juice to start, with a bowl of fresh fruit and cream, followed by three eggs, over-easy, with slices of smoked ham, link sausages and rashers of lean bacon; deliciously tender breasts of pigeon in gravy—one of the specialities of the place—with both whipped potatoes and hash browns; a pot of refried beans, with a dish of mixed chilies, and a side salad with a bittersweet cheese dressing. The whole thing was served with corn bread hot from the bakery.

Despite his boast of coming back for seconds, Ryan struggled to finish the meal, finding that his appetite had outrun his stomach. In the end he had to leave one of the pigeon breasts and some of the potato.

But by the time he'd washed the food down with a couple of mugs of passable coffee sub, he was ready to tackle a few slices of whole-wheat toast and a variety of homemade conserves.

The meal was mostly eaten in silence, prompting Doc to give a barking laugh as Ryan sipped at his third mug of coffee sub. "That is the sad thing about modern Deathlands. Food is killing the art of conversation."

DURING THE LONG MORNING and through into lunch, the tales were told on both sides.

Ryan spoke of the days and nights of deep coma, waking to find himself in the filthy hut of Paddy Maxwell, and the adventures during the next few days, then the trip toward Twin Forks and its tragic conclusion for Ryan's rescuer.

Krysty told of their search and the encounter with the stickies. "Seems that slaving's going on around here, using the muties."

Ryan leaned back in his chair, nodding. "Brings back memories of Wolfram and the Magus, doesn't it?"

J.B. nodded. "Names from the past . . ."

"Is bad blood between you and them?" Jak asked, nibbling on a blueberry muffin, which he said was essential to carry him through until lunch, even though Toby had promised the meal within the hour.

The Armorer answered. "Goes back to Trader." He took off his glasses and polished them on his napkin. "Bad blood? Could call it that, Ryan?"

"I don't much like picking at old wounds. Just say that things that Trader and J.B. and me did harmed both Wolfram and the Magus. Harmed them badly. Have you actually heard that they're involved in slaving?"

Mildred leaned forward across the loaded table. "Haven't heard anything about who might be behind it. But are you just going to leave it at that? Not tell us the whole story?"

She turned to J.B. "Come on, John . . ."

Ryan shook his head. "One day, mebbe. Not now. I want to hear about the Montana Queen."

He spoke to Jak and the Armorer. "Good to see you've both got an honest job for once."

By the time everyone was up-to-date with what had happened and was happening, it was time to set out clean cutlery and glasses and bring in the lunch.

"You got any of that bubbly wine?" Krysty asked.

"We have some of the finest champagne in this or any other ville," Toby replied, beaming, wiping his hands on his apron. "You would like a bottle?"

"Yeah. I reckon we've got something to celebrate, don't you, folks?"

Toby carefully unwrapped the wire and eased out the cork, letting it go with a soft popping sound, the wine foaming into the crystal flutes that he'd brought out specially.

"Absent friends recovered," Krysty said, raising her glass, chinking it against Ryan's and against the others.

"I'll drink to that toast." Doc sipped at the wine. "Not quite Moët & Chandon, but perfectly adequate. Can we afford this luxury?"

J.B. patted his jacket. "Got a jack bonus last night from Dolores Stanwyck. Some miners in late figured that they were entitled to some freebies with the girls. Had to convince them otherwise. Managed it without breaking any bones."

In the end they had two more bottles of wine with the meal. An unusual treat for all of them. One was a *grenache* from the islands of California, with a delicious pink color. The other a tart chardonnay from Oregon.

Even Doc, who fancied himself as something of a connoisseur of wine, sat there licking his lips and admitted that they were both excellent.

The quality of the food was a lot better than adequate, though with some of the dishes it seemed as though Toby had been a little bit ambitious.

Ryan chose a fish main course, rainbow trout, grilled off the bone and served in a pastry shell stuffed with a creamy sauce and crayfish. Krysty picked the quail, roasted and brought to the table with a rich sauce of cream and brandy. Mildred fancied the lasagna, which came in a large earthenware pot, though she found the meat was a little fatty for her taste. J.B. spent ages pondering the menu before finally picking the same main dish as Ryan. Jak went for some underdone veal, served with a fried egg on top and an extra side order of fries. Doc also spent an eternity trawling through the long list of dishes, reading out some of them aloud, head on one side, pondering his selection.

"Squab? I confess that I have never taken to the name. Too abrupt to be tasty. Turkey and cranberry sauce. I think that I am not in the Thanksgiving vein today. Salmon served with pasta and a bean sauce. A trifle heavy, perhaps. Specially as I may select the heavy trifle for dessert. Red mullet from the Gulf, with a prawn and octopus ink sauce. Too black by half."

"Doc," Ryan said, "I'm getting dust on my shoulders, and my stomach's in overdrive. A spider's weaved its web between my knife and fork. Speed it up, will you?"

"My dear fellow...of course."

He turned to the patiently waiting Toby. "I shall essay the lobster with..."

"Real sorry. Lobster's off today. Never got the fresh delivery."

Groans erupted all around the table.

Doc smiled, showing his perfect set of white teeth. "Worry not, cupbearer. Then I shall choose the roast beef, well-done and sliced wafer thin, cosseted by the chef for my dining pleasure, having been fed on lush meadow grass."

The main courses all came with a selection of vegetables. Boiled potatoes, a little undercooked and served without any salt or butter. Carrots and broccoli with sliced beans, and a large side salad that was heavy on wilted lettuce.

But it was still a great meal by Deathlands's standards, and they all cleaned their plates. Mildred, Krysty and J.B. passed on the creaking dessert trolley that Toby wheeled proudly up to show them.

Jak, Ryan and Doc didn't.

"Those chocolate balls with cream," Jak said, watching the serving of the profiteroles with great attention. "More than that. Better."

Ryan pointed at some round dishes with a kind of crust on top. "What's that?"

"Lemon *brûlée*. A sorbet of lemons covered in brown sugar that's baked quickly under a very hot grill."

"I'll have that."

Doc nodded. "I believe that I shall join you in that selection. I remember sampling a similar delicious in Del Greco's on Fifth Avenue at an anniversary meal with my dear Emily. I trust this lives up to my memory."

Ryan wasn't a great gourmet, partly because there were precious few opportunities in Deathlands to sample quality food. But he actually sighed out loud at the first mouthful. His spoon broke through the baked crust of molten sugar, into the ice-cold lemon sorbet beneath. It was a truly exquisite combination of hot and cold, of sweet and bitter.

"Fireblast! But that's good."

Doc leaned back, eyes closed, savoring the taste sensation. "By the Three Kennedys! It is perfection. Every bit as delicious as my memory of the dish."

In the end they had to order another round so that everyone could sample it.

After they'd settled the check, using up all of Jak and the Armorer's bonus and then some, they staggered out, well stuffed, onto the quay, blinking in the bright afternoon sunshine.

"That was a meal and a half," Ryan said. "Reckon I've put back every ounce I lost during my time with Paddy."

Jak leaned on an old iron fence that protected the edge of the dock, his red eyes scanning the port. He turned his head, the gentle breeze tugging at his mane of snowy hair, and froze suddenly, staring across the river.

Ryan caught the movement. "What?" he asked.

"Flash of reflected light. Sun off glass. Round tower at top big house. Don't all look! Watching us."

Ryan glanced sideways, seeing the jagged spear of silver from the room. It flickered and vanished, showing that the glass had moved.

"We saw someone watching from there earlier. Just before you arrived, lover. Remember, Doc?"

"Indeed, yes. We thought we could make out a figure . . . or two . . . up there."

"Room's empty now," Krysty said. "Whoever it was up there's gone."

Ryan sniffed. "Wonder who in Twin Forks is interested in us? And why?"

J.B. turned away. "Most likely it's just some lonely old lady with nothing better to do. Forget it. I could use a kind of lie-in for an hour, to get over that meal. Anyone else coming back to the rooming house for a spell?"

Ryan nodded. "Why not." He watched as one of the stern-wheelers approached them from the north, its steam whistle blowing, calliope tooting out a merry polka. "Wouldn't mind a trip on one of those beauties," he said.

WITH SURPRISING AGILITY for such an enormously fat man, Gert Wolfram descended the spiral staircase from the tower room, the Magus picking his way delicately after him.

"I have lost count of the number of times that our paths have crossed," Wolfram said.

The Magus laughed, a thin, humorless, metallic sound that echoed up the staircase. "And now this will be the last."

Chapter Ten

"Jack's almost gone," J.B. said, sitting on the end of the bed shared by Ryan and Krysty.

"Guess we have to work out what we're going to do next." Ryan rubbed sleep from his eye. "Slept so radblasted well last night. Best night for an age."

"We staying or moving?" Krysty asked, the sheet pulled up to her shoulders, covering her nakedness.

"Only been in the ville a day," Ryan yawned. "Like to look around for a day or so."

"Take a trip on one of the stern-wheelers, like you said? I heard the biggest and wildest of them, the *Golden Eagle,* is due in tomorrow. Day to turn around. She goes back up the Sippi the next dawning." Krysty ran her fingers through her hair, producing electrical sparks. "Goes up as far as Crosstown, Wisconsin. Way north."

"Near the Lakes?" Ryan scratched his chin, feeling the heavy stubble. "Got to shave," he muttered.

"How about the boat?"

He looked at Krysty. "Yeah. Why not? But we'll need plenty of jack for that."

Jak knocked on the door and stuck his head into the room. "Don't forget Dolores wants us in noon. Meeting merchants in ville. What call it? Convention. That's name. From all over. Coming to saloon lunch and girls. Reckons they could get out hand.''

Ryan sucked at his teeth thoughtfully. ''Gang of merchants in town. Trouble in saloon. Bound to be jack-heavy, fat bastards like that.''

J.B. grinned, pushing back the brim of his fedora. ''You thinking what I'm thinking, bro?''

''Could just be.''

Krysty sighed. ''Stealing!''

Ryan patted her on the arm. ''Be a real hot pipe, as Dean would say. These guys come in with their swollen bellies and loaded wallets. Leave their little wives behind while they get drunk or drugged and lay every gaudy slut they can find. Sort of people it'll be a pleasure to relieve of some of their surplus jack.''

He turned to J.B. ''I'll come and meet this Dolores and recce out the saloon. Noon, you said, Jak?''

''Yeah. She said that had to be tactful. Not like usually with riverboat crew and trappers.''

Ryan laughed. ''Tactful! She wants you and J.B. to be tactful. Does that mean warning them politely before you slit their throats open from ear to ear?''

The Armorer looked offended, drawing himself to his full five feet eight inches. ''Dark night, Ryan! I can be just as tactful as the next man. Even more so.''

''Sure, sure. Main thing is that we get a plan together for... Come in.''

There was another knock on the door, and in came Mildred, followed by Doc, the old man looking spruce with a carnation in his buttonhole.

''Lovely day,'' he boomed. ''Sun's roasting out your eyeballs, Master Cawdor and Mistress Wroth.

Even the laggard Dr. Wyeth here has been up and broken her fast before you."

"Been planning, Doc," Ryan said, "and I still haven't recharged all of my sleep batteries yet."

"Planning," Krysty echoed disgustedly. "You should know this, both of you, because he's bound to suck you into his 'planning' at some stage."

"Any plan of the dear boy's is going to be hunky-dory with me," Doc said. "He has only to ask."

"We're going to rob some of the merchants visiting the ville for their convention."

"What?" Doc frowned.

Krysty laughed at the shocked expression on his face. "It's true, Doc. Thought you said any plan of Ryan's was all right with you."

"Why?" Mildred asked. "Why do we need so much jack? Aren't we leaving to get back to the redoubt and the gateway?"

"Not yet." Krysty looked at Ryan at her side. "He wants to take a trip on a riverboat."

"Stealing. Upon my soul!" Doc looked at Ryan, sitting in the bed. "I confess to some doubts about this, old friend. 'Thou shalt not steal' is what the Good Book says. Then again, it says something about not killing, and we break that commandment often enough, almost on a daily basis."

"Not talking about chilling, Doc. These guys'll have too much jack, and we won't have enough. Just sort of restoring the balance a little."

"What an equivocator, Ryan. You would have made an excellent attorney, my dear friend. Truly you would."

Ryan laughed. "Sounds like being a terminator, Doc. Can't argue with you if that's what it means."

Doc shook his head. "Not quite, old friend. I cannot in truth say that I lend my approval to this proposed act of grand larceny." He lowered his head to sniff at the flower. "So delicate. What was I saying? About the stealing. I confess that in my youth I always wanted to pass a little time on one of those magical vessels that plied the Mississippi. The tales of Mark Twain inspired such an interest."

"So we're going for it?" Ryan asked. Nobody spoke and he laughed. "Well, you don't disagree. Then you can all get out so we can dress and launch the day on the road."

RYAN HAD MET WOMEN like Dolores Stanwyck before, often running places like the Montana Queen. His guess was that she'd likely started as a low-grade gaudy slut, and used her native wit and intelligence to better herself, built up a store of jack and used it wisely, investing in property. Gaudies and saloons.

Now she was set up in Twin Forks like a queen herself, looking thoroughly respectable in a long black dress, fringed with white lace at collar and cuffs. A single strand of pearls circled her throat. A wide smile of welcome was on her powdered cheeks, Sierra ice in her blue eyes. She sat alone at a table with a shot glass of whiskey at her elbow.

"Good to meet a friend of John and Jak," she said, giving him a firm shake of the hand, measuring him with a direct stare. "You want work, Ryan?"

"I don't reckon, but thanks for the offer. We're planning taking a trip to Crosstown on the *Golden Eagle.*"

"Need plenty of jack."

"We got it. Partly what John and Jak have earned from you. Mostly what we had saved."

She finally let go of his hand. "Heard you made a hole in your savings at Toby's last night."

Ryan laughed. "Guess you hear anything that moves in Twin Forks."

"Guess I do." She turned to Jak and J.B. "You boys in at noon today? Might need you for these stupe merchants. Kind can give you real trouble when they've sniffed the cork and glimpsed some of my girls."

The two men both nodded. J.B. answered, "We'll be there, Miss Stanwyck."

"Good. See you around, Ryan."

DOLORES WATCHED the outlanders leave her saloon and sighed, aware that a thin film of perspiration covered her body and her pulse was racing.

Around 4:00 a.m. the previous morning, when she'd been fast asleep in her locked and barred apartment above the Montana Queen, which was also sec locked, she had been awakened by two shadowy figures standing by her four-poster.

Intruders were a constant menace, as she kept the saloon's jack locked in a huge wall safe in her room, and she had always carried a blaster tucked snugly beneath her pillow.

It was a compact Smith & Wesson Model 669, holding twelve rounds of 9 mm parabellum ammunition. It was a short-recoil weapon with double-action trigger and an inertia firing pin. The slightly unusual feature was the serrated recurved trigger-guard bow.

Dolores had fumbled for it, trying to lie still, faking sleep, feeling her heart pounding.

Her fingers touched the cold metal of the butt, and she started to withdraw it. To her surprise, the figures still hadn't moved. One stood close to the window and one at the foot of her bed. As far as she could make out in the filtered moonlight, neither was carrying a blaster.

"Please God..." she said under her breath, closing her hand on the Smith & Wesson, finger going for the trigger. She always kept one round under the hammer, despite the risk of an accidental misfire, and she knew that the safety was off.

Dolores powered herself upright, finger tight on the trigger, keeping the barrel of the powerful blaster moving between the two figures. "One breath and you're fuckin' history," she said firmly.

For a few moments nothing happened.

Then the tall figure by the window laughed, a frightening sound because it brimmed with confidence. He was looking down the barrel of a 9 mm automatic and he could laugh like that. "Pull the trigger, lady," he said in a sinister, whispery voice.

"I can shout for my sec men."

"Do it."

"You'll get chilled."

Now it was the much bulkier man at the bottom of her bed who spoke. From his silhouette he was incredibly fat, something over three hundred pounds, and he had a voice to match. Soft yet intense, like a stiletto slicing through honey.

"You have no sec men on the premises. One patrolled outside and one slept in the back, on two-hour shifts."

Dolores noted the use of the past tense. "What's happened to them?"

"Both sleeping," the fat man said. There was no need for him to elaborate.

Dolores wasn't frightened to use violence. It went with the job. And if she'd carved notches on her blaster for every man and woman she'd killed, there would have been eight or nine of them.

It seemed that she held the best cards, but in her heart a part of her knew that something was wrong. But she couldn't work out what it was.

"I'll take you both out," she warned.

The fat man seemed to suddenly lose patience. "Enough," he snapped, starting to waddle toward her. "We've come to talk to you about some visitors in the ville. Things we need to know. Things you can do to help. When you've told us what we need to hear, then we'll go away. Leave you alive. More useful to us. But if you were to reveal to anyone that we've been here..."

"Particularly to these outlanders..." the skinny intruder added.

"Then we shall return and we will hurt you horrible so that your own mother would weep to see what an ugly corpse you've made. You see how easy it is to reach you, past all the bolts and bars and locks.''

Dolores was terrified. In panic she tugged on the trigger and heard the dry click of the hammer striking an empty chamber.

She repeated the action, again and again, then started to weep.

The fat man found all of this tedious. ''I said it was enough. Can you not even tell by its weight that your precious blaster is empty?''

Then she knew. She placed the automatic on her coverlet, lying back, hands up in front of her face to protect herself from the expected attack.

He loomed over her, smelling of a mixture of perspiration and scented lotion, his huge hands poised.

''Just talk,'' he said. ''Talk about Ryan Cawdor.''

Chapter Eleven

The Allied Merchants' Federation of Deathlands had come from far and wide for its annual three-day convention in Twin Forks.

Because of its site at the confluence of the Big White and the Sippi, most had come by river, while others had come along the dusty coach roads. It seemed to Ryan that all of them were cast from the same mold: middle-aged, white, overweight, in suits that were a little too tight across the stomach, carrying leather cases and wearing large badges that proclaimed their names and firms and where they came from.

And all of them had eager, sweating smiles pasted on their highly colored faces.

They reminded Ryan of an assortment of pigs disguised in human clothes.

Dolores Stanwyck's concern was well based.

Ryan had gone along to sit quietly in a shadowy corner of the Montana Queen, minding his own business, eating a bowl of chili and sipping at a schooner of beer. He watched as the delegates to the convention set to enjoying themselves, which involved drinking too much too fast, insulting the barkeeps, puking in the sawdust, upsetting the regulars and harassing the hardworking girls, all in between complaining about the high prices and poor quality of everything from the ten-minute rooms to the imported liquors.

Dolores herself was doing what she could to keep the atmosphere pleasant. She wore a low-cut brocade dress and her highest heels, keeping a smile in place despite all the aggravation, circulating through the bar, offering a free drink here and there to keep a particularly noisy group sweet. She constantly turned her head to spot trouble brewing, making sure that her bouncers, including Jak and J.B., were on their toes and in the right place at the right time.

There had been several minor scuffles, with a hideaway pistol drawn in one of them. But the sec force kept the lid on it, taking away the blaster, unfired, from the staggering-drunk merchant without triggering more trouble.

One incident happened right by Ryan's table, handled by J.B. and Jak.

Five of the conventioneers had been trying to persuade two of the older gaudy sluts to go upstairs with them and give them a special discount.

"Five of you want fucking, then you pay the fucking price for five," said the taller of the whores, a Mex-looking woman with olive skin and cascading black hair.

"I give a good discount in my store up in Oregon," said one of them.

"That's fine, but we don't here in the Montana Queen. Check it out with Miss Stanwyck."

The man, whose badge proclaimed that he was Jerry Ettinger, laughed loudly and unpleasantly. "Suppose we just take you out back, and that way you give us a hundred percent off the price.''

Suddenly, unnoticed, Jak and J.B. appeared at the merchants' table.

"Having trouble, Maria?" the Armorer asked.

"Yeah. These gentlemen—" she invested the word with contempt and loathing "—say they're going to drag us both out back and rape us.''

Aware of the sec men, the merchant changed his tune a little, falling back on fake jolliness. "Hey, boys, we was just having some sporting with the hookers. They kind of got the wrong end of the handle.''

"That so?" J.B. said quietly. "Then best let them go about their business, and you stick to enjoying the rest of the pleasures of the Montana Queen.''

One of the other men at the table, even fatter, whose name badge had fallen off, was struggling to focus his rolling, poached-egg eyes on Jak. "Hey, this snow-head son bitch's some kind of mutie freak," he eventually pronounced. "We don't take no shit from mutie freaks.''

Ryan smiled grimly, watching as the white-haired teenager made his move.

His hand darted to the small of his back, coming out with the glimmer of polished, razored steel. The needle point of the throwing knife was pressed against the merchant's throat, shutting his mouth like a trap.

"Not freak. Not mutie," Jak gritted, pushing the blade hard enough to draw a trickle of blood down the sweating neck. "No more talk. Just drink. Quietly. Understand?" A jerk of the knife punctuated his words. "Understand?"

"You're killing him," the original speaker gasped. "Leave him be. We made a mistake and we're real sorry. Leave us be."

Jak's knife vanished again into its concealed sheath. The man swallowed hard, fumbling for a kerchief to mop away the streak of crimson, staring at it with wide eyes as though he'd never seen blood before.

Ryan sipped at his beer, checking his wrist chron. It would be close on an hour before they activated their plan.

TWIN FORKS CONTAINED a number of main streets, linked with a maze of alleys. The Montana Queen had a row of three outhouses that stood in a dark courtyard, opening onto one of the narrow lanes. Even at midday it was a gloomy place, ill lit and noisesome.

Ryan had been waiting out there for four or five minutes, standing patiently behind an untidy pile of empty ale casks. To anyone coming from the bright oil lamps of the saloon, he was completely invisible.

Doc was in the alley with Krysty and Mildred as backup, if it was needed. J.B. and Jak would remain in the saloon, drawing attention to themselves so that there was no danger of their being implicated in the robbery.

It was Ryan's plan, and he was ready to activate it.

He'd borrowed Doc's swallow's-eye kerchief and knotted it around his lower face to help muffle and disguise his voice. A balaclava, bought from a busy maritime-supply store, was pulled down over his head, concealing the missing eye.

Normally the outhouses were busy, but nobody had come out for several minutes. Doc appeared in the entrance, calling to Ryan in a loud, piercing whisper.

"Is all well, my dear fellow?"

"Yeah. Get back outside. Call you if I need any help."

"Just that several minutes have drifted by and—"

"Nobody's come out. Get on back and keep quiet."

"Of course, of course. Leaving right away, old friend. Right away."

The rear door of the Montana Queen swung open, letting out a rectangle of golden light across the cobbles of the yard, then clattered shut.

Ryan drew the SIG-Sauer and peered into the blackness, making out a man alone, walking unsteadily toward the nearest of the outhouses, going inside and trying to tug across the bolt. He cursed under his breath when it wouldn't shut properly. That wasn't surprising, since Ryan had levered it loose with the tip of his panga only a half hour before.

The steel tips on Ryan's combat boots breathed across the damp cobbles. Though the sun was at its height, very little light filtered through into the yard between the steep walls of the surrounding buildings.

The merchant in the outhouse was whistling to himself as he went about his business. Ryan glanced around, making sure nobody else was leaving the Montana Queen, then took the rusting handle of the door in his left hand and tugged it sharply open.

"Someone in here!" the man snapped out angrily. "Close the door, will you?"

Ryan wrinkled his nose at the foul smell coming from inside, then stepped in closer, half shutting the door behind him, pressing the barrel of the SIG-Sauer against the chubby man's cheek hard enough for the foresight to break the skin and draw a warm thread of blood.

"What the—?"

"Quiet." Ryan adopted a harsh voice, giving it a bayou twang. "Just gimme your jack and you live."

"You can't—"

"One more word and you go headfirst into the shit with a bullet in your brain. Gimme now." He pushed harder, making the merchant yelp in pain and fear.

"Sure, sure... Just move the blaster out of my face, will you, mister?"

Ryan eased the pressure a little, bracing himself against the door. Behind him he heard feet moving across the yard, someone going into the next outhouse along. His victim also heard it and stiffened, holding his breath.

Ryan leaned forward until his mouth was only inches from the merchant's ear. "Just a word and you die. Also means he'll die, as well. All for nothing. Just get out the jack."

"I got an idea, mister."

"What?"

"I'm Todd Keillor. Come from Lubbock in Texas."

Ryan knew his predark rock and roll. "Buddy's birthplace," he said.

"Wouldn't know him, I'm afraid."

"You got an idea?"

Next door the man had only stopped for a noisy piss, sounding like a stallion staling into a deep pool. The door slammed shut, and the footsteps faded away back into the Montana Queen.

"Your idea?" Ryan repeated.

Some of the terror had faded away, though the voice was still shaky. Now there was a trading note in it, the hope of doing a deal.

"I got some jack on me, but some of those good guys in there are loaded. And I mean loaded."

"So?"

"I mean, there's a dry-goods man from Topeka, Big Nate Newcomb, carrying a wad of jack big enough to sink the *Golden Eagle*. Says he's goin' to blow it all on sluts."

Ryan was becoming impatient. It was only a matter of time before a group of merchants decided to come out to take a leak together. And they would want to use all of the outhouses at the same time. "So what?"

Eagerly now, glimpsing light in his horrific darkness, Todd Keillor spilled his words over one another. "Let me go back and I can tell him—I mean not tell him about you—someone wants to see him out here. One of us conventioneers like, and then he'll come out and you can take him and you'll get more jack than I got. A lot more. Lot more, mister. How about that for an idea? Good one, huh?"

Ryan shook his head. "Friend of mine from way back had a saying. Blaster in your hand's worth a whole armory locked away in the ville. Give me what you got and don't hold back."

"Oh, but—" He squeaked in alarm, making no move to remove his billfold.

Ryan clipped him across the cheek with the SIG-Sauer, hard enough to knock him sideways on the seat of the john.

"Jack," Ryan said.

"All right, mister. No call for that." He reached out in the stinking darkness, pushing a thick roll of jack into Ryan's left hand. Without seeing it, he knew that it was a sizable pile, enough for their plans to ride the stern-wheeler.

He stuffed it into his coat pocket, keeping the blaster steady on Todd Keillor's chest. "Good move," he said. "Means you get to stay alive to enjoy the convention."

"You won't chill me?"

"No."

"Won't hurt me?"

"Ah, can't promise that." Ryan reversed the automatic and clubbed the man with a short, powerful blow, hitting him above and a little behind the right ear. The merchant gave a small sigh of surprise and slumped forward. Ryan steadied him on the seat, leaning him back so that a casual glance would make it seem as if he had fallen asleep while doing his business.

Ryan backed away from the outhouse, pushing the door closed, walking quickly across the yard into the alley, where he collected Doc, Krysty and Mildred.

"All right, lover?"

He nodded at her. "Fine. Go and get our tickets when the boat docks tomorrow." He pulled off the

balaclava and unknotted the kerchief, giving it back to
Doc. "Let's move."

J.B. AND JAK RETURNED to the Grits and Greetings
boardinghouse for their supper break at about seven.
Ryan and the others were waiting for them to learn
what had happened back at the Montana Queen.

The Armorer grinned, throwing his fedora on the
bed, removing his glasses to start polishing them.
"Got lucky, friends. Four of the good merchants got
themselves mugged during the day. Two on the upstairs landing and two out back in the courtyard.
Sounded to me like the masked man who pistol-
whipped the fat bastard could have been you, Ryan.
Hope you weren't the one with the razor. Chilled his
man."

"I laid him out. Todd Keillor from Texas. Guess
he's got a headache, but he should live. He tried to
betray one of his friends he said had more jack than
he did. But he had enough."

Jak laughed. "So we're going up Sippi. Looking
forward. Could be real exciting."

Ryan nodded. "Yeah. Sure could."

Chapter Twelve

Jak and J.B. went to the Montana Queen after an early
breakfast to tell Dolores that they were quitting. With
nothing else to do, Ryan went along with them.

First thing he noticed was that the woman seemed
edgy, not wanting to look him in the eye.

"Sorry to lose you guys. Lent some steel and muscle in here. Handled yesterday well."

"Shame about the deaths," Ryan said.

She laughed nervously. "Happens. Law in Twin
Forks couldn't punch their way out of a wet paper
bag. You get a serious problem and you have to deal
with it yourself, best way you can. And that doesn't
always mean doing the right thing. Just the safest
thing. Way of living."

Ryan nodded. "Way of the world. Same in most
places in Deathlands."

"You're going to take a trip upriver on the *Golden
Eagle*? to Crosstown?"

J.B. answered her. "Yeah. Something we've all
fancied, one time or another. They say the *Eagle* flies
higher than the other stern-wheelers."

Dolores was idly shuffling a pack of cards while she
spoke, but she stopped and looked directly at the Armorer. "Flies high... Sure does. But..." She hesi-

tated a long moment. "But it's a rare trip that bodies don't go over the side."

Ryan felt the short hairs prickling at his nape. Over the years of surviving on the knife-edge, he'd learned to listen for the unspoken thoughts that lay behind the spoken words. There was something going on with Dolores Stanwyck.

"You think we shouldn't go?"

He watched her hands. For a moment they froze, and her knuckles whitened. Then she took a deep breath and carried on shuffling and cutting the deck, her gaze back on the table. "No. Not my business what you do."

"You got something more to say, Dolores?" he asked, pressing her, leaning over, hands on the green baize. "Best you tell us if you know something. Or it might go hard with you when we come back and find you lied to us."

"Hey, mister, just back off." Her angry reaction made Ryan realize two things: that he was right in having a suspicion, and that he'd played it wrong by trying to pressure her.

Jak looked at him, obviously surprised by the turn events had taken. "Ryan?"

"It's all right. Just got a feeling. See I was wrong. Sorry, Dolores."

She was flushed, blinking fast, looking past him to a trio of her girls who were laughing at a private joke over by the bar. "All right, Ryan. Don't like being accused of something I haven't done. And I've done nothing."

"Sure, sure." He turned away. "Mebbe we'll call in and see you on the way home again." He made sure that she heard the threat in his voice.

"WHAT THAT ABOUT?" Jak asked as they walked back toward the boardinghouse, where the others were waiting for them. "Picked on her. Seems good woman to me. Tough. Honest."

"Won't argue with that, Jak. But there was something going on under the surface. She was tense and nervy. I just got the feeling that something had happened that made her like that, and it involved us and going on the paddleboat. But she's been around too long to give it up easy. And I didn't feel confident enough to try dragging it out of her."

They were walking along a street that ran parallel to the river.

"Listen," J.B. said, checking for a moment. "Sounds like a big boat coming in."

There was the muffled sound of a stern-wheeler, its huge rear paddle thwacking at the surface of the Big Muddy. And then the mournful blast of its whistle echoed around the ville.

"*Golden Eagle?*" Ryan glanced at his wrist chron. "Said it would dock some time this morning. Sails upriver dawn tomorrow. We should go aboard and book our cabins early. They reckon that she fills up fast."

RYAN ALLOWED an hour and a half for the boat to discharge her passengers and freight, then went along on his own to make the bookings.

When he came out onto the quay, he was impressed at the sheer size of the vessel. She loomed over the warehouse, her twin funnels trickling a pillar of dark smoke. Ryan guessed that they probably kept the large boilers stoked with wood even when she was in port, saving the tedious process of cooling down and refiring.

There was a steady stream of men working up and down three gangplanks, and a steam-powered hoist was swinging netted boxes of cargo into the bright morning air. A sign pointing to a fourth walkway read Tickets.

Ryan walked onto the boat, feeling the spring of the gangplank under his boots.

Away on the far side of the river, in the round tower, the sun glinted off the telescope as it moved lazily around to focus on the *Golden Eagle*.

A stocky, bare-headed man in a dark blue pea jacket, a line of gold braid on his cuffs, was leaning against the iron rail, smoking a black cheroot. "Morning," he grunted. "Booking on with us for tomorrow?"

Ryan nodded. "Yeah. Where do I go?"

"Along to the second companionway. White door, number 7 on the right. Along the passage and down the first stairs. See a green door on your left. Purser, it says. In there. You're good and early, mister."

"Heard you get busy."

The man spit into the river. "*Golden Eagle*'s always busy. She's the best. What's your business? Don't look like a car man. Goin' up river to hunt the stickies?"

"Just for pleasure. Me and five friends. What's the word on the stickies?"

"There's mines and plantations up-water. Rumor has it that the fat man's involved."

"Wolfram?"

"They say." He shrugged his shoulders. "Say the Magus is with him. But nobody ever seen them in the flesh. Just whispering and shadows."

Ryan nodded. "What always happens with them. And they got trouble with stickies?"

"Lot of breakouts. Killings. Difficult to keep them working, even chained. Muties like that got no regard for their lives. Makes it tough to hold them under."

"I heard that." A couple of young women, wearing too much makeup, pushed past him with a wink and a grin at the officer, who returned their greeting. They went along in the direction that the man had indicated for purchasing tickets.

"Regulars aboard?" Ryan asked.

"Dolly and her sister, Jolyanne. Kind of hardworking girls, if you take my meaning."

Ryan nodded. "Sure do. Well, best get my cabins booked. See you around."

The purser was only about fifteen, making a valiant effort to grow a beard, which led to his being ruthlessly teased by the pair of whores.

"Why try and cultivate those straggly little hairs, sonny, when they grow wild around your ass?"

The lad blushed ferociously.

One of the women noticed Ryan and nudged him. "Fancy a cabin-share, honey? Bunk up together all the way to Crosstown. Show us some generous jack, and

you could have me and my sister together. Just to
yourself. Best deal in Twin Forks.''

"Already got me some company, ladies, but thanks
for the offer.''

The Trader used to say you should always be polite
to waiters and whores.

After they'd gone, Ryan made his bookings, taking
the recommended top-deck berths, near the stern on
the starboard side. He reserved a row of three inter-
connected outside doubles, handing over more jack
then he'd anticipated.

"Cabins don't come cheap on the *Golden Eagle*.''

"Nothing does, sir. Here you are. Two meals a day
included. Liquor's extra. Your tickets. Sails at dawn.
That'll be around six tomorrow morning. Don't be
late. Get your baggage aboard today if you can. The
Golden Eagle doesn't wait for nobody.''

THEY PASSED THE DAY quietly wandering around the
ville, finishing up with a much cheaper meal at Toby's
and retiring early.

Jak slept badly that night, with dark dreams of a
mob of stickies pursuing him through dank caverns.

The captain of the *Golden Eagle* had a pair of unexpected and deeply unwelcome visitors at two in the
morning, though sufficient jack changed hands for
him to smother what remained of his conscience.

Chapter Thirteen

They ate a fast breakfast, with the windows of the dining room in the Grits and Greetings reflecting their own faces against the darkness outside. Despite the early hour, they were offered a full fry-up with eggs, bacon, ham, grits, hash browns, toast and coffee sub.

Ryan settled their final bill, and they gathered their weapons and clothes and set off into the cool morning. The sky was just beginning to lighten with the false dawn, and the streets and alleys were thronged with fellow passengers, all making their way out onto the quay to join the long lines at the gangways. In the gloom the brightly lit boat seemed even bigger.

"She's enormous," Mildred said. "Just like the old pictures I've seen of them back in the 1800s. Like a dream come true."

"Looks like there's some real swift and evil bastards and bitches coming along with us," J.B. muttered as they joined the line.

Ryan had already noticed that. A good half of the men and many more of the females looked as if they earned their jack by dubious means. There were also some of the departing merchants, leaving after their ill-fated convention, visibly a little uncomfortable among the proliferating lower classes, keeping to themselves in small, nervous groups. Whores and gamblers and a variety of stone-eyed opportunists thronged the noisy, bustling decks when they finally got aboard the vessel.

An overworked purser peeked at their tickets with the aid of a flickering oil lamp, pointing up a ladder and toward the back of the immense boat. "You're all on the starboard side. Thirty-one to thirty-three."

"How long before we sail?" Krysty asked.

The man glanced at a silver turnip watch dangling from a chain across his midriff. "Should be six. Crowd we got coming on, it'll be nearer to seven."

"We get to Crosstown...when?"

The man pointed irritably to a schedule printed on a large board behind him. "You got eyes, lady. Use them."

It showed Cairo, Illinois, at the junction of the Ohio, in a day and a half. Another day and a half to St. Louis, where they stopped over for twenty-four hours. And one more day to Crosstown, just over the line in Wisconsin.

"Long way," J.B. said. "Guess we can make a good speed all the way."

Doc had been counting on his fingers. "Five days in total."

"Depending on the weather and the river," the sailor said over his shoulder. "Best allow at least a day, one way or t'other. And there's been bad trouble with gangs of muties all along the Sippi the last month or more. We haven't been attacked. Not even triple-stupe muties would try that. But smaller craft and some settlements been hit. And hit hard. See the smoke for forty miles or more across the levees."

Above their heads the whistle sounded in a long, menacing call. And they could hear the steam engines pounding, making the deck vibrate.

"That mean we'll soon be off?" Ryan asked.

The man laughed. "Means he's pissing steam at being late. Now, get moving, folks."

EVEN CYNICAL DOC WAS profoundly impressed with the grandeur of the *Golden Eagle*. "By the Three Kennedys!" he exclaimed. "But she is undeniably a floating gilded palace. I have never seen such magnificence."

They walked through some of the public areas as they made their way along passages and up wide staircases toward their own cabins. Several of the main sections were obviously set up for some full-time gambling, the roulette, poker and crap tables covered in off-white dust cloths.

One corridor and a set of steps was closed off by a thick maroon velvet rope strung across, and four armed sec men stood on casual guard, directing passengers around.

"Staterooms closed off, folks, for the duration. Sorry for any inconvenience, but you can get to where you're going real easy by taking the next stairs."

All very polite and very coldly efficient. Ryan wondered just who it was traveling on the stern-wheeler who employed men of that caliber. Maybe some powerful baron? Be interesting to find out a little later.

But the main thing to do was to get to their own accommodation. They could feel the engines working harder and faster, and shouts from the deck indicated they were ready to sail.

Everywhere Ryan looked he saw a slightly tawdry opulence. Gold leaf overlaid ornate carvings of cherubs and angels and languid, half-naked women carrying spilling horns of fruit. The overhead lamps were almost all crystal chandeliers, though some of them needed a good cleaning. The carpets were a little faded at the corners, but they were thick and soft underfoot. Deep armchairs and long sofas, mostly with silk and satin pillows, were scattered throughout the vessel.

"Down here," Jak said, leading the way. "These are high twenties."

"I believe that this is the larboard side of the ship." Doc peered out over the rail. "Yes. We need to be over on the river side. And they are seemingly getting ready to cast off the stern and bowlines. Let us make haste. It would be a disappointment to miss our sailing."

Jak disappeared around a sharp corner, beckoning them after him, moving past a section of open deck with a low rail backed by the huge stern-wheel. It was moving very slowly, barely rippling the surface of the river, easing the *Golden Eagle* against her moorings. It was as though the captain was letting her strain at the leash, eager to finally get sailing up the Sippi.

"Here. Thirty-one to -three."

The keys were in the heavy oak-paneled doors, with the numbers painted on in thick gold paint. Ryan turned the handle and stepped into the room.

"Fireblast!" Even the luxuriant furnishings of the public areas hadn't prepared him for the stylish elegance of their suite. "Like the classiest damned gaudy in the biggest ville in Deathlands," he said.

"Dump the stuff and let's get out on deck," Krysty urged. "We got plenty of time to admire it later."

The whistle was blowing again, and they heard the thunderous sound of the big paddle wheel beginning to turn with serious intent. Ryan laid the Steyr rifle on the ruffled coverlet of the double bed, along with his traveling pack, and followed Krysty into the cool morning air.

The others came out moments later, all of them exclaiming at the quality of their accommodation. Even the taciturn Armorer couldn't restrain himself.

"Triple-class, bro," he called after Ryan. "Worth the risk of getting the jack back at the saloon. Never traveled so high on the hog." He ducked as a wall of spray blew up over the stern rail, splattering across his glasses. "Dark night! Have to watch myself out here!"

There was a surprisingly large crowd lining the dock as the big boat slowly pulled away, the narrow gap of water widening, the river turning to churning froth as the white-and-crimson paddle beat harder and faster.

Ryan leaned on the rail, finding a gap between a tall old man with a long white mustache, gold rings glinting on every finger, and what looked like a blond, ringleted child of twelve, in a schoolgirl's short, lacy skirt and straw hat. Only when Ryan glanced sideways at her did he realize that the whore wouldn't see thirty again.

"There's Dolores Stanwyck," J.B. said, leaning on Ryan's shoulder.

"Where?"

"Standing by those crates. Looks kind of like she's trying to hide and look out for us." He waved his hat and shouted out the woman's name. But there was far too much noise, and she continued to peer up, short-sightedly, not managing to see any of them on the deck.

Gradually they pulled out into midstream, turning around with a ponderous elegance, so that the blunt bow pointed toward Crosstown.

A SAILOR WALKED around, calling out for passengers to retire to their cabins for an hour while the ship was cleared away and made ready for the cruise, reminding them that lunch would be served in the three restaurants from noon onward. He cautioned that passengers traveling steerage on the lower decks were limited to the Bronze Room only for dining.

"We eat in the Gold or Silver," Krysty said, pushing the door of their room behind her, closing out much of the noise of the stern-wheel.

"How do you know?"

She picked up a heavily embossed invitation card from one of the mahogany-and-ormolu tables that perched on dangerously thin legs in a corner of the chamber. "Captain's table for supper," she said.

"Really?"

"Look." She held it out. "'Captain Melville Huston welcomes you to dine at his table this evening at seven of the clock. Casual clothes would not be fitting.'"

"I've only got casual clothes," Ryan protested. "They want evening dress?"

"Your clothes are clean and neat, lover. I can't see them turning us away."

"Think the others have all got an invite from the captain, as well?"

Krysty put the card down again on the polished, veneered table. "Ask them later."

They had a small balcony with sliding doors, and Ryan opened them and stepped out onto the narrow strip of deck. With partitions at either end, they had a surprising amount of privacy, and a wonderful view, high up out across the diminishing skyline of Twin Forks.

"Hey, this is something," he said, checking automatically to see what was above them. But the side rose sheer to what he guessed had to be the top-price staterooms, the ones guarded by the cold-eyed sec men.

"What are we going to do for the next hour, lover?" Krysty glanced around the overelegant room. "There's a big bowl of complimentary fruit and a bottle of wine. Could make a start on that."

Ryan looked across at her, smiling at the sheer beauty of the shafts of sunlight spearing through the louvered windows, setting fire to Krysty's blazing red hair.

"Got a better idea," he said quietly, walking and turning the key in the lock.

"Sure you're up to it? Still probably weak from your time down the river, lover."

He shook his head. "Best kind of medicine I ever heard of. Shall I pull the drapes?"

Krysty was already sitting on the bed, tugging off her blue-and-silver Western boots, letting them clunk on the carpet. "No, leave it. Nice to have both some light and some privacy."

THEY MADE LOVE TWICE in the idle hour.

The first time was urgent, clawing at each other, Ryan driving down with all his strength, making her moan with delight. She kissed him, an arm locking him to her, her tongue piercing between his lips. Her fingers dug into his back, making him buck with the delicious pain.

The second time was slower, more studied, with both of them taking time to offer pleasure with lips and tongues, sucking and licking, tasting sweat, tangling, hair matted.

They lay pressed together like spoons in a drawer, feeling the gentle rocking of the boat, the background of the rumbling wheel, pushing them upstream at a surprisingly fast rate. Ryan glanced out the window, seeing a wooded shore drifting by.

He was firmly inside Krysty, from behind, arms around her, cradling her superb breasts, face buried in her nape, her sentient hair seeming to caress his skin.

"Good," he whispered.

She nodded, voice muffled by the pillow. "Very good, lover. Time out of war for us. Think we all need a break from the running and the chilling."

He began to move slowly, her buttocks firm against his thighs, feeling a slight discomfort from the recurrent wound in his leg, though it was almost healed again.

Krysty was easing against him now, sighing, green eyes closed.

They worked together in unison, feeling each other's need, knowing when to hold back and when to give, coming together at the same moment that the ship's whistle gave out a long blast. They broke into laughter, hugging each other tight.

They heard a megaphoned message from the passage outside. "Decks clear now, folks. All welcome in all parts of the *Golden Eagle*. And gaming's begun."

"Gaming's just finished here," Ryan joked, peeling himself reluctantly away from Krysty, feeling the coolness of perspiration already beginning to dry on his own skin. "Time for a quick shower, then we can go explore."

"I'm after you with the shower," Krysty said, lying back on the bed, pulling the top sheet over herself.

The water was warm, the complimentary bar of soap heavily jasmine scented, and Ryan scrubbed at himself, getting rid of dirt, some of which he suspected might still have come from his time with Paddy Maxwell. The foaming water began gray but quickly became cleaner, and he was soon out, drying himself on one of a pair of large, fluffy white towels.

Krysty followed Ryan, offering a swift peck on his damp cheek as she bustled by.

Ryan dressed, standing by the window of their cabin, staring vaguely out at the banks of the Sippi. He looked up at the sound of someone walking heavily on the floor above him, in the guarded stateroom. It struck him in passing that the walker must be a big man to make so much noise.

Then Krysty appeared, drying herself, and he forgot about their neighbor above.

He buckled on the gun belt, with the SIG-Sauer matched by the weight of the panga on the other hip.

"Ready?"

"Nearly, lover. Go see if the others are ready, and we can go look around."

"Sure. And start some real relaxing."

Chapter Fourteen

The *Golden Eagle* was something else.

The six friends walked around her together during the long, sunny morning, their shadows thrown sharp and hard on the scrubbed deck. The wind was from the north, in their faces as they stood in the bow, leaning into the fresh breeze that was exaggerated by the speed of the boat.

They strolled around the port side, ending up by the pounding stern-wheel, a popular spot for idlers. They could watch Tennessee vanishing behind them, the foaming wake remaining like a chalk line on the muddy surface of the Sippi, attracting the predatory birds.

But it was the interior of the paddle steamer that was most impressive.

"It is an odd thought," Doc said, "but it reminds me curiously of a high-born and enormously wealthy and stylish member of the decadent Russian court, fallen on hard times. Just a little frayed and tawdry around the edges, despite all the glitter and brilliance that catches the eye."

Ryan understood what the old man was saying.

The *Golden Eagle* obviously deserved her reputation as the grandest and most expensive of all the stern-wheelers that plied the big river.

Everywhere was luxury.

The luncheon was mainly an extensive buffet with iced melon and wafer-thin sliced salmon, roast beef, tenderloin of lamb, rainbow trout smoked to perfection, breast of duck with wild cherries, quail and pigeon, crystal bowls of mixed vegetables, with a variety of delicate sauces, and a variety of sorbets and ice creams in all flavors imaginable.

They all went back twice with loaded plates, to their reserved table with printed name cards: Ryan Cawdor And Party. Silver-plated cutlery and good quality china bore the name of the vessel and a small reproduction of it on every plate and cup and saucer and bowl. The same picture of the *Golden Eagle* was engraved on all of the glassware.

Though the food was included in the overall cost of the tickets, the waiters and servers reminded all the passengers that wines and spirits had to be paid for.

And they weren't cheap.

But that didn't stop the assorted high rollers who dined in the Gold and Silver restaurants from imbibing staggering quantities of liquor.

After lunch the companions retired to one of the gambling saloons to sit in brocaded armchairs and drank real coffee from tiny porcelain cups, included in the price of the tickets.

Though the long trip upriver had been going on only for about six hours, the gamblers, of both sexes, were already locked into their pleasures.

Roulette wheels spun silently, the white balls rattling and bouncing, the faint slap of cards and the muttered instructions of the croupiers sounding like acolytes of some obscure religious ceremony.

"None of them look like having fun," Jak commented. "Like convention morticians."

Ryan sat back, watching the surface of the dark coffee vibrate gently, like everything on board the boat, vibrating, taking its time from the ceaseless turning of the giant paddle wheel at the stern.

Krysty laid her hand on his arm. "Feel good, lover? Relaxing a while?"

"Yeah. Can't deny it's a classy operation. And I can't deny that I'm already enjoying taking it easy. Last few weeks have been ice on granite for me."

"Me, too. The worry when we thought that we weren't going to be able to find..." Krysty's voice cracked, and she fell silent. Ryan glanced sideways, seeing a single tear glistening in the corner of one of her brilliant emerald eyes.

He laid the empty cup on the table in front of them and squeezed her hand. "That's over now," he said quietly. "And we're together again."

Doc was sitting in a sunlit chair, his lids drooping, gnarled hands unfolding around the lion's-head hilt of the ebony swordstick.

"Someone's ready for an afternoon sleep," Mildred commented. "Can't say I blame him. Something about the rhythm of the boat that lulls you along."

She patted J.B on the arm, making him start. "How do you feel about the idea of retiring to our cabin for an hour or so, John?"

The Armorer blinked, pushing back the brim of his fedora. "I'm not going to be able to stand the pace of another three days upriver, then all the way back again. Too much high living. Just not used to it."

Ryan grinned. "Don't have to come all the way back to Twin Forks. Been looking at the map. We can leave at Crosstown and then cut across country back toward the redoubt in Tennessee. Or travel halfway south again. Might make it easier."

Krysty put down her cup. "Gaia! I can't believe you, Ryan, I truly can't. We are having our first good time in…in a long while, halfway through the first day you're talking about making plans to get off and vanish into Deathlands again. What is the point of all this?"

"All right, all right. Sorry, love. You're right. Just that I get kind of prickly sitting in comfort with all this fat, tricked-over food. Not really my style."

Doc blinked. "Putting on the style, are we? By God, but we are, my trusty companions. We'll go no more a'roving, so far into the night. Or should we? This floating gilded palace of sin brings back so much of my early life that I almost expect to see my dearest Emily poised at the head of the grand staircase, in her finest ball gown of salmon pink silk, her tiara glittering, osprey fan in gloved fingers, her kind eyes seeking me out." He shook his head. "It is enduringly painful, dear friends. As though the fragile temporal curtain between us had grown more thin and opaque, and I could reach her with but a single step."

Mildred reached out and took his hand. "I know what you feel, Doc."

"Do you, Dr. Wyeth?" He nodded slowly. "Perhaps you and I are the only ones left in all Deathlands who share the knowledge and the feeling. That we live while everyone we ever knew is a hundred years in the cold, cold ground. Nearer two hundred years in my own sorry case." He levered himself upright, grunting with the effort. "I think I shall go and rest awhile."

He spoke to Jak. "If you should choose to come gamboling and somersetting in during the afternoon, pray attempt do it with some quietus, dear child. Let an old man have his requiem."

"Sure. Going to recce, Doc. Won't wake you."

"Want some jack for the machines, Jak?" Ryan asked. "Or play a little cards?"

The teenager grinned at him, ruby eyes glinting. "Not cards. Seen too many sharps look like got aces up sleeves. Might try machines. Cheat you honest."

Ryan felt in his pockets and handed over a fistful of small jack. "Spend it unwisely," he said.

"Will do."

They were so unused to the array of rich food that all five finally decided to go to their cabins for a couple of hours of rest and relaxation, leaving Jak to explore the *Golden Eagle* on his own.

RYAN KICKED off his combat boots and slumped on the soft bed, fumbling to loose his belt. He dropped it on the floor, the hilt of the panga clattering against the leg of the bed. He had already removed the SIG-Sauer and tucked it under the pillow.

Krysty had opened the window, letting in the afternoon warmth, breathing in the fresh air. She had stripped to a pair of pale blue silk panties and a plain white T-shirt. Following Ryan's lead, she put her own blaster, the short-barreled double-action Smith & Wesson 640, beneath her own pillow.

As they lay side by side, in that deliciously comfortable world between waking and sleeping, they both heard the sound of ponderously heavy steps from above their heads, walking slowly up and down the guarded stateroom.

"Sounds like a giant in a kid's fairy story," Krysty said dozily.

"Real big man. Don't think I can recall meeting a baron who weighed in over the three-hundred-pound mark. From the guards, it's got to be someone with serious power and jack. Be curious to see who it is. Might ask around the crew."

"Doesn't matter," Krysty said. "Long as he hasn't captured the lost twins and is holding them in a cage of gingerbread and spun honey, waiting to crunch their bones to make his bread. Or boil their hearts to give himself everlasting life. Anyway, might just be a lonely, fat old lady, promenading up and down with a sour expression on her rosebud lips."

Ryan coughed. "Go to sleep, love."

JAK WAITED TO TRY his luck on three or four of the beautifully restored slot machines that lined several of the main gambling rooms. Most of them dated from the mystic days before the long winters and before the brief nukecaust of skydark, and had been adapted from the ancient quarter and dime slots.

The *Golden Eagle* was fitted with the finest electricity-generating system, based on both the wood boiler and the use of the stern-wheel itself as a power source. And for decorative and aesthetic purposes, there were hundreds of polished oil lamps in the main corridors and public areas, casting a more gentle, golden glow over the hectic proceedings.

The machines were electric powered.

Some of them were of a model that Jak had occasionally seen before, back in his childhood among the dirt-poor settlements of the bayous. They had a metal head of a Native American on the front, polished by constant contact of tens of thousands of eager gamblers, who would hold it or rub at it while pulling the chrome handle with the black plastic knob at its end, setting the tumblers turning and the display of fruits changing in the three rectangular glass windows.

Jak wandered slowly along, gazing at them, deciding that the odds weren't worth the playing. And they looked so boring, with no excitement to them.

Occasionally there would be the tinkling of a bell and the whispering cascade of metal counters spilling out as someone had a modest win. The teenager noticed that it was mainly women playing the slots. Mainly older women.

Some looked as if that was all they did, ignoring their beautiful surroundings, never glancing sideways to admire the scenic view out the floor-to-ceiling windows. Each wore a glove on her right, pulling hand, to protect it from blisters, slipping in the jack, tugging, barely waiting for the result before setting the operation spinning again.

"Seems like Hell," Jak muttered to himself.

The frail little lady, in a respectable dress of dark green wool, at the nearest machine had to have had sharp hearing, as she caught his murmured words above the endless chattering of the slots.

"Hell, young man?" she asked quietly. "This is not Hell. Hell is a closed room. Hell is other people. Hell is to play and not to win. Hell is not to play at all. Hell is stinking mutie bastards with freak snow hair trying to distract decent folks from their funning."

The last sentence was spit out at him with ferocious venom, a thread of spittle striking him full in the face. Jak had a razor-edge temper, and he actually had his fingers on the hilt of one of his knives before sense broke through. He wiped off her saliva and managed a smile.

"Lotsa slotsa luck, lady," he said, eyes glittering like a poised cobra's.

He walked away, ignoring the curious looks that his appearance brought from some of the promenaders and gamblers.

In the next room, which was busy with six tables crowded with men and a few women attempting to beat the house odds at blackjack, Jak found some slightly more modern machines, mostly looking as if they dated from only just before skydark.

These were like something from Mission Control, Houston, with dazzling lights and colors and a constantly changing, comp-activated display screen. There were switches and buttons that allegedly controlled the destiny of the winning combinations, though Jak pri-

vately doubted if they had the least effect on the ultimate results.

He looked around the room, taking in the mirrors
that were scattered all across the domed ceiling, which
was covered in a cunningly painted classical-style
mural, showing an array of overweight and under-
dressed gods and goddesses, carousing and making
merry. And making explicit love. The interior of the
Golden Eagle was like a luxurious maze, and it was all
too easy to lose track of exactly where on the vessel
you were. Jak's guess put him on the same deck as
their cabin, or a half deck below it, directly beneath
the most expensive and exclusive staterooms.

He decided to play for a while, using the jingling
pocketful of loose jack that Ryan had given him.

The albino teenager won a little, then lost some and
won a little more and then lost the rest.

It was all gone in less than a quarter of an hour.

He walked out toward the deck, whistling to himself, amused at what a waste of time the gaming had
been and how devoid of pleasure.

Some of the mirrors in the ceiling were two-way
glass. Behind one of them, two faces were pressed together, watching Jak. One was a fat, multijowled face,
the other as thin as a cutlass blade.

Both faces smiled, and the both smiles never got
within a country mile of the stone-cold eyes.

Chapter Fifteen

Violence was always close to the surface on board the *Golden Eagle* as she plowed her way at high speed, north, along the dark brown Sippi River.

It was late afternoon, while Ryan was washing to be ready for their dinner invitation at the table of Captain Melville Huston, when he heard the sudden uproar on the deck just outside, below their balcony.

"Trouble?" asked Krysty, who was brushing out her crimson hair in front of a gilded, scallop-edged mirror. Ryan had been watching her out of the corner of his good eye, convinced that he could actually see fiery sparks fountaining from the brush into the washbasin below.

"Yeah."

They went out together, peering down over the wrought-iron railings onto the deck below, where two men were engaged in a furious argument. One was short, skinny and dapper, with a waxed mustache. They noticed immediately that he had the scarlet imprint of fingers, livid on his pale cheek. The other, who had done the slapping, was taller and older, with a fringe of thin hair. He wore an elegant suit, with a beautiful embroidered vest and highly polished knee-length boots. A small crowd of passengers held them apart.

"Nobody, nobody says that of me," the little man yelped. "Upon my honor, they do not!"

"Honor." The other spit over the starboard rail into the river. "A word that soils your lips, you shit-eating piece of scum."

The little man was overtopped and outweighed, but he refused to back off. He pointed an angry finger at his opponent. "I demand satisfaction from you."

The other man laughed. "A little bantam like you. What are your weapons? A stun gren and a pair of stilts?"

The other man was almost apoplectic with rage, eyes popping from their sockets. "You refuse to fight me?"

A uniformed officer had appeared, pushing through the growing crowd, calling out for order and silence.

"I heard a demand for a duel," he said, voice ringing out over the sudden stillness.

"This pig fucker said that—"

"The lady he spoke of was—"

The sailor wore a sword and he half drew it, the blade shining in the bright sun. "It is of totally no matter, gentlemen. Affairs of honor are carried out in the half hour before the evening meal commences. This is normally at half after six. On the foredeck. An officer of the *Golden Eagle* acts as witness so there will be no problems with the law in the event of a chilling. What are the weapons to be?"

Krysty nudged Ryan. "Got it real well organized, don't they, lover?"

"Must happen most days on a place like this. Combination of cards and women and drink."

The taller man half bowed. "I am the injured party. I choose swords."

There was a murmur from the watching crowd, many of whom seemed to know both the protagonists.

The little man shrugged. "All one to me. I shall be there." And he spun on his heel and walked quickly away.

The officer saluted the tall duelist and also stalked away, back along the deck, in the direction of the bridge. Ryan guessed he was going to report the incident to the captain.

At that moment Ryan was aware of a familiar feeling, a cold prickling at his nape, and he looked around, seeing Krysty also look behind her.

"What?" he said.

"Shadow over the sun. Someone walking over my grave. Got the sensation of being watched."

Simultaneously they both looked above and behind them, but the blank wall of the guarded stateroom shielded them from any unseen observer.

"Going to watch the fight?" Krysty asked.

"Likely. J.B. and Doc'll probably want to check it out. And young Jak."

THERE WAS a public-address system installed throughout the *Golden Eagle,* but it often seemed to be crackling and generally unreliable. At about twenty minutes past six, a message was carried around the boat by a half dozen of the sailors, reminding all of the passengers that an affair of honor was about to be resolved on the foredeck.

Ryan and the others had gotten there early, securing a good viewpoint from one of the higher decks, not far from the calliope, which had been playing a bright melody of old folk tunes throughout the afternoon but had now fallen silent. Just a few wisps of steam trickled from the gold-and-silver pipes.

Mildred had been the least enthusiastic, but had reluctantly agreed to join the others. "Maybe they'll ask if there's a doctor on board, and I can volunteer. I always wanted to do that for real. I was once in a theater for an amateur performance of *Cymbeline*. Halfway through the first act, a man rose from his seat and asked if there was a doctor in the place. Of course, the play stopped dead. I thought it was an emergency and stood, saying I was a doctor. He stared up at me and said, 'Isn't this a perfectly rotten production, Doctor?' Well, I felt such a fool, standing there."

The duel was extremely well attended. It seemed that virtually all of the passengers were thronged there, though Jak reported that the little old ladies were still playing the slot machines down below.

The small man, who they'd learned was called Diego Kahla, was stripped to shirtsleeves, waiting patiently by the starboard rail. Neither of the fighters bothered with seconds, though a young officer stood nervously between them to observe fair play. The other man, who gossip reported was the bastard son of a notorious baron from Georgia, traveling under the assumed name of John Carradine Gatewood, was chatting to a brace of high-price whores, seeming oblivious to the pressure of the fight.

"Betting's odds are against the Mex," J.B. said. "Seems Gatewood's already chilled better than a dozen men in fights like this. Rules of the boat says the winner gets the loser's jack-poke. Kahla's done well at five-card stud this afternoon."

"You mean to say that the fight was provoked?" Mildred said, shocked. "That's just a sort of legalized murder and robbery. It isn't fair."

"Nobody ever said life was fair," Krysty protested. "We all know that."

"Gatewood's picked swords," Ryan said. "Look at the size of the blade he's selected. Saber. Sort of cutlass. Huge blade. Kahla won't be able to even lift it."

Jak grinned. "Saw him with his sword. Using rapier, like Doc."

Krysty looked at the teenager. "Really! That's unfair. He'll likely get butchered."

Jak rubbed thumb and forefinger together. "Want bet, Krysty? Reckon little man wins inside minute."

Knowing the albino youth's extraordinary expertise when it came to close-contact fighting, Krysty chose not to risk a wager against him.

The gleaming ship's bell, tinted orange by the setting sun over the western bank of the Sippi, rang a single deep note to indicate the half hour.

The officer cleared his throat. "Duel will begin on my signal. Any apology?" He hardly waited for the possibility of an answer. "No? Swords. No other weapon. I'll shoot down any man breaks the rules or interferes.'' He waved a .32-caliber Taurus revolver in his right hand. "Ready? Start.''

Only then did the crowd become aware of the discrepancy between the two men's chosen weapons.

Gatewood, tall and lithe, wore a white suit, with a vermilion vest that sported mother-of-pearl buttons. He swished the long-bladed saber that Ryan recognized as resembling a nineteenth-century light-cavalry officer's sword. It was nearly three inches wide, single-edged, with a needle point to it and a ponderous brass basket hilt.

Kahla, jacketless, wore a dark vest and pants over a white shirt with loose, baggy sleeves. His rapier was less than an inch in width, probably Spanish in origin, several inches shorter than the saber, with a delicate, silver-chased hilt.

"My support is with the swordsman rather than the clumsy artisan,'' Doc whispered.

Ryan's first gut reaction had altered. Trader used to say that biggest and strongest was best, and it generally was. But there was also a case in this kind of combat to be made for fast and light and deadly.

Apart from the fluttering of the ornamental bunting that was strung all about the upper decks of the boat, the only sound was the steady, monotonous pounding of the stern paddle wheel, which Ryan noticed was moving a little more slowly than usual, as the evening light began to fade.

Gatewood made no effort to launch his attack on the sailor's word, contenting himself with planting a kiss on the cheeks of each of the blond sluts, half bowing to them, an unworried smile on his lips.

Kahla shuffled a couple of steps across the deck, as though he were testing out the footing, the rapier held loosely at his side, point trailing.

"Fuck'n get on with it!" someone yelled in a flat Yankee drawl.

A number of the watching whores started to giggle and clap their hands, eager to see some action.

Gatewood waved the enormous saber with a great flourish over his head, bowing and smiling, gradually edging a little closer to his much smaller opponent.

"Three to one on the colonel," shouted a stout man who had dragged a chair out to give him a place in the front row. At those odds he didn't get many takers, showing where the mood of the passengers lay.

"Take him up, Jak," Ryan whispered, slipping a small bundle of folded notes to the teenager, who grabbed them and wormed his way through the crowd, keeping an eye on the fighters. He did the deal with the gambler, who looked surprised to have any wagers in on Kahla.

"Are you ready to meet your death, my tiny amigo?" Gatewood called, closing in, making Kahla step back toward the rail of the boat.

"As ready as you," said the small man in a high, squeaky voice, like a pompous mouse, which brought a ripple of laughter around the deck.

Without any further warning, Gatewood was on him, swinging the massive saber with his enormous strength, bringing it hissing down, aiming at the neatly parted hair.

But Kahla wasn't there.

To a gasp of shock from the watchers, he had ducked under the murderous blow and jinked sideways, pinking his opponent in the top of the right thigh with his whiplash rapier as he moved past him. He continued to stand with his back to the crowd, the blade trailing on the planks again. A tiny bead of crimson dripped from it onto the white wood.

"Touché!" Doc called out delightedly. "Tapped his claret for him."

In that split second the whole atmosphere changed as the knowledgeable passengers realized that the duel now had a whole different scenario.

Gatewood also backed away, cursing, rubbing a hand at the small wound. "A mere nothing," he said with a sneer, but his face had grown pale, his eyes flickering nervously from side to side. Ryan noticed beads of sweat on his forehead.

"The next will not be nothing," Kahla riposted, his confidence visibly grown.

What happened was so fast that even Ryan couldn't be certain just what he'd seen.

The crowd behind the little Mexican jostled and pushed violently, and there was a volley of curses, followed by a woman's scream.

And the thin metallic sound of steel snapping.

"Someone broke his blade," J.B. hissed. "Stamped on it. Bastards. I didn't see who..."

Time froze.

Kahla was holding the hilt of his fencing sword, with only a couple of jagged inches left of the blade. His jaw dropped, and he saw his death advancing.

Gatewood grinned wolfishly, moving fast, the saber half lifted.

Ryan reached for the SIG-Sauer, but the sailor was swinging around with his Taurus. "No blasters," he shouted. "I'll chill the first man draws a blaster. It's only swords and—"

For once in his ilfe Doc reacted with lightning speed, drawing his own rapier from its ebony sheath and throwing it toward the trapped man. "Take it," he called. "And use it with honor."

The Toledo steel caught the burning rays of the dying sun, glinting like a flash of molten blood, spinning across the deck. Diego Kahla snatched at it, dropping his own sabotaged sword, flashing a smile at Doc.

"Cheating!" someone roared, possibly the man in the chair. And the sailor spun toward Doc, finding himself looking down the muzzles of five blasters.

"No cheating," Ryan yelled. "Swords!" The officer nodded slowly and thoughtfully, then reluctantly lowered his own weapon.

It was Gatewood's turn to back away, driven toward the rail by the weaving web of deathly steel.

Kahla used the perfectly balanced blade like the master he obviously was, cutting the bigger man three, four times, across the arm, the knee and on both sides of the face. Blood streamed over the white suit, invisible on the crimson vest. Gatewood was breathing raggedly, trying to keep up the guard of the heavy saber. But his strength was being sapped, and the end was coming.

"Do him!" whispered a slut in the front row, who was sporting a swollen black eye.

The saber lifted in a last, desperate attack, but Kahla was in under it, arm and wrist straight in the perfect lunge. His blade went in under the fifth rib on the right side, sliding through clothes and skin, flesh and muscle, piercing the heart. He twisted his hand as the blade was withdrawn, doing irreparable damage, blood gushing from the long, narrow wound.

Gatewood dropped his useless sword, which clattered on the deck, loud in the breath-held stillness. The setting sun concealed his deathly pallor as he slumped to his knees. "Tell my father, Judge...that..." Then he fell facedown in his own blood.

"Get our winnings, Jak," Ryan said in a normal conversational voice.

THE SIX FRIENDS SAT around a plain Amish table in the roulette room, each with a large crystal glass of finest imported brandy in front of them.

Diego Kahla stood opposite, his own balloon glass raised in his left hand, right hand still holding Doc's bloodied rapier. He peered down at the delicate fluted engraving on the Toledo blade.

"'*No me saques sin razón, no me envaines sin honor.*'"

Doc smiled. "It means—"

Kahla bowed. "I know what it means, my dear comrade. 'Do not draw me without good reason and do not sheathe me without honor.' I hope that I followed those rules."

"Indeed you did, my dear fellow," Doc said. "Most wonderfully well. It was an honor to watch you at work."

"And you made us a fistful of jack," Ryan said with a grin, lifting his glass.

"I made a small profit myself," Kahla admitted. "Though, as you might expect of a mongrel like Gatewood, his appearance grossly exceeded his value. But—" he shrugged "—I am wealthier than I was this morning."

He turned to Doc, offering back the rapier. "I would gladly pay a small fee for the hire of the sword, Doctor. No? Most kind. Perhaps you will dine with me this evening?"

Ryan answered for them all. "Sorry. Got an invite from the captain tonight. Got to go get ready soon."

"Tomorrow?"

"Sure. Thanks."

BUT IT WAS NOT TO BE.

His undoubted skill as a duelist didn't save Diego Kahla from the thin flensing knife in the back that took his life at some time during the dark hours of the night.

His bloodless, naked corpse, already prey for fishes, waited to be spotted by the dawn watch, bobbing along the overnight mooring of the *Golden Eagle,* floating among the empty bottles and rubbish.

Chapter Sixteen

Ignorant of the man's murder, Ryan led the others through the maze of stairs and corridors to the main saloon to dine with Captain Melville Huston. The oil lamps glowed bright gold along the passages, bringing out the rich colors of the heavily padded furniture.

In the gambling rooms the brilliant chandeliers threw their electric light over the green baize, heightening the crimsons and yellows of the playing cards that flickered across the tables. The whirring of the roulette wheels and the constant ebb and flow of conversation from gamblers, whores and dealers almost drowned out the pounding of the stern-wheel, driving the boat along to her evening berth.

On the way down to eat, they passed the roped-off staircase to the upper grand stateroom. Two sec men in smart suits stood alertly at the bottom of the stairs, and Ryan, glancing sideways, saw two more armed men at the top, in front of a locked door. Whoever was up there ran a tight force and was seriously into keeping hold of his or her privacy.

Ryan picked his way through the noisy throng, reaching the dining room a little before the hour of seven. The head waiter's name was Eduardo, printed in dark Gothic lettering on a neat white card on his lapel. He was heavily built, swarthy, with a pronounced Mex accent and dressed in a smart maroon tuxedo.

He looked disdainfully at the casually dressed group, glancing down at a list on a small table. "You would be Mr. Ryan Cawdor and party?"

"We would."

"If you would care to walk this way?" He led them between the half-full tables, stepping with a peculiar gait, tight at the thighs and loose at the knees, feet in polished pumps turned outward like a duck.

"If we would walk that way, then we would have no need of talcum powder," Doc muttered, as runic as ever.

"Looks to me like he's carrying a raisin between the cheeks of his ass for charity," Mildred riposted, making herself and Doc break out into muffled laughter.

Eduardo appeared not to hear them, shimmering along with immense dignity, reminding Ryan of a full-rigged galleon beating against the wind.

"Here we are." They reached a long table at the center of the room. Ryan quickly counted twelve seats down each side, with one at the head and one more at the bottom. "Three of you on each side. It would be agreeable if the ladies could be split on either side. And you, Mr. Cawdor, here, close to the head. Captain Huston had expressly asked for you to be positioned near to him."

"Mighty kind of him. How's he know me?"

Eduardo gave him a brief, wintry smile. "The ways of the captain of the *Golden Eagle* are mysteriously his own, Mr. Cawdor. It is not for a lowly creature like myself to question him on that sort of matter. I might find myself being towed behind the *Eagle* over the shoals at the end of a knotted rope. Pray take your seats, and a waiter will soon be with you to determine your presupper drink requirements.''

Krysty sat next to Ryan, with Jak next to her. J.B., Mildred and Doc Tanner picked the three seats opposite, leaving empty seats near the head and bottom of the long, polished table.

''First ones here, lover,'' she whispered.

''Mebbe means we can be the first ones to leave. I can't say I like formal occasions like this.''

''When did you go to formal meals?'' Jak asked.

''With Trader. Some of the time, not all of the time. When we had important meals with powerful barons. Never liked them. Least we don't have a death threat here like we often did. Look at all these forks, knives and spoons. Never knew which are the proper ones to use.''

''Begin at the outside and work your way inward,'' Doc offered, overhearing Ryan's worry. ''And watch what other people are doing.''

A tall, saturnine waiter appeared silently at Doc's elbow. ''Would any of you care for a drink while waiting for your host to join you?''

''That would be splendid. Most awfully kind. What can you offer us, my good man?''

''Most guests will take a glass of French champagne.''

Doc nodded. ''That sounds admirable.''

He looked around at the others. "Six glasses of bubbly? Yes?

"Champagne all around, if you please."

The other guests were arriving, filling the remaining seats, introducing themselves to Ryan and his companions. All of them showed every evidence of wealth, power and position.

The seat at the bottom end of the table, opposite the empty captain's chair, was taken by a red-faced elderly man in a black evening suit and white bow tie, pulled so tight it seemed close to strangling him. He introduced himself as Colonel Willoughby De Vere, who owned several thousand acres of best bluegrass country near Bowling Green, in the old state of Kentucky, where he bred racehorses.

He was traveling with his neurasthenic daughters, both in their late thirties. The colonel explained that their family doctor had urged them to take a vacation and get some fresh air. The pale-faced, pinched women sat silently, gazes fixed to the table, taking only a small glass of mineral water each. Their father asked for a mixture of brandy and champagne.

Two more guests were a husband and wife from Oregon, Baron Edgar Hooren and his wife, Deborah. They were in their late fifties and formally dressed, looking askance at the casual attire of Ryan and his party, though the baron was intrigued by the esoteric mix of blasters that they carried.

Ryan glanced at his wrist chron, seeing that it was ten minutes after seven. The only vacant seats were now the captain's at the head of the table, and the ones on either side.

Eduardo came and asked if anyone wished for more refreshment, explaining that Captain Huston sent his apologies for his late arrival. "He sees over our mooring for night."

"How about those two?" Mildred asked, pointing at the empty pair of seats.

The maître d' looked flustered. "Book top chambers and you get invite every night to eat with captain. But we believe that honored guests are seeking privacy. They sent message don't want stinking invitations." He shook his head sorrowfully. "Seems plenty rude to me to say that. But we kept seats. Now I'm going to bring two other guests to take them. Very rude to Captain Huston to have empty places for dinner on first night out."

The replacement guests were two brothers, with such pale skins that Ryan wondered whether they might be albinos, like Jak. Their eyes were pink hued, and their hair was almost pure white, with just a hint of light gold. They introduced themselves as Troy and Randall Mills, twins aged twenty-five, owners of a large copper mill over the border in Canada. They explained that their main purpose in taking the *Golden Eagle* north was to investigate some of the mines that lay close to the Sippi, ones that they understood were worked largely by stickie slave labor.

Captain Melville Huston himself appeared a couple of minutes later, bustling through the dining room, bobbing, weaving, ducking and bowing to his passengers, arriving at the head of his table and looking at his guests. He stood there as though he were waiting for something.

Doc reacted fastest.

Pushing back his chair, he made a small bow. "Honored, Captain," he said in ringing tones.

Huston was short and stocky, in his forties, around five feet six and one-sixty pounds, with a weathered complexion. Ryan noticed that the man's eyes were a light blue, but the left one was clearly false, moving haltingly. He was dressed in a dark blue uniform, with layers of gold braid around collar and cuffs, and he smiled faintly as he returned Doc's bow.

"Glad to have you aboard the *Golden Eagle,* Dr. Tanner."

The captain watched as the others around the long table also rose to their feet.

"Good to meet you all. Pray sit down, and we can begin to dine." He cleared his throat, dropping his voice, muttering an apology for his tardiness. "Problem with a shifting mud bank, obstructed mooring. Always a difficulty on the river. But we shall be stopping quite soon."

He sat and tucked a long linen napkin into his collar, beckoning to one of the team of hovering waiters. "Let's get started," he called.

The food was excellent, accompanied by a range of fine Deathlands and imported wines.

But the conversation was faltering. The captain seemed preoccupied, and half a dozen times Ryan caught the pale blue eyes turned in his direction. The De Vere women never spoke, except to ask for the salt to be passed or to refuse any alcoholic beverage. They picked at their food like sparrows, hardly lifting their eyes from their plates.

Their father dominated the table, relating long anecdotes about his horses, what they'd won, what had sired what, pedigrees and lineage, the importance of weather on the feeding, trotters and pacers. Names of his favorites: Citation, big Man o' War, the Old Campaigner, a fine horse that he'd driven stone-blind.

Ryan was content to let the talk flow, concentrating on his own food: a rich clam chowder, spiced with chilies, accompanied by a very dry white wine; smoked trout, baked in a lattice crust of golden pastry, with a prawn-and-cream-and-leek sauce; a choice of thin-sliced cold ham with capers and a mixed salad, or glazed pork with a ginger-and-honey sauce, or a haunch of buffalo with squash and okra. Ryan chose the roast beef, served with spiced red mash and pickled beans.

There was a wide choice of desserts, ranging from steamed puddings with molasses or a creamy custard sauce, to fresh melons in a brandy sauce with mangoes, and baked grapefruit with brown sugar and strawberries. Ryan went for a mix of delicious sorbets: coconut, banana, apple and cinnamon, decorated with powdered sugar, whipped cream and blueberries.

It was one of the best meals that he'd ever had.

Halfway through he felt a change of movement, and Captain Huston half rose. The rumbling of the sternwheel slowed and stopped, and the forward momentum of the huge vessel gradually came to a gentle halt.

"Night mooring, Captain?" he asked.

Huston resumed his seat. "Indeed, yes, Mr. Cawdor. Once across that sandbar, I was happy to entrust her to my trained officers."

After the dessert the De Vere ladies withdrew, followed by the taciturn Baron Hooren and his wife, leaving nine guests in all to relish the decanters of fine port and brandy that were circulated with the tiny porcelain cups of real coffee.

The Mills twins were interested in the mines they hoped to visit, and pressed Captain Huston for information. "I believe that you have two important guests who are deeply involved in the business. So we have heard," Randall said, toying with a slender silver fruit knife.

The captain didn't answer for several seconds, gazing into his full glass of ruby port. Finally he said, "I fear that the personal details of my passengers must remain private and confidential, if that is what they have chosen."

"So, we cannot meet with them?" Troy pressed. "That is a shame."

The captain sipped at his drink, his gaze flicking to Ryan, then away again. "You may approach them yourself, though I think it will prove a waste of time. They have made their wishes very clear in this matter."

"Can't we even know their names?" J.B. asked, pouring himself another glass of brandy.

Huston shook his head slowly. "Set aside any rumors, Mr. Dix. Speculation can only be harmful. Perhaps even dangerous to those who attempt to pry where they are not wanted." He looked around.

"Now, if you will forgive me, I have essential business connected with the mooring. Please stay and drink as long at my table as you like. There is a good cheese board on offer and some fresh-baked biscuits."

He rose quickly, bowed and walked away through the mostly empty dining room.

Colonel De Vere belched suddenly, putting his hand over his mouth and flushing an even deeper shade of crimson. "My apologies," he mumbled. "Dined well but not too wisely. Pray excuse me. Must join me gals."

Making a staggering exit, he walked with the exaggerated delicacy of the very drunk.

Ryan watched him go, aware that he himself was well stuffed with food and that another glass of port or brandy would be one glass too many. The Trader used to say that a man who remained too long at the saloon would likely be staying the night in the graveyard. "Turn around the deck, and then back to the cabin," he said. "Gone ten o'clock."

Krysty patted him on the arm. "Had no idea that so much time had gone, lover. That was a great meal."

One by one the friends rose to their feet, except for Jak, who stayed in his place. The Mills brothers also stayed where they were.

"Said something about some cheese," the albino teenager muttered.

Randall nodded. "And some more coffee. Help to become jober as a sudge."

"Take care, Jak," Ryan warned. "Night wears on, there's likely to be some cold-hearts getting busy around the decks, looking for easy jack."

"Sure thing. Be along soon."

Doc was steadying himself with the swordstick. "I would be most obliged if you came in as quiet as a mouse fart and didn't disturb a slumbering old man. My pate is somewhat addled, and my intestines full to overloaded. What I need most is a good night's rest, and I shall be a new man in the morning."

Mildred touched him lightly on the shoulder. "Hope the new man's an improvement on the old one, Doc. Or is that too much to hope for?"

He snorted and stared at her, watery eyed, mouth opening and closing like a gaffed marlin. "I confess that I . . . I am a tad lost . . . for words, madam."

"Makes a real pleasant change, Doc." She offered her arm to him. "Care to promenade me around the deck? And watch out for the skeeters."

The dining room was almost deserted as they left. Ryan glanced back, seeing Jak's white hair, glowing like a magnesium beacon in the general darkness, under the spilled pool of light from the crystal chandelier over the captain's table. He was tucking into a large sliver of golden cheese, watched in silence by the Mills brothers.

THE TWINS SPENT a little time in a drunken inquisition of Jak, trying to find out exactly what he and Ryan and the others did for a living, where they'd been and where they were going. But the teenager was sober enough to hold his tongue, offering them virtually no information at all.

Eventually they became tired of his stubborn silences and left the table, tottering off, arm in arm, heading for the roulette tables.

Jak picked himself a slice of a strongly flavored goats' cheese, cutting it up and spreading it on a slice of soda bread. He drained his cup of coffee and waved away the waiter who came to offer him more food and drink.

"Enough, thanks," he said.

He didn't want to go straight back to the cabin he shared with Doc, favoring some fresh air first. He walked through the gambling saloons on his way out, being careful to try to avoid being sucked into the action around the tables.

The only moment of trouble came when a fat, scented, overdressed fifty-year-old man wearing florid clothes and a rakishly tilted wig, approached him.

"Care to keep me company, my pretty little boy?" One hand was on his arm, the other groping toward Jak's groin.

"No," the youth replied, pushing him away.

But the powdered queen was too drunk or too hopped up on jolt to see the danger and hear the threat in the teenager's voice, persisting.

"Got a good cabin, laddie. You can do anything you want to me. Like leather, and I could lie on the floor and let you..." His pocked face pressed close to Jak's cheek, so that the young man could taste the rancid breath.

Jak didn't hesitate. His hand went like a striking rattler to the concealed sheath at the small of his back, coming out with one of his leaf-bladed throwing knives. He slid it close to the man's body, so that none of the men and women around saw what was happening, touching the needle tip to the flabby wattles of the lecher's throat.

"Walk away quiet or I slit you open," Jak hissed.

"Didn't mean . . . Pay you well if you're nice. Can treat me mean . . ."

The knife dipped in harder, drawing a stream of crimson. "Shut fuck up or chill you," the albino snarled, feeling the warmth of blood across the back of his hand.

"All right, all right . . ." The man recognized the reality of the situation and his imminent danger of dying under the steel of the ruby-eyed, crazy kid. Backing off, he reached for a kerchief and dabbed at the bleeding gash in his throat.

JAK WENT ON DECK, looking out at the tree-lined shore where they were moored for the night. It was near-dark, with tendrils of mist hovering over the water of the Sippi.

He was on the port side of the stern-wheeler, toward the rear, relishing the cool dampness of the air after the smoke-filled interior of the boat.

There was nobody around Jak as he leaned on the iron rail, watching the ripples of the big river passing along the flank of the boat. Listening to its whispering.

"Good evening, young man." The dark voice was soft and sibilant.

Jak spun, finding himself surrounded by two sec men with drawn blasters, an enormously fat man, smiling at him, teeth white in the dim light, and a tall, skinny man with eyes that oddly reflected the rising moon.

He recognized them from Ryan's descriptions.

The Magus and Gert Wolfram.

Chapter Seventeen

"You're sure it was them?"

Jak nodded. "Told you what looked like. What you think, Ryan?"

"I think it *was* Wolfram and the Magus. Can't be two other men looking like them in all Deathlands."

Jak was sitting on the double bed in Ryan and Krysty's cabin. J.B. and Doc and Mildred were in the room, either perched on the sofa or standing around, listening to the deeply disturbing account of the encounter on the deck.

"Never said names. Talked about how knew you from times past. Seemed to know all of us. Knew I was from bayous. Knew Mildred had been frozen. Knew Doc was time-trawled."

"They mention Dean? Being in the school up in Colorado?" Ryan asked worriedly. The thought that such a notorious and evil couple had come gibbering out of the past filled with such dangerous knowledge was deeply disturbing. There were profound blood scars between Wolfram and the Magus and himself and J.B., back from the days with the Trader. And if they knew that he had a son, and where he was living, then the boy could become a vulnerable pawn in a murderous game.

Jak shook his head, brushing an errant ivory white curl from his eyes. "No. Don't think knew about kid. But knew most everything else."

Ryan bit his lip. "Tell me again what they said."

"Wasn't much. Just letting know what they knew about us. And why they were on the boat."

"It sounded like a poorly veiled threat to me," Doc said.

"Where those two are concerned, just being close by them is a serious threat," J.B. replied.

"Tell us again," Krysty said.

The teenager closed his eyes for a moment, putting his memory into gear. "Sec men kept blasters drawn on me. Smith & Wessons. Couldn't see too well in dark. Looked like Model 586 double-action revolvers, .357s. Both had laser scope-sights. Handled them like they knew their business. Never gave a half chance."

"Magus or Wolfram carrying?" the Armorer asked.

Jak shook his head. "Couldn't make them. They kept to one side, out of line of sec men. Careful and professional." He shuddered. "They're one triple-sick pair. Magus acted almost like android. Part human. Had sort of steel gloves or nails on hands. Tapped his eyes, and it was like metal on metal."

Ryan nodded. "Word is that the Magus is partly prosthetic. False hand or hands. Face got messed up by Trader, long years ago, somewhere in south Texas or over the border. Story was vague. Had his skull rebuilt by some old surgeon. Metal contact lenses, they say. Steel teeth. That's how I remember him. You got anything to add, J.B.?"

"No. Long and narrow, while Wolfram was big and round."

"Huge," Jak said. "He did most of talking. Said how they'd known you and J.B. in old days. Kept smiling a lot. But not smiling inside. Made me want throw up. Tell truth . . . more scared than ever been."

Ryan nodded sympathetically. "I can believe that, Jak. Why were they on the *Golden Eagle*?"

"Wolfram talked a little about their plantations and mines upriver. Spoke about problems with stickies. Rebelling and escaping. Magus interrupted and said wanted strong overseers. Foremen. Run sec side and stop trouble. Asked if we'd be interested."

Krysty shook her head, laughing. "They sure got a nerve asking that."

Ryan looked grave. "Not funny, lover. Not at all. What I remember of them, they don't waste words. And what they say is like the blank surface of a muddied pool. Looks placid and calm. Got all manner of evil and danger hidden just out of sight. Raw head and bloody bones."

"What else did they say?" J.B. was leaning against the door of the cabin, cradling the Uzi. They had closed the shutters over the cabin windows, giving them a degree of privacy.

"Not much. What didn't say was worse. Didn't threaten chill or kidnap. Only hinted vengeance. Like you said, Ryan, all below surface. Both seemed friendly, apart from drawn blasters. Said they reckoned that we'd be seeing something of them during journey. Mebbe eat together sometime."

"That'll be the day, pilgrim," the Armorer said. "Trader used to say that if you ate with Wolfram or the Magus, you used a damned long spoon."

"I suppose that it could be just a coincidence that they're on the same boat as us," Mildred commented.

Ryan stood and walked to peer between the slats of the shutters. "No way, Mildred. Trader used to say that a coincidence was just a well-hidden plot. Mebbe we should leave tonight and head back overland toward the redoubt."

"We're having such a good time up to now, lover," Krysty protested.

"Sure. Up to now. Up to now we didn't know that two of the most dangerous butchers in Deathlands were traveling with us. Men who would cherish a grudge to their hearts like the coals on a winter fire."

"Now we know that the villains are aboard, can we not keep an extra watch?" Doc stretched out on the sofa. "I confess that I am greatly relishing this trip thus far. It would be a deep sorrow if we had to abandon it."

Jak also stood, walking nervously around the cabin, hands tangling like a nest of snakes. "Why not get in firstest with mostest?"

"Take them out?" Ryan glanced at J.B. "It's an idea. But they're well guarded. We don't know how many sec men they've got up there."

The Armorer nodded slowly. "If we'd seen them first off, it could have been a possible. Have to remember how many enemies those two must have throughout Deathlands. Yet they're still living, and most of their enemies aren't.''

Ryan sighed. It was a difficult decision. His combat sense told him that Wolfram and the Magus were probably on the boat for a reason linked to their own presence aboard. And that reason would only be malign.

But there were six of them, well armed and experienced in chilling, which should be more than enough to deter the two protagonists and an unknown number of their sec men. He didn't see how either side could possibly hope to have a clear-cut victory, except at the cost of much blood spilled. Kind of a Mexican standoff.

And it was an odd fact that the fat man and the Magus should have chosen to come out of their secret stateroom closet and deliver such an explicit warning to Jak. That wasn't normally their way.

In the past the two men were notorious for slaying from hiding. The bullet in the back. The garrote in the night. The stiletto in the groin. The poisoned chalice.

Krysty was at his side, her hip pressed against his, hand light on his arm. ''What do you reckon?''

''Can't decide.''

''What would Trader say about it?''

''Trader was a man for playing safe. Only take chances when you had no choice.''

''We got a choice here.''

There was a gust of wind, strong enough to make the mighty vessel rock slightly, tugging at her moorings. From the saloon below them, they heard the faint squealing of whores at the sudden and unexpected movement.

Ryan looked at Krysty. "This trip means a whole lot to you, doesn't it?"

She nodded, the golden light from the lamps heightening the brilliant fire of her hair. "Yeah, it does. A little comfort and luxury kind of charges up the batteries. Gets us ready for what comes next along the highway."

"Sure. But if we have a run-in with those two evil dogs, there's likely to be some of us traveling on the last train to the coast."

J.B. had been listening to their conversation. "Could put it to the vote, Ryan."

"We don't work as a committee," he replied. "Not the way we operate. Never have and never will. Comes down to a big decision like this one, I make it and you either go along with me or you walk."

Doc sniffed. "It seems a good way to make sure that our circle gets broken, old friend. At least you should take our view into account."

Ryan considered his words for several long seconds. "Right. I say we run a serious risk by staying aboard the *Golden Eagle* all the way to Crosstown. Wolfram and the Magus must be up to something. To something against us."

J.B. was busily polishing his glasses. "I agree. But for some reason they've laid down a good hand that favors us. Given us a free warning. We stick close together and keep a good watch, then I don't rightly see how they can hope to get to us. Not with so many people around."

"That's a vote for going on?" Ryan asked.

"Yeah. It is."

"I'll go with John," Mildred said quickly. "I've never known anything like the *Golden Eagle*. Everything about it is amazing. Food. Gamblers. Decoration. We'll likely never get another chance to ride a stern-wheeler. Like John says, we can keep an extra watch out against the ungodly."

Ryan turned back from the window. "Two for going on. Guess you're three, love?" Krysty nodded, unsmiling. "Doc, how about you? And Jak?"

The teenager leaped in first. "I say try and waste them. Then we can ride on north with no worries."

"What if that's not possible?" Ryan pointed a finger at Jak. "We're not talking some drunken drummer with a rebuilt Saturday night special stuck in his back pocket. These are, arguably, the two single most dangerous men in all of Deathlands. Bear that in mind and decide what we should do."

Jak hardly hesitated. "Then I say we quit boat while we're ahead. Can't enjoy trip knowing their shadows stand in corner of room."

"Three to one," Ryan said.

"Three to two, surely. Lover?" Krysty looked at Doc. "Got the chance to hang up the jury, Doc. You for going on or for quitting?"

"Ah, me, I hate choices! Selecting and rejecting. Decisions that might prove correct or might prove fatally wrong. If only one were blessed with twenty-twenty foresight instead of flawless hindsight. But mankind is so fallible—and womankind, of course, my dear Mistress Wroth and Dr. Wyeth. To stay, perchance to die. If these rogues are out to get us, then surely they might try and follow us, even if we take to the terra firma.''

Ryan rubbed his finger against the side of his nose. "Can't argue with that, Doc. They might."

"Then might we not be safer if we stay here? As has been pointed out, we are surrounded by people."

"Scum of the earth, Doc."

The old man nodded. "Possibly so. But it could be that even the scum of the earth might offer us some scant protection from these wicked folks. To flee into the wilderness would, mayhap, lay us open to an ambush at any moment. They might know the terrain hereabouts far better than we do."

Ryan grinned. "Your combat planning's improving, Doc. Can't argue too much with what you say."

"And I admit that I am relishing this soft, rich life for a few days, Ryan, my old friend."

"Yeah, me too," he admitted. "Well, I'll swing my vote behind staying aboard the *Golden Eagle.*" He shook his head at the general smiles from his companions. "But we have some tight rules while we're sailing north."

"Stick together and keep eyes open," Jak offered. "Those rules?"

"Sure. No going anywhere alone. Men like Wolfram and Magus won't do what you expect. They'll strike like lightning from a clear summer sky. Fast and totally lethal."

Krysty hugged him and kissed him gently on the cheek. "Glad we're going to see the vacation through, lover. It'll be all right, you'll see."

ALMOST DIRECTLY above them, the grossly fat figure of Gert Wolfram was stretched out on a silken sofa, chasing the jolt dragon through a silver pipe, eyes closed, a beatific smile smeared across his jowls.

"So far so good, my dear Magus," he whispered throatily. "Will you not participate?" He gestured with the onyx mouthpiece of the ornamented bong.

The skinny man was standing by one of the side windows, looking out into the starlit night. He waved the offer away. "You know I keep my brain clean and my hands steady and my eyes open, Gert. You would do well to remember who we are going against. Not some backwoods gang of careless chillers."

"I know that, old friend. Ryan Cawdor and his scummy companions might be the most dangerous of our enemies—our living enemies—in all Deathlands. I shall be ready and alert when the moment comes to put our plans into execution. But there is time to relax before that."

The Magus reached up to scratch his right eye. There was a grating sound of steel on steel. A thin smile stretched the seamed muscles of his rebuilt face. "True, there is still a little time before we strike. A little, little time."

Chapter Eighteen

The night passed peaceably.

From everything that Ryan knew about their two enemies, he considered it unlikely that they would make their attack in some crude, brutal way. It wouldn't be hard to smash in the shutters over the windows and lob in a handful of frag grens or flamers or implodes.

But that wasn't usually the way of Wolfram or the Magus.

When the moment came for them to take their awaited vengeance against Ryan and J.B., it would be something unexpected, something more subtle. The point, not the edge.

Nonetheless, Ryan made sure they all bolted their windows and doors.

There was no point in taking chances in case Wolfram and the Magus came up with a cunning double bluff, chose a full-frontal attack. All things were possible.

THEY HEARD THE NEWS about the killing of Diego Kahla from one of the busboys.

"Stripped and stabbed," said Richard, a short, crop-headed blond lad in a spotless white apron, his name printed on a card pinned to his T-shirt. "Nobody heard a thing."

"Robbed?" Ryan asked.

"Sure was. Winning his duel didn't do the poor sucker no bastard good."

The thumping of the powerful engines had begun a little after dawn, building up a good head of steam to take them upriver for their night's scheduled stop at Cairo. Not all that many of the passengers had bothered to rise early to come down for breakfast. From the singing and shouting going on into the early hours of the morning, it seemed as though a lot of them would be suffering hangovers.

"Three killings altogether," Richard said as he poured out glasses of sparkling ice water for everyone.

"Three?" J.B. repeated. "Who were the other two?"

"Gambler named Sweetwater Rickets and a breed whore. Called herself Baby Martinez. Shared a cabin down the port side, in the steerage class. Purser found them this morning. Word of a shot in the dark. Sweetwater's knife was in her heart, and a .22 ball from her little pearl-handled over-and-under derringer in his temple. His wallet was open, and a handful of jack was still clasped in her thieving fingers."

"This paradise of a vessel holds too many serpents aboard it," Mildred said. "Maybe we should have taken to our other plan and cut and run."

Nobody answered her.

A wispy young blond woman appeared at their table. "Hi, I'm Sprite and I'll be serving you breakfast. Assisted by Richard here. You ready to order?"

After consulting the menu, everyone went for the same order. Fresh-squeezed orange juice, followed by the Eye-Opener Starter Breakfast: three eggs over-easy, a monstrous mountain of rancheros hash, which was chunks of fried potato with a liberal helping of onions and thick-slicked peppers, red and green and orange; a side order of avocado-cream dip, spiced with chilies; six strips of back bacon and three link sausages, backed up with whole-wheat toast and grape jelly and washed down with several helpings from a bottomless jug of steaming coffee.

"That was magnificent," Doc said with a sigh. "It has quite eased away all thoughts of that poor murdered man. The *Golden Eagle* is a wonderfully dangerous craft. A most luxurious, dark ferry that carries us to Heaven or to Hell."

Sprite appeared again, offering more coffee, but everyone—even Jak—refused.

At that moment they all felt the familiar rumbling of the huge stern-wheel, starting to thrust them away from their overnight mooring. Water foamed under the stem, and they heard the clanking of the windlass, tugging up the double-fluked anchors from bow and stern.

"On to Cairo," Richard said, collecting a bowlful of dirty plates and cutlery.

"What's the forecast for weather?" Krysty asked. "Looked fine and bright this morning."

The busboy hesitated. "Think I heard of a wind rising from the south. But they tell us not to worry passengers with such things. The *Eagle* can stand up to most weather."

THEY MADE GOOD steady progress up the Sippi during morning.

It was a little after noon when the *Golden Eagle* steamed across the old state line, taking her into Kentucky. The river twisted and turned endlessly, like a sun-warmed cottonmouth, between sandstone cliffs and past tree-lined bluffs. They steamed past cutoff oxbows, occasionally saluting small settlements with the steam siren.

The main rooms were quiet, with only the fruit machines seeing much business. The more serious gamblers stayed in their beds, saving themselves for the evening gaming. Just a few of the hardened players leaned against the poker and blackjack tables, idly turning cards with the weary dealers, counters chinking. The pit bosses endlessly walked around the saloons, their cold eyes darting into every corner of every table, ever alert.

Ryan had insisted on sticking to the plan of not splitting up, leaving anyone alone and vulnerable. He went with Krysty, Jak and Doc, while Mildred and J.B. chose to stay in their cabin for a while.

"Would there be any objection if we were to play a hand or two of poker?" Doc asked.

"Why not? Just don't get carried away and spend what we don't have. We'll sit here and watch." He gestured to an inlaid beech-and-walnut chaise longue, situated near the green baize gambling tables.

A bow-tied waiter quickly came to take their orders. Ryan chose a straight malt. Krysty picked a gin and tonic, and Jak opted for a cola and rum.

Doc eased himself into one of the high stools, nodding at the five men gathered around. "No objection to a newcomer joining you?" he asked.

"Five-card stud, ten for openers, no limit," the dealer snapped.

"That sounds jolly fun." He fumbled in the deep pockets of his antique frock coat for a handful of jack that Ryan had given to him. "I'm in, gentlemen."

J.B. AND MILDRED HAD MADE slow, gentle love in their locked cabin, kissing and touching, bringing each other sighing pleasure.

It was only after the second coupling that Mildred got up to wash at the basin in the en suite bathroom, becoming aware that the steady movement of the steamer had altered in the past hour or so. They were pitching much more roughly from side to side, the waves jolting under the bow. The soapy water swished in the basin, slopping over the rim onto the floor.

"Getting unsteady, John," she called.

"Yeah." He stood and peered between the slats of the shutters. "White water breaking on the banks," he said. "Choppy waves, coming from behind us."

"Think we'll have to stop?"

"Boat this size should be able to cut through most weather." He put on his glasses in order to be able to see better. "But the sky's black as pitch."

RYAN AND THE OTHERS had also noticed the menacing change in the weather.

The glasses had begun to slide on the polished wood, and waiters were going around raising the slotted sides of the tables to prevent things falling to the floor.

Ryan stood and went to see how Doc was getting on. He'd been playing steadily for well over an hour, and his pile of chips was the largest of any of the players'.

"The gods smile upon me, Ryan, my dear friend," he said, clasping his hand to his chest. "When I have lost I have lost small, and the few winning hands have been big ones."

"Shut your flapping mouth and play, you lucky old fart," barked a heavily built man with a nicotine-stained mustache and rings on every finger.

"Take it easy, mister," Ryan warned, easing back his coat to show the butt of the SIG-Sauer.

"I'll raise ten," Doc said.

Two of the players dropped out, leaving the man with the mustache and a younger, red-haired gambler, dressed as a priest. Both went along with Doc.

Ryan leaned over his shoulder. "Show me," he whispered.

Doc slowly fanned out the five cards: ten of diamonds, king of hearts, king of clubs, ten of spades and the king of diamonds. High-ranking full house.

"Raise another twenty," he said, leaning back in his chair.

The priest folded, but the mustached man pressed on. "Your twenty and another twenty. See what kind of balls you got, old-timer."

"Big enough, I believe. Your twenty and forty."

This brought a long hesitation. Krysty and Jak joined Ryan at the table, watching to see how the gambling was going. Behind them, at a roulette table, a young female croupier was trying hard to attract some morning attention to her wheel.

"I offered a rise of forty," Doc repeated. "Did I not hear some comment about showing the size of my genitals? I've shown you mine. Now you show me yours."

The man gnawed at the ends of his mustache. "You're fuckin' bluffing me, you outlander retard!"

"Pay to see."

The house dealer was looking a little worried at the growing anger, glancing behind him to see if any of the wandering pit bosses was nearby. The wind outside was now rising audibly, and the movement of the *Golden Eagle* was gathering, making glasses rattle, the chandeliers tinkling.

"It's a bluff."

Doc was losing patience. "A gentleman at the gaming table does not willfully keep another gentleman waiting."

"Shit!" He threw his cards on the baize, revealing three eights.

Doc leaned forward to stack his own cards, unseen, but his opponent reached for them. "Let's see what bluffing shit you was pulling on me."

The dealer opened his mouth to check this piece of appalling behavior, and Doc Tanner began to stand. But Ryan was the quickest. He drew his blaster and pushed the muzzle into the angry face of the beaten player.

"Let it lie, friend," he said quietly. "Doc won fair and square, and you don't have a right to see what cards he was holding."

The man dressed as a priest held out his hands in an attitude of prayer. "No need for violence, brothers," he intoned piously. "It's only a game, after all."

"Fuck that!" Despite the threat of the 9 mm automatic between his eyes, the man's hand was inching toward the holstered revolver at his hip.

"Another inch and your brains get to decorate the wall behind you," Ryan warned. Though he wanted nothing less than to squeeze the trigger and blow the man away, trouble was always something to avoid when possible.

The red mist had come down, and the gambler was blind to any danger. His fingers brushed the walnut butt of his big, rebuilt Army Colt.

Ryan sighed and smashed his left fist into the center of the man's face, crushing his nose, breaking the bone and spreading the septum into bloody pulp. Crimson streamed out over the mustache, down into the open mouth and onto the table.

Suddenly security was everywhere. A stocky pit boss carrying a snub-nosed .32 pistol jammed it into Ryan's ribs from behind, his own face blanching in turn as he felt the muzzle of Jak's big Colt Python Magnum grating against the center of his spine. And there, in the doorway of the gambling saloon, balancing awkwardly against the swaying of the boat, was J.B. with his Uzi at the ready.

"Everyone keep calm," the Armorer said.

To the sec men he added, "Best tuck away the blasters, friends. That way nobody's goin' to get hurt."

The gambler had slithered to the thick carpet, coughing blood, hands clasped to his face.

Captain Huston appeared from nowhere, hands folded behind his back, his good eye surveying the violent scene, the drawn blasters.

"Trouble, gentlemen?" he asked quietly. "Like to hear what went down here."

It was the priest who answered, bowing toward the skipper of the stern-wheeler as though he were one of the disciples. "I saw it all, Captain."

"So, tell me."

"Old gentleman been winning and winning well. Feller on the floor got steamed up and tried to grab at his hand, see what he'd been holding. Guy here—" he pointed to Ryan "—with the one eye, stepped in. Warned about what he'd do. Drew his blaster. But the man with the mustache there ignored him. Started to draw. Gotten coldcocked. My view is that he had it coming, and he was lucky not to have his skull blown apart. God and his blessed angels smiled upon him."

Huston nodded, swaying at a violent shift from his boat. "Getting skittish," he muttered, looking around the saloon. "Seems that you acted for the best, Mr. Cawdor."

He turned to his sec men. "Take this gentleman up and stop him ruining our fine carpet. Show him the brig for a few hours to gentle him down." He clapped his hands. "And that's it. Now, the weather's getting restless, ladies and gentlemen. We're going to have to clear public areas and close the decks. Real sorry. Need to find a quiet shelter and moor up, so if you could all return to your cabins. Only for a couple of hours. And there'll be complimentary drinks this evening.''

The roulette wheels stopped spinning, and the cards vanished into the discard slots on the tables. Slowly and reluctantly the room cleared, leaving a faint haze of cigar smoke hanging around the crystal lamps.

Ryan holstered the SIG-Sauer as the semiconscious gambler was hauled from the bloodied floor and carried away, toes dragging across the carpet.

Captain Huston looked at him. "Seems you did the right thing, Mr. Cawdor. Glad to hear that. Wouldn't have wanted to go against… Well, upset anyone's plans for the rest of the voyage." He put his head on one side, listening to the wind rising as one of the shutters on the port side ripped loose with a deafening crash of torn timber. "Best get to the bridge. Worsening. Take care on your way to your cabins."

He spun on his heel and stalked off. The boat's movements were becoming increasingly violent, and Ryan reached out to steady himself on a fixed table. "Heard the man," he said. "Let's go, friends. Before we get blown away."

WHEN THEY REACHED their deck level, Krysty hesitated, staring at the door to the stormy outside. "Would like to take a look there," she said, voice raised against the screaming of the wind. "Sounds a sight worth the seeing."

Ryan shook his head. "Let's go back inside, lover."

Mildred and J.B. were already at their own cabin door, hanging on to each other against the pitching of the deck. Jak was steadying Doc, who was jingling the jack in his pocket.

"Thanks for your help, my dear Ryan," he called. "Incidentally did I show you that I had the winning hand?"

"You did, Doc, you did."

Krysty tugged at his arm. "Come on, love, get a life. Don't always have to play it safe. We can hold on to the rails if it's too bad."

Somewhere a door was slamming remorselessly back and forth. And it felt as if the *Golden Eagle* was slip-sliding in a half circle, her bow pointing toward the starboard shore of the Sippi.

The other four had all made their minds up, retreating into their cabins, leaving Ryan and Krysty alone in the shadowy corridor, where the polished oil lamps swung and clattered on their brass gimbals.

"Come on. Just for a minute. We can wash up and get dry in the cabin. Be fun."

Ryan closed his eye for a moment, knowing in his heart that this was a bad idea, but not feeling quite strongly enough to stop Krysty from going out onto the deck.

As she turned the white handle, the door was ripped out of her hand, crashing back, letting in a wave of wind-torn spray that flattened her hair, tugging at her clothes. Krysty laughed exuberantly at the violence of the storm, turning to beckon to Ryan. "Come on, lover!" The words were mimed against the bedlam of the hurricane.

She vanished and he followed her, ducking and blinking against the driven water. The sky was like pewter, with no trace of light, making the river look supernatural and menacing, its muddy surface whipped with the crests of white waves a dozen feet high. The banks were invisible through the drenching rain and spray. Though the massive stern-wheel was only a few feet away from them, it was both invisible and inaudible.

Ryan felt that the boat was drifting sideways, and he realized for the first time that she was actually out of control, a toy of the raging storm.

Krysty was on the starboard side, clinging to the rail, beneath a canvas canopy that was blowing wildly, looking as if it were about to tear to shreds at any moment.

Ryan flattened himself against the superstructure, beneath the overhanging balcony of the stateroom where he guessed Wolfram and the Magus would be sheltering, maybe even watching Krysty and himself in this stupe venture.

"Come back in!" he yelled, but her face was turned away, eyes squeezed shut against the primal force of nature. Her head was thrown back, relishing the power and the danger.

He took a half step toward her, reaching out against the wind, when there was a deafening crack, screaming over the typhoon's raging. The canvas ripped across, flapping loose from its mooring above Krysty, plunging down on her with a malevolent intent, like a giant manta ray.

It wrapped around her head and shoulders, plucking Krysty off balance, tipping her against the rail, her legs flailing for a moment as she tried to grab for support.

But the storm had her in its thrall, whirling her up and over, toppling back toward the churning wheel at the stern of the helpless vessel.

Ryan was after her, feet skidding on the wet planks, blinded by the spray. One hand reached for the slippery rail while the other grabbed helplessly at the torn canvas shroud that held his lover.

His fingers brushed it, and he saw it snag for a moment on a stanchion on the edge of the stern. The one-eyed man snatched the moment to lock his hand in the rough, soaked material, steadying it for a couple of seconds on the brink of the drop, feeling Krysty's weight tugging against him.

Agonizingly it was shifting him, as well, lifting him, pulling him up and over the rail, following Krysty toward the thrashing, whirling paddle, and Ryan knew that they would be both sucked and crushed into the dark water.

He was over, managing to twist like an acrobat and grab the iron stanchion, hanging on to the suspended canvas with his other hand. He clung there, poised between life and death, aware that nothing could now save them. In a few seconds his grip would go, and they would be doomed.

He had closed his eye, then opened it once more—to find that he was staring, inches away, into the blankly incurious steel eyes of the Magus.

Chapter Nineteen

Time stopped.

Ryan wasn't even aware of the ripping, howling wind that tore at him, or the grinding strain on his arms, one holding the ragged canvas that enveloped Krysty, the other gripping the slippery iron stanchion on the corner of the rail. He knew that the whirling stern-wheel was slicing through the spray, only a few inches away from Krysty's dangling boots.

But none of that had the same reality as the glittering face of the Magus, streaming with river water, leering at him from the safety of the deck. The angular skull, remembered from years long gone, was so close that Ryan could see every pore in the smooth skin, see the effects of the sophisticated, heroic surgery—the best available in all of Deathlands—carried out in the past, which had saved his life, leaving him to survive with prosthetic add-ons to his hands and his face.

The teeth were a strange, mottled mix of plastic and titanium steel, sharp pointed, with serrated edges that Ryan knew could snap through reinforced cable.

And the dead eyes of the Magus, sheathed in metallic lenses, were impenetrable in their deep-set sockets, staring blankly into Ryan's good eye.

A distant phrase, barely recollected, came into Ryan's memory at that spine-chilling moment. Something about becoming death the destroyer of worlds. That was what he saw there, in that crazed, alien face, aware that this was the last living being that he would ever see.

The pressure on both his arms was becoming unendurable, and Ryan knew that the last train was about to pull out for himself and for Krysty. Nothing and nobody could save them now. He felt his fingers slipping off the cold iron, the pounding stern-wheel eager to drag them both down and under. The noise and the spray boiled about him, numbing what remained of his senses.

"Ryan Cawdor." The voice slid through the maelstrom that whirled around the *Golden Eagle*. It was unbelievable that Ryan could hear his name being whispered from the cruel mailbox slit of a mouth. The face of the Magus, so close to him, showed no human emotion.

The artificial hand lifted and brushed against Ryan's cheek, wiping away the blown spume, making him wince in expectation of the blow.

Ryan tried to spit his hatred into the passionless face of the Magus, but the wind blew the thread of spittle away into the shrieking darkness. Krysty was limp and still, a deadweight in his arms.

Suddenly the Magus moved, reaching over and gripping Ryan by his other shoulder, the artificially powered fingers digging in so hard that muscles creaked, making Ryan gasp in pain. Then he was being lifted, with unimaginable strength, back over the rail, Krysty wrapped tight in her sodden shroud of colored canvas, trailing behind him.

Both of them were safely on the water-washed deck planking, lying there helpless at the feet of the Magus.

Ryan fumbled for the butt of the SIG-Sauer, glimpsing a ghost of a chance to take the creature out. But the Magus was quicker, his boot crunching on Ryan's wrist, pinning him motionless, his dull, leaden gaze piercing into his face.

The boat was jerking and quivering like a mortally wounded animal, its timbers grinding out a shrieking protest at the storm's treatment. The sky seemed a little lighter, viewed through the great veil of opaque spray, whirling off the top slats of the spinning stern-wheel.

Ryan could just feel Krysty's movement, weak and helpless like a sickly, newborn calf, kicking to try to free herself from the enveloping awning.

The Magus leaned down toward Ryan, his index finger touching just below the undamaged right eye, making him shrink again. He pushed at the soft, wet skin, hard enough to bring a frisson of terror that Ryan was about to be blinded.

"Not now," the Magus whispered. "Not now. Later. Yes, later, Ryan."

And he turned on his heel and vanished along the deck into the clouding spray.

Chapter Twenty

"I say go whack them," Jak stated, pounding his right fist into his left palm.

"Could take them at St. Louis." J.B. crossed his legs and looked across the cabin at the others.

The worst of the storm had eased, and the paddle steamer was once more making her steady way upstream on the Sippi. Over two hours had slithered by since the bizarre encounter with the Magus on the stern deck.

"They've got all the sec men, and I reckon that their stateroom'll probably be barricaded." Mildred was washing her hands in the basin.

There had been a number of injuries during the typhoon or hurricane or whatever it had been, and she had offered her help, setting broken limbs and bandaging cuts. Her first care had been for Krysty, who had been nearly knocked unconscious when she was carried over the railing. There was a deep swelling under the fiery hair, just above the right ear, and several purple-crimson bruises all along her legs and arms and around her ribs. It had taken Mildred some time to make certain there were no fractures. Now she rested on the bed, looking pale and washed-out.

Doc paced up and down the room, the ferrule of his swordstick rapping on the boards and then making a more muffled sound on the carpet. He was biting his lip, fingers constantly stroking the silvery stubble on his chin.

"Upon my soul! But this is a damnably strange experience. These two villains are seemingly set on a course of action destined to allow them some vengeance for some old and ill-imagined slight. But they are prepared to wait for it."

Ryan laughed mockingly. "Believe me, Doc, there's nothing ill imagined about their vengeance. Days we rode with Trader, me and J.B. stepped on some toes. And some faces. Left some smoldering villes. Some weeping widows and plenty of red-eyed orphans. More than a handful of widowers, as well."

"Magus and Wolfram got more claims against us than most," the Armorer said. "Wolfram's business of trading in stickies was ruined by us. He got some wounds in that action. And the Magus... Well, he'll never again be the man he was."

"Finding them both here." Ryan shook his head. "Damn, but my clothes are still wet."

"You fieldstrip and clean and oil the SIG-Sauer?" J.B. asked.

Ryan nodded. "Sure. Thing is, the bastards got a plan. No doubt. Can't be a coincidence they're here. I wonder if they might've been watching us from back in Twin Forks. The steel-eyed fuck-head had me right in the palm of his hand." He gestured, squeezing his fingers together. "Like that. But he just said that it would come later. Confident. Real confident."

He stood and stretched, feeling the stiffness in his arms and wrists from the battle to save Krysty's life, wincing at the strain of the deep black bruise where the unnatural grip of the Magus had plucked him from a watery tomb.

"I've changed my mind," Krysty said quietly.

"About staying aboard?"

She took a long, slow breath, managing a pale smile at Ryan. "It's a woman's prerogative, isn't it, lover? If it had just been an ordinary sort of ambush..." She let the words trail off into the stillness, a stillness that was only broken by the regular pounding of the stern-wheel a few yards away from them.

"I don't know." Ryan sat by her and squeezed her hand. "There's things a man shouldn't run away from."

"Very runic and old West," Mildred said, half teasing, half serious. "Very John Wayne. A man's gotta do what a man's gotta do. Even if he ends up in Boot Hill."

They all froze, every head turning upward when they felt rather than heard the sensation of someone moving above them. Ponderous, slow feet, very heavy.

"Wolfram," Jak said. "Shitter's letting us know he's there."

The crackling intercom was suddenly switched on, and they all listened to the distorted voice of Captain Huston.

"Storm did some damage to the superstructure of the *Eagle,* but we've got that in hand. Soon have the old lady looking as fresh and good as new. Worst was the calliope got mostly blown away. We carry some spare pipes so, the Good Lord willing, we'll be tuning up some music for you in a day or so. Main thing is that we've lost some time.''

Ryan checked his wrist chron, surprised to find that the battering didn't seem to have damaged it at all. ''Running well late,'' he said.

The voice went on. ''Pride ourselves on this run that we keep time. Means that we won't hit Crosstown on schedule unless we take in a tuck here and there. Easiest is to pick up at St. Louis. Sorry to disappoint those passengers looking forward to a whoop and a holler in the ville, but we'll be stopping only for about three hours to stock up on water and provisions and carry out some of the main repairs. Then we'll move on. Problem is that a storm like that one will have changed the course of the Sippi. New sandbanks and bars and shallows. Have to go slower the rest of the way.''

''I was looking forward to some time on shore,'' Mildred said. ''Visited old St. Louis in the days when I was doing competitive pistol shooting.''

Ryan smiled. ''Find it changed. Got badly nuked. Old city more or less vanished, and the site of the settlement shifted by miles. Just a black, rad-hot hole in the ground where it was. The big river moved, as well. New St. Louis is a neat little ville. Not unlike Twin Forks.''

''Really!'' She shook her head. ''Still, seems a shame that we won't have much time there.''

The intercom coughed and barked again. ''We're real sorry about this. Every passenger can enjoy a complimentary drink of either wine or beer with their meal this evening. The storm means that we'll hit

Cairo much later than we wanted. Probably during the dark hours. We suggest that passengers stay aboard. Some mean folks move during the blackness in Cairo. Place where the vicious animals come out at night. Then, soon as we get past St. Louis, everything's back to normal. Any questions, all of you feel free to approach any of my officers. And if they can't help you, then I'll be glad to do my best for you."

AT THE EVENING MEAL Ryan noticed that there were again two seats empty at Captain Huston's table, Wolfram and the Magus choosing to stay hidden in their own set of rooms.

The maître d' offered Ryan and Krysty the seats, but they chose to stay with the others and dine at a smaller table set off on the port side of the saloon, not far from the main-entrance doors. The food was less exotic, with a smaller range of dishes, and less well cooked.

But it was still better than adequate.

Ryan had examined their cabins, finding that there were interconnecting doors concealed behind Oriental hanging drapes. For extra security he unlocked them, giving them all free access to one another's cabins and to a better escape in the event of any sudden attack.

But his gut feeling was that the twin enemies weren't planning anything like that.

The whole thing seemed in their hands, and Ryan was uneasily conscious of time passing, as though he and the others were already just puppets of Wolfram and the Magus. But however hard he tried, Ryan couldn't perceive any direct threat.

There was still time to ask Huston to pull alongside the rain-drenched shore, and they could all be off safely in a couple of minutes. But Ryan suspected that the evil brains of the pair would already have seen that possibility and laid specific plans to counter it.

It seemed that all they could do was sit and wait and keep alert.

THE NIGHT PASSED BY without any incident.

Ryan had woken from a bizarre dream involving an elderly woman attempting to deliver a flock of geese to a house where he was in hiding. He lay still, on his back, eye probing the darkness. The boat was still moving slowly, its ponderous engines turning the powerful wheel at the stern, thrusting it upstream against the swollen waters of the Sippi.

Once the threat had been established from the Magus and Wolfram, he had suggested to the others that it would be a good idea not to sleep nude. Not that Doc ever did. Best to keep mainly clothed, with just the boots kicked off. Blasters needed to be very much to hand.

"The last time that I slept unclothed, as nature intended, bare-nekkid, nude, stripped, peeled ... My apologies for wandering a little. Not since I was in hospital for a minor operation when I was in my early twenties, in Egremont, Illinois. Then it was forced upon me."

"What minor op, Doc?" Mildred asked.

He had colored, huffing and puffing. "I think that falls into the region of being my business."

"Means it was either prostate or piles, Doc," she replied, grinning wolfishly at his discomfort. "And if I staked the family fortunes on it, I think I'd go for piles. Were you riding tall in the saddle, Doc?"

The old man glared across the cabin at the woman, fists clenching. "It is truly no matter for jesting, you sneering harridan!"

"Doc!" Krysty admonished him. "You don't have to—"

But he was off and running. "I can tell you, madam, that it was far from amusing. One of the most severe pains that I have ever suffered. It was akin to having a child's flayed fist protruding from my rectal orifice. Had you offered me a thousand dollars, *Dr. Wyeth*, to sit down, I should not have been able to do it."

Mildred held up her hands, palms outward. "All right, all right, Doc. Mea culpa. Shouldn't have made a joke about something like that. I've seen patients with that problem, and I know how agonizing it can be for them. Sorry."

He looked at her, gradually relaxing. "I accept your apology. Ye knew not what ye spake. But I must insist—"

Ryan laid a hand on his shoulder. "I think that's enough, Doc," he said quietly. "We got us plenty of trouble without any falling-out together."

The Armorer nodded. "That's true enough, Ryan. I can't think of worse enemies in all of Deathlands to have against you than those two. The Magus and Wolfram.''

WHEN RYAN WALKED barefoot onto the dew-wet deck, the sky was just brightening from the east. He looked above him, toward the barricaded stateroom deck, and caught a glimpse of one of the hard-faced sec men, leaning over, staring down at him.

"Morning, friend," Ryan called, waving his left hand. His right dropped to the cold butt of the SIG-Sauer, already holstered at his hip.

The man's expression didn't alter, and he slowly drew back out of sight.

"Yeah, and fuck you, too," Ryan whispered to himself, resuming his watch over the river.

The great paddle wheel was turning at a good rate, the rudder holding the *Golden Eagle* safely in the middle of the Sippi, which was, Ryan calculated, close on half a mile wide at that point, up above Cairo.

The banks were wooded, with a mix of conifer and deciduous trees, and there was no sign of life anywhere on either side of the river.

Ryan was aware of someone moving behind him and he spun, seeing Jak a few paces from him. The teenager grinned at his friend's speed of reflex.

"Fast as ever," he said.

"Man gets slow, also gets dead," Ryan replied, quoting one of the Trader's most frequent sayings.

"Trader also said man moves too fast gets dead," Jak said, the morning wind tugging at his tumbling white hair, blowing it over his ruby red eyes.

"Yeah, he did, didn't he? Well, nobody ever said Trader was the most consistent man on this planet."

"Think he's alive?"

"Likely not." Ryan considered it. "Think we'd have heard some word by now if the old lion was still living."

A small boat shot out from the starboard bank, propelled by a couple of young boys, rowing together, heading toward the center of the stream.

Captain Huston, or whoever was on the bridge, spotted them and gave them a warning blast on the steam whistle. The loud, melancholy sound echoed across the Sippi, deadened by the thick forest all around.

The boys were both laughing and they stopped rowing, standing up in their rocking boat, dropping their breeches, mooning the huge paddle steamer.

Ryan leaned over the rail, watching the capering lads as their boat receded astern, into the tumbling waves caused by the passage of the *Golden Eagle,* then he caught a familiar sound—the muted cough of a silenced rifle, from somewhere behind and above him.

Jak had also been watching the boys, smiling at their dawn high spirits. He gasped and Ryan glanced back in time to see the taller of them, a ginger-headed youth, throw up his arms and topple silently into the muddy waters. He rose once and then vanished in a small ripple.

The blaster coughed above them once more, and the second lad went down, blood blossoming from his face, joining his dead companion in the river while the empty boat drifted on southward.

"Son of fucking bitch!" Jak swore, half drawing his own Magnum. "Those shit-eating bastards. Came from—"

Ryan heard the laughter from the closed-off stateroom deck and recognized the high, grating metallic sound of the Magus's voice.

He touched Jak on the shoulder, aware that the teenager was quivering with the ferocious tension of white-hot anger. "Let it lay," he said.

"Cold murders."

"And nothing we can do about it. Not now. Likely nobody else saw or heard a thing. Silenced hunting blaster. Noise wouldn't carry above the sound of the engine and the paddle wheel. Kids are dead. Nothing bring them back."

"Like a chance at venging them."

Ryan nodded. "Can't argue with you on that, Jak. Just have to hope the chance comes."

HE DIDN'T TELL KRYSTY or the others about the bloody double murder. There wasn't much point. The only thing that really mattered to them was self-preservation.

At breakfast they were entertained by a tall, skinny musician, with greased back hair and a vivid floral waistcoat. He plucked a long-neck banjo and sang a mournful and beautiful song about guerrilla fighters running the ridges of their green homeland of Tennessee.

He bowed at the round of applause when he finished the song. "Many thanks, y'all," he said. "That was a predark melody from the talented pen of a great writer called John Stewart, one of the immortals."

Mildred clapped loudest. "I know John Stewart. Got several of his albums. Well, I mean that I used to have them. Love him. Amazing to hear one of his songs here, like this. Amazing."

Ryan urged them all to eat as large a breakfast as they could manage. "Never know what's going to go down and when we might get another chance of a good meal."

Not that Jak needed any urging.

There was a serve-yourself buffet, and Ryan watched incredulously as the snow-haired teenager seemed to be in perpetual motion, coming to the table with a platter heaped high with hash browns, eggs and bacon. Moments later he was up and moving back toward the long table of food, peering under the polished metal covers, helping himself to baked trout and a mixed-pepper omelet.

Ryan finally raised a hand as Jak stood, ready to begin his fourth trip to the buffet. "Don't take what I said too literally," he said. "Three helpings should be enough for anyone."

"Still got couple small gaps that'd fill up nicely some fresh fruit salad."

Ryan grinned. "Just don't make yourself sick. Need all the health we got."

Krysty put down her empty coffee cup and dabbed at her lips with a linen napkin. "Think that all of this could be mind games, lover?"

"You mean that the Magus and Wolfram don't actually intend to do anything hostile? Just scare the shit out of us?"

She nodded. "Yeah."

Ryan rubbed his finger down his chin, thinking. Finally he shook his head. "No," he said. "No, I don't think so."

Chapter Twenty-One

"By the mark three . . . by the mark twain."

The elements were combining against the *Golden Eagle*. After the violent storm, they now encountered a dense fog that had come drifting out from the forest to the east, layering itself over the sullen waters of the Sippi. Ryan and the others stood on their section of deck, leaning on the cold, wet, iron rail, watching as the banks disappeared from sight.

Captain Huston had immediately slowed the paddle wheel, dropping the speed of the huge vessel to a bare walking pace. And he had put a leadsman into the blunt bow, swinging his weighted line, hauling it in and reading the depth of water beneath the shallow keel.

"By the mark twain." There was a pause as he coiled the line, heaving it ahead of the slow-moving boat, the splash muffled as the lead hit the river. "By the mark twain. Coarse sand." His voice echoed around the silent stern-wheeler, up to the captain, who stood huddled in a dark blue pea jacket on the bridge.

Mildred had her arm around J.B., her braided hair glistening with the crystals of mist. "One of the first things I remember when I started schooling is learning that the writer, Mark Twain, took his pen name from working on riverboats. I never thought that I'd ever ride one and hear them calling out the depths like this.''

"I might be in error, but it seems to me that the vaporous murk is becoming thicker. I can no longer make out the line of the shore on this starboard side," Doc stated.

"And we're slowing down more," Krysty said. "Paddle wheel's hardly turning at all."

One of the officers was passing by and heard her. "It's the hurricane, madam. Something as bad as that can change the course and shape and depth of the Sippi and make all the charts out of date and useless. Captain has to feel his way along or risk running her aground."

"What's that?" Jak had his head on one side. "Thought heard powerful engine."

Everyone listened, but the sound, if it had been there in the first place, wasn't repeated.

The badly damaged calliope was in the middle of being repaired, and every now and again there would be a brief burst of music from the shrouding fog.

First it was a shredded version of a blaring Sousa march, followed by a melancholy, bass-heavy attempt at the predark weepy "I Will Always Love You." Now they heard a florid half verse of "Shenandoah."

"Away you rolling river." Doc said mournfully. "Not that you can possibly locate the damned river with this fog. The way it progresses, you won't be able to see a hand in front of your foot."

"What?" Jak said.

"I said you would shortly be unable to make out your knee in front of your ears. No, I am getting fearfully confused. What an addle-brain I have become." He closed his pale blue eyes and concentrated. "One will not see one's hand in front of one's face. That is it."

The calliope had broken into a lively version of "Dixie," steam rising from the pipes of the organ and mingling with the layers of fog.

One of the crew of the *Golden Eagle* had been working at the davits of a lifeboat, slung close to where Ryan and the others had been standing. Now he was almost invisible in the fog. Ryan turned and found the man was staring at him, hammer poised, starting to pound at the davit with great vigor.

Krysty sensed something wasn't right and also turned. "What is it, lover?" she asked quietly.

"Think that man's been put there to watch us," he replied. "Could be in Wolfram's pay."

"Sure you aren't getting paranoid?"

He managed a half smile. "Mebbe. When you're dealing with people like the Magus and Wolfram, then a touch of paranoia isn't a bad idea."

THE ORNATE BOAT WAS barely crawling along. The banks were totally invisible, and Captain Huston was using the mournful whistle at regular intervals, warning anyone else foolish enough to be out on the Sippi that the *Golden Eagle* was in command of the center of the current.

It hadn't made any difference to the gamblers.

The little old ladies with gloved hands still battled endlessly with the fruit machines, the whirring of the gears interrupted occasionally by the soft tinkling of jack spilling into the winning trays, to be swept by the eager players into the waiting plastic cups.

Roulette wheels spun, the ivory balls rattling and bouncing from slot to slot, and the croupiers carried out their business with the solemn reverence of acolytes, worshiping at the shrine of the great god Chance.

The air was thick with expensive cigar smoke, reeking with the scent of brandy and whiskey. Outside, on the slippery decks, the long rows of multicolored lights that draped the vessel glowed dimly through the mist, showing the diminishing outline of the *Golden Eagle.*

A pair of officers loomed from the fog in front of them, both saluting smartly.

"Ryan Cawdor?"

"Yes."

The taller of them had a long, drooping mustache that was dripping with water from the mist. "We have a problem, and Captain Huston wondered whether you and your companion, John Dix, might be able to help us."

"Problem?" the Armorer repeated. "What kind of problem are we talking about?"

"Best the skipper tells you himself. But it could involve some shooting."

Ryan laid his right hand on the butt of the SIG-Sauer. "We're ready."

"Sure are," J.B. agreed, showing the Uzi to the two officers.

"I'll come," Jak said.

"We can all come," Mildred added.

The officer hesitated. "Captain said he didn't want to start a panic. Asked if just the two of you could come. Might need the rest of you later."

Ryan considered the request. His first thought was that it might be part of some dark plan of the Magus and Wolfram, but it didn't seem likely. He would back himself and J.B. against any sec-man ambush they might try.

He turned to the others. "Be back soon. Go straight down to our cabin and keep the doors bolted."

Krysty tugged at his arm. "Don't like this, lover. Got a bad feel."

"Got to take some chances," he said. "They could have chilled us any time, before we knew they were aboard."

"Quick as you can, sir," the mustached officer said, glancing at a gleaming silver half hunter that dangled from a chain across his midriff.

Ryan nodded. "Don't forget. Keep the bolts across. And if we aren't back in sixty minutes from now—"

"No harm'll come to you or your friend, sir," the other officer stated. "I reckon we can more or less guarantee that."

"Glad to hear it." He kissed Krysty on the cheek, tasting the fog in her hair. J.B. kissed Mildred, and the two old friends followed the sailors across the deck. Within ten paces they'd vanished into the mist.

J.B WAS ALONGSIDE Ryan. "You sure you're sure about this, *compadre?*"

"We're ready for anything they might try."

"Guess so."

One of the officers turned to make sure they were following him, smiling encouragingly.

The calliope was still going at full blast, pumping out a jazzed-up version of "This Land Is Your Land," drowning out any other sounds.

A set of iron stairs loomed out of the swirling mist ahead of them, and they climbed to a higher deck, continuing toward the high bridge.

"She's stopped," J.B. said, head on one side. "Feel the vibration. Paddle's not turning."

The sun was veiled, and the morning was as dark as late evening. It was also bitterly cold, and Ryan decided that he might go down and indulge in a brandy once they'd finished with whatever it was that Captain Huston wanted from them. He hurried along the deck, shoulders hunched against the cold.

"Nearly there, sir," one of the sailors called. "One more lot of steps."

The higher they went, the thicker grew the fog. Ryan remembered Doc's saying about not being able to see your hand in front of your face. It was very nearly true.

"In here." The officer stepped aside from the half-glassed door onto the control area of the *Golden Eagle*. It was flooded with light from several oil lamps, and Ryan and J.B. blinked, dazzled by the brightness. They were able to make out the stocky figure of Captain Huston, gold braid glinting on his uniform, standing by the sailor at the huge wheel.

But there were other people standing on the bridge of the stern-wheeler. One was enormously fat, another skinny with metallic gloves, a cruel smile slashed across his reconstructed face, and three or four sec men, all with drawn and cocked blasters.

Ryan felt his heart sink. It was a trap after all, though he couldn't quite see the scope of his enemies' plan yet. He was aware of J.B. tensing at his side, half lifting the Uzi.

"A hasty action would be regretted by everyone, John Dix," Wolfram said in a warm, buttery tone, "and would mean the deaths of your friends."

"Your absent friends," the Magus added.

The calliope suddenly stopped playing, and they all heard the noise that it had been masking, the noise that Jak thought he might have heard a few minutes earlier.

It was a powerful engine, revving up somewhere on the port side of the *Golden Eagle*.

Then Ryan saw the plan.

"They've lifted Krysty and the others," he snapped. Pushing one of the burly sec men out of his way, he threw open the door and ran out into the fog, going to the port side, peering past the red navigation light in the gloom. J.B. was at his shoulder. Oddly nobody had tried to stop them.

They could just make out the source of the noise. A flat-bottomed boat was roaring away, its white wake visible against the blackness of the river. The fog was too thick to make out who was aboard, though Ryan thought that he spotted a splash of brilliant red that had to be a woman's hair.

Then the boat was gone.

Wolfram's voice insinuated into the mist from behind them. "Do come in out of the cold, Ryan, my old friend. We have a great deal to talk about."

KRYSTY WATCHED the bright lights of the boat disappear into the clinging mist. It had been so easy, the snatch done with admirable efficiency by the half-dozen sec men.

They'd been waiting patiently in the shadows of the deck as she had led the others toward their cabins, all holding cocked automatics.

There was a shout above the noise of the thundering steam organ. "Got you cold!"

Jak stepped back and drew his Magnum, and was immediately clubbed to the deck from behind, falling unconscious at the feet of his attacker. "Don't nobody else try to get fucking triple-stupe, and you all stay living and unhurt.

"Pick up the kid," he said to one of his colleagues.

"He's not a kid," Krysty told him, aware of what a feeble response that was.

"Don't give a fuck, Krysty," said the apparent leader of the ambush. "Keep your hands high while we take away the blasters. Then move on around the back of the boat to the left side."

"Port," Doc said mockingly.

The man laughed, the sound devoid of any humor. "That so? Best keep your flap shut, Doc, or you'll be on the deck with the kid."

The guns were removed with professional ease, though Krysty noticed that they had missed some of Jak's knives. And they ignored Doc's swordstick.

"Move it."

"Could dive for it," Mildred whispered. "Never hit us in this fog."

"Shut the fuck up, you black bitch!"

Mildred turned instantly on the man, and he backed away from the flaming anger in her face, even though he was the one holding the gun.

Krysty thought about Mildred's suggestion, and blanked it. Jak wasn't a strong swimmer, nor was Doc. And they could easily get lost in the mist, in a river that was at least a half-mile wide. It wasn't a gamble worth the taking.

She laid a hand on Mildred's arm, calming her rage. "Later," she breathed.

They moved around the stern of the vessel, along the port side, where Krysty saw a boat waiting, with a double outboard engine, tied to the lowered gangway. It began to look as if they were victims of a complex conspiracy that probably involved Captain Huston and some of his crew, including the invisible musician pumping away at the calliope, covering the noise of the boat's engine as it had arrived alongside the *Golden Eagle.*

Three more armed men were already in the boat, one holding the tiller. The leader of the sec group gestured to Krysty, Mildred and Doc. "Down the ladder and into the boat. Quick and easy. Any of you make a break, the others die that moment."

It was done smoothly. Jak was dumped, moaning feebly, in the bottom of the boat, while the engine revved up. Krysty stood in the stern, peering up toward the dim spot of golden light that was the bridge of the stern-wheeler, wondering if Ryan was there. If Ryan was still living.

At that moment the calliope stopped playing, and the boat moved away into the center of the Sippi. Krysty watched the *Golden Eagle* vanish behind her.

FOR A MOMENT Ryan considered plunging off the bridge into the river, but there were too many reasons not to risk it. The powerful motorboat was gone, and he could easily lose his way in the fog in the enormously wide Sippi. Also, the bridge was around sixty feet from the water.

"Please don't make me have you both shot, my dear Ryan," Wolfram urged.

Slowly he turned and followed J.B. into the brightly lit bridge, pulling the door shut behind them.

Chapter Twenty-Two

"Looks like we owe you a vote of thanks for looking after us so well, Captain," Ryan said bitterly. "Carrying on the great naval tradition, huh?"

"Won't forget it, Captain," J.B. added. "Worth our remembering."

Huston's ruddy face was pale, a line of strain etched deep around his eyes and mouth. He shook his head at the two prisoners. "Not my fault," he muttered. "You don't know what they said they'd do if I didn't—"

The Magus patted Huston on the shoulder, and the captain jumped as though the man's touch were tainted with high voltage. "Man has to do what other men tell him to do." The curiously dead metallic eyes turned toward Ryan. "Just the kind of thing our dear mutual comrade the Trader would have said."

"Better if you give your blasters to us," Wolfram suggested jovially, as if he were asking them if they wanted to take off their coats before eating.

"And his knife," the Magus hissed. "The long, honed butcher's blade. And search the Armorer with a very special care. I recall his pockets were sometimes filled with delicious toys. Plas-ex and grens."

"That was then, Magus, and this is now," J.B. said, holding out his arms sideways, allowing the lean, part-android to search him. "Wasting time. Those days of explosives and implodes are long, long gone."

"Prefer to spend your time with time-jump black bitches, do you?"

J.B. didn't rise to the sneered taunt. "Better person than you could ever be, Magus," he replied calmly.

Wolfram giggled. "This is so like olden times, is it not? So many memories that we share. Some truths and some false memories. How given we old men are to the vice of lying, Ryan Cawdor. I have a question for you, my old comrade-in-arms."

"Ask it. Doesn't mean I'll answer it."

"Where is your little boy, Dean? We sadly lost track of him some weeks ago. It would have been so nice to have the mongrel cur of that she-panther, Sharona."

Ryan was shaken to the core as he realized how the two cold-hearts had been following him and the others through Deathlands. And how much they seemed to know. "Boy ran away, down near Death Valley," he said. Least that was one thing they didn't know. Wouldn't ever know.

Wolfram nodded, still smiling. He reached to tug out a large black satin kerchief and wiped sweat off his high forehead. "A lie, of course. But we shall find time to ask that and so many, many questions, Ryan."

"Go fuck a dead scabbie, Gert."

"You will answer," the Magus said, pointing at Ryan's good eye with his gleaming nail. "Nothing on this blighted earth is more certain."

"What'll make us talk?" J.B. asked, moving closer to Ryan, spotting the vein that throbbed across his friend's temple and the way the great cicatrix of the scar in his cheek was purple and twitching. They were dangerous signs that Ryan's temper was slipping from his control.

"How to make you talk, friends?" Wolfram threw back his head and bellowed with laughter, his jowls quivering, belly rippling. Opening his mouth, he sang in an unexpectedly high, pure lyric tenor. "'If you had wings like Noah's dove, then you'd sail up the river to the ones you love.'" He stopped, his jolly face turning to greasy planes of wind-washed bone, eyes narrowing with anger. "But you don't have wings, like Noah's dove, do you, Ryan Cawdor? Do you, John Barrymore Dix? No, you do not."

Neither man answered, though the truth of Wolfram's mocking was unanswerable. Krysty, Mildred, Doc and Jak were gone, spirited away either up or down the big river, out of reach into the drifting fog, helpless prisoners.

"Get to it," Ryan said wearily, trying not to show his own despair.

The Magus turned to the captain. "Do you have the private dining room ready?"

"Yes."

"There will be no need for you to join us, Captain."

"Fine with me."

"And in another few hours you will be rid of us forever. Does that not bring a smile to your wrinkled old cheeks? As well as a purse of jack for your devious aid."

Huston nodded at the Magus. "Guess it'll be good to move on without you and all your trouble."

Ryan was still fighting against the surging, blood-red rage. "Just fucking tell us what your plan is! You going to chill us, then do it. But you could let the others go."

Even as he said it, Ryan recognized the futility of trying to do any sort of deal with men like Wolfram and the Magus. You might as well ask a striking rattler to show mercy.

Wolfram laughed again. "Do I detect the first teensy sign of begging, Ryan? I think I do, yes, I think that I do. But it is not necessary."

"No?"

He shook his head. "We will discuss this over luncheon. But be assured that if all goes as my partner and I wish it, then you and the Armorer will do us an enormous favor that will help us to a serious quantity of jack. And at the end of it, perhaps in a month or so, you will all go free. All of you."

"Haven't seen any pigs flying by lately," J.B. said. "Hard to believe."

"Yet true."

Huston stood by the wheel, shuffling his feet. "It's difficult and dangerous holding the *Eagle* here like this, in thick fog in the middle of the Sippi. You gentlemen don't mind, I'd like to get her moving again upriver."

"When will we reach the dropping-off point, Captain?" the Magus asked.

"This evening, just before full dark. If all goes well and this damned weather clears. The landing's on the starboard side of the river, about five miles past the ruins of a burned-out mill. Good landmark."

Wolfram sighed. "I had asked you to be discreet about the precise position of our destination, Captain Huston. Telling Ryan and John Dix where we are going is not very discreet. I fear that we might need to give you something of a spanking before leaving your excellent floating gin palace."

Huston's face went several degrees paler. "I thought...thought that you said it...it wouldn't matter after you'd lifted the others and got them safe. Thought that's what you said... Sorry if... Real sorry."

The Magus clapped his hands. "Wasting time. Captain's right, Gert. Less they want their friends tortured slowly to death, they'll do like we say."

"What is it you want?" Ryan asked.

Wolfram smiled at him. "Over some food, I think, my old comrade. Over some food."

RYAN'S ADVICE to the others still held good. There was no way of knowing how and when they'd eat again. So he and the Armorer, despite their worry, anxiety and anger, tucked into the luncheon in the private room of the stern-wheeler.

Wolfram sat at the head of the table in an ornately inlaid mahogany carver that looked as if it had been built with someone of his bulk in mind. The Magus sat next to him, bolt upright, picking at his food, limiting himself to vegetables: some creamed squash with

fresh peas, and a dish of baked eggplant with a layer
of cheese on the top.

Ryan faced Wolfram, and J.B. was across from the
Magus. The saloon had a beautiful crystal chandelier
that vibrated and tinkled in time with the movement
of the boat. The fog was clearing slowly, and they were
moving upstream again, a little faster than walking
pace. There were lookouts in the bow and up on the
wings of the bridge, as well as a pair of lead men
working in unison. "Mark twain . . . mark four and a
half . . . Soft mud."

The first course for everyone but the Magus was
wafer-thin layers of smoked salmon with lemon, and
elegant slices of brown bread and butter, with the
crusts cut off, followed by a bowl of thick, rich soup,
made from lentils and shredded carrots. Then came
the fish course: delicious fillets of fresh trout, covered in bread crumbs and baked with sweet potatoes
and lima beans, with a rich cream sauce that was flavored with coriander and nutmeg.

Wolfram would have taken the edge away from the
voracious Jak in a dining contest, helping himself to
two portions of the salmon, two of the soup and three
of the fish.

The silent waiters next served a round of delicate
fruit sorbets decorated with thin slices of fresh strawberries and melon and guava.

The meal was proceeding in almost total silence.

The only sound was Wolfram's noisy eating, gulping and snuffling like a hog rooting for truffles. Outside, Ryan was aware that Huston was speeding up a

little, which presumably meant that the fog was clearing more.

Now that they knew where their destination was, five miles past the burned-out mill, Ryan considered whether they might try to break for it. But the sec men were armed and watchful, while they had lost their blasters.

"You are thinking of going over the side if we give you the chance," the Magus said, his harsh voice breaking the stillness of the private room.

Ryan didn't respond, though the man's perception had shaken him.

Wolfram laughed, beckoning with a snap of the fingers to the waiters to bring in the main, meat course, which was a large turkey, stuffed with a chicken, stuffed with a quail, with an array of mixed vegetables, including pumpkin and superb roasted potatoes, golden brown, and a thick gravy.

"Surprised that we can keep on second-guessing you, Ryan? We been studying you for long enough. Know the way you'll jump. But you mustn't bother about trying to escape. No need."

He turned to his colleague on his right hand. "I believe that the time has come to explain our plan, has it not, Magus? Serve yourself to your veggie meal, while we attack the luncheon speciality of the *Golden Eagle*. Captain Huston has done us exceedingly proud and has well earned his reward."

Between mouthfuls Wolfram explained to Ryan and J.B. just what they intended, while the bleak-faced Magus interrupted now and again with extra details.

It took a long while.

RYAN DIDN'T specially favor very sweet food. Home-made ice cream could usually tempt him, but cream *gâteaux* and sugary cobblers weren't his special favor-ites. But he was now stirring in the fifth spoon of part-refined brown sugar, whisking it slowly into the creamy coffee in the large porcelain mug, knowing that he would be needing every atom of energy over the next few days. To his left the Armorer was doing the same.

"Your comments, my dear fellow?" asked Wolf-ram, who was forking away at a third slice of choco-late cake with almond butter and chopped pecans.

The Magus had passed on the desserts and was sip-ping at a small cup of black coffee, toying with a sin-gle, wafer-thin peppermint cream.

Ryan tasted his own coffee, carefully placing the cup back in the saucer. "Let me see if I've got this straight, Wolfram," he said.

"By all means. I shall be surprised if any detail has passed you by."

Ryan nodded. "You hold Krysty, Jak, Mildred and Doc, keeping them all snugly locked up and well fed and unharmed."

The Magus had taken out one of his metal contact lenses and was washing it carefully in a goblet of wa-ter. The shadowed socket appeared to hold the rem-nants of an eye, bloody and cavernous, though Ryan was sure that he could make out tiny wire filaments in the darkness.

"And they go completely free once you've done what we're asking from you."

It was Ryan's turn to nod. He considered removing the patch over the raw socket of his own missing left eye, to match the Magus, but decided against it.

"And you want us to act as foremen, or charge hands for you on your plantation."

"And in the mines," Wolfram prompted, smearing chocolate on his sleeve.

"And in the mines." Ryan finished his coffee and replaced the empty cup on the saucer. In between courses the waiters had been sent out so that they didn't hear any of the conversation, though the sec men stood, still as marble statues, eyes not moving from J.B. and Ryan.

The Armorer continued. "You used stickies as slaves. Like old times, Wolfram. And now they've revolted. Rebelled. Run away. And you are well and truly fucked."

Ryan cut in. "And you want us to pluck the chestnuts out of the fire for you. Appropriate when you're dealing with stickies, isn't it?"

"They've kidnapped three of our foremen. Vanished from the mine and the fields. Gone into the hills and the forest. Not a trace of them. Just whispers and rumors and the occasional burned-out homestead."

Ryan looked across at the Magus, who had readjusted the metal lenses. "You've got some triple-good sec men. Why not promote some of them or send them out on the trail of the stickies? Teach them a lesson."

The Magus favored him with a smile as thin and polished as a steel needle. "We are talking as many as a hundred stickies, and we believe they are attracting more numbers every day. And some other muties, perhaps.''

"And you think me and J.B. can regain control for you? On our own?"

Wolfram pushed back his chair, levering himself upright on the creaking table, glaring down at Ryan. "Let us be clear. What Trader did to us both cannot be forgiven. He is gone. You were his trusted, able lieutenants, and you now carry the blood price. My heart says to chill you and all your companions very slowly." A faint froth of pink bubbles gathered on his fleshy lips, and his small eyes were wide with hatred. "It has been a very long time, this moment for us."

"But you need us," Ryan said.

"Yes," the Magus said, kicking back his chair so that it tumbled on the thick carpet.

"And you will set aside the feud and let us go. Let us all go if we can destroy the uprising and return some of the stickies to you again?"

"Yes," Wolfram replied. "We will give you seven clear days to get away from us afterward, then the feud will begin again, to the death."

J.B. calmly poured himself some more coffee, took off his glasses and polished them on his discarded napkin. "Sounds fair, don't it, Ryan?"

"It does."

But he knew in his heart that he could never trust the Magus and Wolfram. They were deeply, inalienably corrupt and evil. But what he and J.B. needed was time. They wouldn't chill Krysty and the others before the attempt had been made on the stickies. That would remove their overwhelmingly strong hand and

would be grotesquely foolish. Neither the Magus nor
Wolfram were stupid. The treachery would come after Ryan and J.B. had done what they could with the
stickies. Failure would mean all six deaths.

And so would success. Unless they got their retali-
ation in first.

"Well?" Wolfram prompted. "Time is passing."

"We will have you dropped off well before we reach
the burned mill." The Magus smiled. "So you won't
need to look out for it and make an escape. And we
will return your weapons."

"With plans of where the mine is. The farm. Our
fortress. And where we believe the stickies have fled."

Ryan glanced down the table to J.B., who pushed
back the brim of his fedora and gave an almost imperceptible nod, sipping his coffee.

"Very well. We'll do it. How long before we get put
ashore off the boat?"

Wolfram looked at his golden chron, the numbers
traced with tiny diamonds and rubies. "If we pick up
speed, it will be in about three hours."

Ryan checked his own chron. "That'll be about
ninety minutes from dusk. Sounds all right. We get the
map and our blasters back before then?"

"Yes."

Ryan stood, followed by J.B. "Then we'll go and
rest up in our cabin. See you later."

The closing of the heavy door sounded uncannily
like the lid dropping on an ornate coffin.

Chapter Twenty-Three

"They must know if they put us over the side a distance from their headquarters that we'll try to get at them. Rescue the others. At least give it a go." Ryan lay on the double bed in his cabin. J.B. stood by the open shutters at their window, looking out over the fog-shrouded river.

"But it's part of their sicko game, isn't it?" he said. "They know they've got the aces in their hands. But this is all about vengeance. What the bastards want is to see us struggle against them and lose. Eventually we might have to play their game. Go after the stickies and try to help Magus and Wolfram get their businesses back together again. Then they'll waste us all. And the game'll be done for them."

Ryan nodded. "True. That's the way I see it, as well. But I reckon we have to try it. They give us a chance on a plate, so we'll recce it. How's the weather?"

The Armorer turned and glanced behind him. "Clearing. I can catch glimpses of the far bank. Wooded. Small hills. All I can make out." He checked his chron. "Must be close to time for them to put us ashore. Haven't given us our blasters or the map yet, like they promised."

Ryan swung his legs off the bed and stood. "What I'd like most is a chance to get back at the treacherous shitter, Huston. Delivered Krysty and the others into their hands, which betrayed us, as well."

"Might get a chance at him one day." Both men turned at a knock on the door. "Yeah?"

It was one of the officers, accompanied by two of Wolfram and the Magus's armed sec men. They carried the Uzi, the Steyr rifle, the Smith & Wesson fléchette-firing scattergun and Ryan's trusty SIG-Sauer 9 mm P-226 with the built-in baffle silencer.

"Your blasters," the sailor said.

"What about my panga?" Ryan asked.

"And the map?" J.B. added.

One of the sec men reached into his belt, drawing out the eighteen-inch blade, and lobbed it onto the bed. His comrade fumbled in an inside pocket and tugged out a folded sheet of paper, throwing it alongside the panga. The officer carefully placed the blasters on the bed.

"How long before we get put ashore?" Ryan asked.

"Soon," the older of the sec men grunted. "Some time in the next half hour."

"We free to walk around the boat until then?"

After an exchange of glances, the man nodded. "Don't see why not. Nobody said not."

"Fine, thanks."

The three men left the cabin, shutting the door behind them. There was a definite speeding up of the huge stern-wheel as the *Golden Eagle* pounded faster up the Sippi.

EVERYTHING ON BOARD was perfectly normal. The afternoon was wearing on, and the sun was setting like a ball of brazen flame far off to the west. All the saloons were busy, crap games, roulette and the jackslots all doing good business. Nobody took any notice of Ryan and the Armorer as they strolled by, carrying their weapons.

They'd already checked out the map, which seemed simple enough. It showed their landing point, the place where the fast boat had taken Krysty and the others, the fortified ville of Wolfram and the Magus, close by the mine, with the plantation a little farther off and a deserted settlement. The map also showed the rough-dotted region where it was believed the fleeing muties had established their own base.

It was carefully drawn, showing the main geofeatures to scale, including rivers and streams, a swamp and a region where there was a warning of mines and traps.

Ryan and J.B. had studied it for several minutes, concentrating all their combat attention on it. They were carrying the map along with them, but both of them could have redrawn it from memory with precise accuracy.

As they passed by a group of gaudy sluts, gathered around a drunken priest who had clearly been a big winner at the tables, waving a wad of jack, Ryan stopped to ask if anyone had seen the captain recently.

A squint-eyed blonde in a low-cut basque gown giggled. "Have a better time with us, honey-bunch."

"Sure that's true. But I need to see Huston for a while. Then we might come right back and take you up on that offer of a better time."

She giggled again. The whore was sitting on the sofa, next to the almost comatose priest, her left hand tucked inside the front of his pants, working hard at trying to raise his interest without much visible success.

"Seen him a few minutes ago, walking the upper deck toward the stern."

It couldn't have been better.

Ryan turned on his heel and led J.B. back toward their cabin, brushing past the throng of gamblers and idlers, who parted like the Red Sea when they saw the grim look on the tall, heavily armed man's face.

THEY SPOTTED the short, muscular figure of the captain, walking alone down the port side of the boat, leaning over the side now and again, staring out toward the banks, where a few stubborn tendrils of mist lingered.

Ryan came up on his left, J.B. on the right, making him start, his face apprehensive.

"Yeah? What can I do for you gentlemen? We'll be stopping real soon now."

Ryan was looking around. Everyone seemed to be inside, and the stretch of deck all the way along to the stern was deserted. He hooked a hand through the man's arm and urged him along. J.B. had casually lifted the Uzi so that the muzzle was pressing into Huston's ribs.

"Let's walk a spell," Ryan said. "Quick talk about what you've done for us. I don't reckon there's much more that you can do for us now."

Huston didn't speak, his body slumping, legs faltering, as though he knew how far the walk was going to be and how it was likely to end.

Ryan stopped when they were right at the stern, the spray from the throbbing paddle wheel hanging in the air, rainbowing in the golden light of the setting sun. Nobody was around.

"Here'll do," he said.

Huston came to life then. "Couldn't help it. They threatened me."

"And paid you," J.B. said.

"Sure. You wouldn't have turned down all the jack they offered me."

"Wrong," Ryan argued. "As wrong as you can be."

He had drawn the SIG-Sauer, letting it hang out of sight at his side.

Huston was twitching, face white as parchment. The cool air was suddenly filled with the hot smell of urine, and a damp patch appeared at the front of his pants, dribbling through onto the scrubbed planking.

"You can have all the jack," he whispered.

Ryan shook his head. "Sorry, Captain. I just don't have the time."

He lifted the blaster, pressing the barrel against the side of the trembling man's skull, just above his right ear, and squeezed the trigger once.

The silencer was still working well, and the only sound was a faint coughing noise, no louder than a dowager clearing her throat before making a speech to the ladies' auxiliary.

The muffled sound was completely drowned by the thundering of the stern-wheel.

A spray of blood and brains splattered on the deck and railing, dappled with tiny shards of white bone. Huston staggered and would have gone down if J.B. hadn't supported him below the arm. The man's mouth opened, and blood trickled out, darkened by the sunset's ominous light. His eyes rolled back in their sockets, and he gave a rattling sigh.

"Gone," J.B. said. "Want him over the back? Good as any, I reckon."

Ryan holstered the SIG-Sauer, making a mental note to reload the spent round when he had a chance. "Yeah. Quick as we can, before anyone comes by."

Avoiding the leaking flood of crimson from the shattered head, they lifted the dead man and dropped the corpse over the damp railing, where it landed on the revolving wheel and was carried down and under.

"Shit!" Ryan said as the draggled, sodden body appeared again, hooked between the white slats of the massive paddle wheel. The eyes looked to be staring at them as the body rolled over, one arm seeming to beckon as it vanished once more.

"What are we going to do?" J.B. leaned over. "Someone's bound to see it."

Ryan didn't hesitate. He climbed over the rail, reaching out his left hand for J.B. to hang on to, waiting until the corpse reappeared, straining over the murderous wheel and heaving at the limp hand. He nearly lost his grip on the cold, wet flesh, but tightened his fingers and pulled, feeling his own shoulder almost jerked from its socket, gritting his teeth and pulling as hard as he could.

"Got it!" the Armorer yelled, seeing the body flop loose from the grip of the paddles and slip under the stern into the whirling thunder of white spray.

They both heard a dull thunking sound, watching as the wheel revolved once more, coming around empty. One section was stained scarlet. Then, thirty or forty yards out in the frothing wake, they saw the black shape of the body of the captain drift away to the south, taking his last journey down the Sippi.

"Close," Ryan said, clambering back over the rail onto the solid safety of the deck.

"Wheel's slowing," J.B. said. "Must be coming toward our landing place."

"Best get back to meet them." Ryan wiped spray from his face, leading the way to their cabin.

THE SEC MEN ESCORTED THEM along the deck. The *Golden Eagle* had come to a full stop on the eastern bank, the first officer holding her in position against the current, while a gangplank was thrown out onto the muddy shore. The fog had cleared, but darkness was galloping across the big river.

"Where's Huston?" Ryan asked. "Like to have said my farewells and thanks to him."

"Seems to have vanished," Wolfram's senior sec man replied, glancing suspiciously at Ryan and J.B. "You two wouldn't know anything about that, now, would you? Like you had a score to settle with him."

The Armorer pushed back his fedora and shook his head. "Not us, friend."

"I ain't your friend, Dix. None of us on this boat are your friend."

"Is," Ryan said. "You should say 'is your friend,' not 'are your friend.' Get it right."

"Fuck you. Won't be so smart when you get among the stickies. You got your map safe? Wouldn't want you to get fucking lost."

Ryan patted his pocket. "Safe and snug," he said. "Just make sure that no harm comes to Krysty or the others. Or there'll be a blood reckoning."

The man put his hand to his mouth in mock concern. "Oh, please don't. You're scaring me to death, Mr. Cawdor." The smile vanished. "Don't you see that you're both dead men, Cawdor? Then your slut, the rest of them. All dead."

"Talk comes cheap," the Armorer said, fingering the trigger of the scattergun.

"Time you was gone. Down the plank and into the woods. We'll see you in a day or so, mebbe."

"If you see us, it'll mean we're likely chilled," Ryan said softly. "But the most likely is that you don't see us. And that's goin' to mean that you're chilled. Think on that when you go to bed tomorrow. Wonder where we are. How close we are to you. And sleep well."

He led J.B. down the bouncy plank, picking his way along the narrow strip of beach, turning as the walkway was removed and dragged back on board the *Golden Eagle,* which gave them a valedictory blast on the whistle.

Ryan and J.B. stood together, watching the vessel depart. "Look," the Armorer said, pointing with the Uzi at the sealed top deck, where two figures were staring at them. One was immensely fat, wearing a white suit. The other was taller and skinny, turning as his metal eyes reflected the dying sun, converting them into pits of living fire.

Ryan, on an impulse, lifted the rifle in salute, getting a farewell wave from the Magus.

"You and me," he said to J.B. Dix. "Like old times. Just the two of us against Wolfram and the Magus. All we need is Trader."

The sun was virtually gone as they walked into the dark, silent deeps of the forest.

Chapter Twenty-Four

From the map it looked as if they had something in the region of thirty miles to cover before they reached the home base of Wolfram and the Magus, through treacherous sections of what used to be the Shawnee National Forest and swamp, on the western flanks of the old state of Illinois. They had to travel past the region where the stickies might be holed up and waiting for any pursuers or intruders, a deserted and mysterious settlement set in a part where the plan showed personnel mines and traps had been scattered.

"Best find somewhere to hole up for the night," J.B. said. "Lord knows what kind of mutie creatures might be stalking around here."

Ryan nodded, slinging the powerful hunting rifle across his shoulder. "Take to the trees?"

The Armorer squinted around. "Good as any place. Kindling's all wet from that storm, so we'd struggle to get a fire lit. Yeah, let's find a place to get off the ground."

THE NIGHT WAS MADE miserable by a drizzling storm that started within an hour of their finding a secure place in the fork of an elderly oak tree and continued well into the early hours of the next morning, soaking both men through to the skin, leaving them cold and miserable as the first pale light of the false dawn penetrated through the branches of the forest.

Ryan had managed a few scattered periods of sleep, waking with a jerk that nearly pushed him off balance, though he had taken the precaution, as had J.B., of slipping his belt around one wrist and buckling it around a stout branch.

He stretched, blinking his eye open, groaning quietly at the aches and pains that ravaged the muscles in arms and thighs, shoulders and back.

The Armorer sniffed and fumbled for his spectacles, taking them out of an inside pocket and trying to wipe them clean with a kerchief.

"Not the best of nights, *compadre*," he said to Ryan, stretching his arms so that the muscles creaked.

"Thought I heard the sound of an explosion, somewhere around two o'clock. Listened for it, but there was no more sound. And there was a noisy pack of coyotes hunting over to the east, coupla hours later."

J.B. nodded. "Heard the animals. Didn't hear any explosion. Must've been during one of the bits of sleep I managed. Few and far between."

"Don't fancy our chances of finding much food in this place," Ryan said.

"There's that settlement on the map, on our line of march toward the fortress." He pulled his fedora from his coat and uncrumpled it, jamming it on his head.

Ryan was unbuckling his belt and readying himself for the scramble down to the soaking ground below. "Try for it. Should get there around the middle of the day."

"REMEMBER TO RELOAD the blaster?" J.B. asked as they started off north and westward.

"Yeah. Before we settled for the night."

They had made good progress. A few minutes after leaving their nighttime refuge, they struck a narrow hunting trail that snaked through the woods, eventually leading to a deserted and overgrown blacktop that ran roughly north and south.

It was marked on their map and appeared to take them directly toward the small ville.

There was no sign at all of the road being used recently, and no trace of any kind of human habitation.

The friends walked alongside each other, talking little, constantly on the alert for any threat.

Ryan brought up the subject of what they'd do if they were unable to rescue the others.

"Have to go along with what they want."

J.B. sniffed. "No choice. Trader used to tell us that when you had no choice, it made things a shit-lot easier. No worrying about making a decision."

"Means getting at the stickies to start the plantation and mine going again."

"Wonder what happened to those three foremen that vanished. Wolfram reckoned the stickies got them."

Ryan stepped around a patch of leprous fungus with pale green spots on a sickly yellow top. He'd come across them elsewhere in Deathlands, knowing that to crush them with your boots released a cloud of almost invisible noxious spores that affected sight and breathing. They nestled in the center of a delicate ring of the ubiquitous, fragile yellow-and-white flowers known as Deathlands daisies.

"Could have done a runner?"

J.B. nodded. "Mebbe. What if the stickies have completely abandoned the area? Means that there's no hope of getting the slave labor to work the mine and the land. What do we do then, old friend?"

Ryan grinned mirthlessly. "Then we go in and do us some heavy chilling."

THEY PASSED a lopsided billboard a little before noon. The board was pocked with bullet holes, leaning down to the left, so badly weathered that it was almost illegible.

Ryan stopped and wiped off a coating of gray green lichen, reading it slowly.

"Three Miles Ahead. Paul Burgess Art Village. Admission Rates Published At Entrance. World-Famous Displays Of This Top Artist's Work."

"That must be the ville marked on our map," J.B. said, slapping at an insect that was buzzing around his face. "Didn't say it was some kind of art show."

"Wonder if it's occupied?"

"Soon find out."

But before they'd covered the three miles, they came across the first sight of the work of the stickies.

RYAN HAD BEEN TELLING his partner about a bizarre dream that had disturbed his sleep.

"Sullen, lead-colored sea, with small breakers. I was watching from the top of a cliff, looking out to where Krysty was doing some swimming. Saw her red hair, like a fire in the water, about a quarter mile off. Everything seemed calm and in the ordinary, then I saw the sharks.''

"Big whites?''

Ryan shook his head. "No. More like basking sharks. But mutie large. Forty or fifty feet long. I saw the flukes first, then they rolled together, showing their tails and dorsals. They were close to the beach below me, between Krysty and safety. She was swimming in, stopping to wave to me. From where she was, the sharks weren't visible.''

On the left they were passing a small sign that drew their attention to a predark historical marker, showing the spot where Lieutenant Zebedee Anstruther had established a trading post in June of 1849.

Ryan continued his story. "I stood and shouted and waved, but Krysty couldn't hear me above the noise of the breakers. She trod water and waved, thinking I was just greeting her. The sharks sensed movement and started toward her, slow and ponderous and menacing. Nothing at all that I could do. Just stood and watched as they got within about a hundred feet. Then they both dived and vanished.''

"Then what?'' J.B. asked, kicking a rounded pebble out of his path.

"Woke up,'' Ryan said tersely.

"Often the way.''

They walked a hundred yards or so in silence, rounding a gentle bend in the rutted, ribboned highway, stopping as they saw the burned-out building.

"Stickies,'' J.B. commented.

It looked as though it had been a roadside eatery, maybe serving burgers, subs and chilie stew. The roof had gone, as had the windows and doors, only a blackened shell remaining. As they drew closer, they could catch the bitter smell of gasoline, laid over the familiar stench of roasted meat.

"How long ago?" the Armorer asked as they stood together a few paces from the ruin.

Ryan shook his head, looking at the damp ashes. "Three or four days. Difficult to tell." He took a few steps over crunching cinders, peering through the shattered front window. "Three bodies inside. One a child."

It was typical stickies' funning.

The fire had covered most of the details of the mutilations, the corpses resembling three charred, crusted logs, with jagged branches that had once been arms and legs. But it was still possible to see where sharp knives had been used to slash and hack before the burning.

"Least we know the sick bastards are still around this neck of the woods," J.B. said.

"Or they were three days ago."

Both men suddenly stared at each other, wordlessly readying their blasters. The forest on both sides of the trail had fallen silent. Totally still, without even the faintest breath of wind to stir the topmost feathery branches of the stately sycamores and chestnuts.

Ryan felt the short hairs prickling at his nape, and his finger was tight on the trigger of the SIG-Sauer.

Something or somebody was watching them from the dark shadows around.

J.B.'s head turned from side to side, and he sniffed at the air, trying to catch the distinctive stink of the stickies' skin.

He caught Ryan's eye and shrugged, gesturing with the barrel of the Uzi to their left, away behind the wrecked building. Ryan shrugged back, indicating his own doubts, doubts that were suddenly removed by a harsh voice from under the trees, a little way to their right.

"Stand real still, outlanders. And put them nice blasters down in the dirt. We got you well covered."

"I don't think so," Ryan called. "We don't mean no trouble, and you got no reason to fear us. Come out and talk."

There was a long pause, and Ryan's skin crawled with the expectation of a bullet. "You seen any stickie fuckers around here, stranger?"

J.B. answered. "Just seen their work right here. Can't mistake it."

"That was Ma and Pa Jode and Tommy. Ran a fast-food joint. Got burned three nights ago."

Ryan bit his lip. "Easier to talk when you can see who's there," he said. "We'll holster our blasters if you come out of the trees."

"All right. But one wrong outlander tricky move, and you get whacked."

There were five of them. All male, all bearded, aged from around sixteen to sixty, wearing a mix of leathers, furs and homespuns. They all hefted self-built muskets, in good condition, and all of them carried long daggers.

Their leader was missing his left arm, and his face showed recent stickie scars, circular, raw wounds where the suckers of the muties had ripped away roundels of skin and flesh.

"You sure you ain't seen no stickies?"

"Sure. Where do they come from?"

"Escaped from a big settlement about twenty miles north of here. Other side our ville. Mines and plantations. Owned by the fat man and metal-eyes. Slavers. Had a revolution, and their muties ran. Ran this way. Circled our place, though we had some skirmishing with them." A hand lifted involuntarily and touched the weeping cicatrices.

"Lost many?" Ryan asked.

"These three. Wouldn't leave and come inside the ville for safety. Paid the blood-and-fire price to the fuckers. Had two women chilled in the first night, before we knew the muties were around."

"Any chance of food and water?" Ryan asked, sensing that the initial moment of tension was passed.

"Why not? Don't have much to spare, but you're welcome to what we got. And if we run into the stickies, those blasters you got could be right useful."

J.B. slapped the butt of the Uzi. "Wouldn't be the first time this beauty's cut down stickies."

THERE WAS ANOTHER SIGN, telling them that they were now approaching the Paul Burgess Art Center.

"Who was he?" J.B. asked.

"Famous artist, predark. Bought up a big warehouse on the edge of the old ville, way before the nuking. Also took some of the stores and houses. Set up to show all his art and stuff."

There was a bitter note in the man's voice that Ryan picked up on.

"Not popular?"

The man spit in the dirt. "Could say that. Turned folks from homes."

"But they reckon he brought a lot of visitors, Ephraim," one of the younger men said.

"Yeah, back then, for a while. All of that ended with skydark and the long winters."

"The art still here?" Ryan asked.

"Sure is. Useless garbage. You can see it after we've given you some passage food. Nobody bothers much these days."

Ryan weighed up the settlement as they walked into it. There was a main drag, with a number of tumbled houses and stores and a church whose spire had toppled down some time in the past hundred years, the shingles spilling from it over the neat gravestones in the adjoining cemetery.

As far as he could judge, it looked as if about twenty of the homes were still in reasonable repair, holding around fifty men, women and children, most of whom came out to peer suspiciously at the pair of heavily armed outlanders.

Two side streets opened up to show allotments and cultivated fields. Corrals pinned close to the backs of the houses held a few scrawny cows and some half-wild hogs.

The leader of the group who had found Ryan and J.B., and had introduced himself as Ephraim Schwarz, pointed out a large building on the edge of the township. "There's Burgess's art stuff," he said. "Building's held together better than most. Likely on account of having more jack spent on it in the first place. Take a look later if you want."

THE FOOD WAS AS POOR and scanty as Schwarz had warned them, thin gruel with bits of fatty pork floating in the transparent depths, with some gritty bread and saltless butter, followed by some bruised windfall apples and a beaker of cloudy moonshine that bit like a cottonmouth.

But Ryan and J.B. forced down as much as they could, thanking their silent, watchful hosts for the meal.

A glance at his chron showed Ryan that it was three parts of the hour past one in the afternoon.

He wiped his mouth on his sleeve and stood suddenly, seeing out of the corner of his eye that one of the younger men had been working his way toward the Steyr rifle, hand creeping out toward the walnut stock. Ryan chose to ignore the attempt, seeing that J.B. had also spotted the movement.

"Go and take a look at the art building, then we'll move on," he said.

Ephraim nodded. "Want any of us to come along with you? Show you the way? Keep the stickies out of your path?"

"Reckon we can find it. Thanks again for the grub. Take care now."

None of the villagers showed much expression, no handshakes or waves or smiles, merely the same surly, watchful resentfulness and suspicion.

A COUPLE OF MANGY DOGS followed the two men along the street. The sun had broken through, and the damp was rising in clouds of fetid steam from the rank puddles. Ryan glanced behind them, but nobody was following.

"Classic frontier pesthole," J.B. commented, easing the strap of the scattergun on his shoulder.

"Not many dumps like this have predark art galleries. Might be interesting. Fine paintings and stuff. Never heard of this Burgess guy, though."

"Me, neither. Here it is. Hope the sec door's open."

"If not, then we'll just carry on north toward Wolfram's headquarters."

The heavy sec door opened easily, and they walked cautiously inside to be greeted by automatic strip lighting that threw a stark white glow over the interior of the old warehouse.

And its contents.

Chapter Twenty-Five

Ryan had seen pictures of old galleries and museums in ancient, crumbling mags, walls lined with delicate paintings in beautiful colors. He'd even seen originals in a few of the wealthier villes, owned by barons with a taste for excess and splendor.

The Paul Burgess collection wasn't like anything he'd seen before. There were no pictures. None at all.

And nothing that resembled any kind of statue or sculpture that Ryan recognized.

"What the fuck is this?" J.B. whispered, his voice sibilant, echoing off the dusty walls.

"Damned if I know," Ryan replied.

They were in a large single room, at least a hundred feet long and about forty feet in width. The walls were painted a matt white that had faded to a muddy cream. The ceiling was the same color.

And the room was filled with scattered rows of boxes, all precisely the same size. Ryan's guess put them at regular cubes with each side close to four and a half feet. Some were dull metal, looking like aluminum. Some were partly of wood and partly of clear perspex. Some were a mix of all three materials with an occasional cube with an empty side to it.

"This is art?" Ryan asked. "I've seen better art on shithouse walls in frontier gaudies."

J.B. began to walk around, examining the boxes. "I don't know. They're real well built, Ryan. Precise. Engineered to a thou, I'd guess." He pressed down firmly on the top of one of the metal cubes. "Solid."

"But they're the same. Deadly boring. What's the point of them?" Ryan cleared his throat, tasting age-old dust, brackish and antique. "I know what I like in art, and it's not this. This isn't art."

The Armorer had walked to a small white notice tacked to the wall. "Says that Paul Burgess was the greatest minimalist artist of the twentieth century. Took minimalist to new heights."

"Depths," Ryan grunted. "I guess *minimalist* means there's almost nothing there."

"There's other rooms out back," J.B. said, threading his way through the irregular rows of cubes.

Ryan followed him reluctantly. "If it gets more minimalist than this, it'll vanish up its own ass."

The next room had a long table at its center, made from the same smooth metal as most of the cubes. Ryan noticed that it tapered about six inches along its total length of around twenty feet. On it were bolted a number of pyramids of chromed steel. All the same size, at regular intervals.

"I know," Ryan said quickly. "You reckon it's nicely made. Sure is."

"Well, it is," the Armorer protested.

"Does it have a name?"

J.B. read another of the neat little notices. "Called 'Construct XLVII, 1995. For Rabin.' Wasn't he the Israeli baron who got chilled?"

Ryan ignored the question, walking through into another room. The building was totally without windows, a single door appearing at the farther end.

The next section had yet more of the minimalist exhibits from Paul Burgess. A partition wall of hardboard had weathered and warped over the decades, inset with a row of identical doors with a peephole at its center and brass handles stained green with age. Ryan tried the first one and found it locked. As were all the others. The printed card on the wall said that it was called Alpha Particles Reversed CLVII.

J.B. followed him, whistling under his breath. "They open or closed?" he asked.

"Guess."

"Closed?"

Ryan nodded. "Right. I think I've seen what I need to see. How about we get going north, J.B.?"

"Sure."

"What's that?"

"Main door opening. Real quiet. Feel the draft coming in from it?"

Both of them were instantly alert.

In Deathlands the only people who tried to approach you silently were enemies.

Ryan glanced around. Apart from the row of locked doors, there was no cover. The back exit might be locked or open, but whoever was coming after them had likely got it covered.

"Run or fight?" J.B. whispered, the Uzi braced at his waist, ready for action.

"Fight. What's in the side room next along?"

The Armorer slid along and peered around the corner. "Set of steel tables. About a dozen of them."

"Fixed or free?"

J.B. disappeared for a moment, then reappeared. "Freestanding. Notice says the viewer should feel free to rearrange them as they wish."

Ryan only hesitated a moment. "Right," he said. "Let's get ready."

MOVING CAT FOOTED, Ryan had gone along the row of doors, using the blunt edge of the heavy panga to knock off all the handles, letting them clatter to the stone floor. He waited after each one to listen, making sure that the intruders weren't advancing on them. But there was no sound. From the stillness of the air, he guessed that the big entrance sec door had been closed again, meaning that the villagers, assuming it was them who'd crept in, were all in the first large room with the mixed sets of cubes. They probably were waiting to work their way in and pin J.B. and himself down at the far end of the art complex.

Ryan swung some doors open, leaving others closed, then called out to J.B. "Get in one of the rooms and keep quiet."

The Armorer picked up on the plan immediately, and in a stage whisper said, "Sure thing, Ryan. You doing the same?"

"Yeah."

Tiptoeing back to the room with the tables, he helped J.B. to lift them and silently place them at an angle that covered the area with the blank doors, setting them on their sides in a random pattern.

He crouched behind one, with the rifle unslung and cocked, lying the SIG-Sauer on the cold floor at its side. J.B. was hunched two tables along, the Uzi ready to fire. He turned and winked at Ryan, the overhead light glinting off the lenses of his spectacles. "Old times," he mouthed.

They waited.

Ryan thought he heard someone testing the lock on the single door immediately behind them and swung around anxiously. But it sounded as if it was locked. He crawled over, cursing himself under his breath for stupidly leaving the door untested, finding there was a simple triple-bar sec lock that opened from their side.

He turned back to cover, giving a thumbs-up sign to the Armorer.

Their attackers were very cautious now they knew that their approach had been detected.

Ryan guessed they were probably into the part of the exhibition with the long table and the row of pyramids, meaning they'd appear any minute now.

It wasn't surprising that they were being so careful, knowing the weight of firepower that the outlanders could lay down against them.

There was the shuffling of feet, and Ryan peeked around the corner of the table, seeing that Ephraim was leading a hesitant move into the room where some of the doors now swung open. The man was ignoring the section of the gallery where Ryan and J.B. were hiding, convinced that they'd taken cover behind the doors.

He had several men gathered behind him and he glanced back, pointing at the doors, then standing and giving a shout of encouragement, charging at them, kicking them open and firing his musket blindly into the narrow rooms, followed by his whooping comrades.

It was like taking candy from a blind child.

Ryan opened fire with the Steyr, while the Uzi burst into life with a noise like ripping silk. The range was less than thirty yards in perfect light, and the villagers went down like bowling pins. Blood sprayed and blasters clattered on the floor. The rooms filled with screaming and panic as the few survivors of the opening blast of lead fought to turn and retreat, boots slipping in the splattered pools of crimson.

Ryan had aimed at Ephraim as the leader, the 7.62 mm full-metal-jacket round ripping into the man's forehead, distorting and spinning, slicing off a circle of bone from the top of the skull, the exit pressure sucking most of the brains from the cranial hollow. The door and ceiling were dappled in overlaid shades of pink and gray as Ephraim went down.

"Out the back, now," Ryan said, slinging the Steyr onto his shoulder, crouching as he sprinted for the door. He slipped the catch and glanced outside.

J.B. was at his heels, snapping off single shots from the Uzi to keep their attackers cringing in the farthest part of the exhibition.

As the exit door opened, there was the crack of a firearm, and a musket ball flattened itself on the frame scant inches from Ryan's face.

He could make out a narrow path, fringed with overgrown ornamental bushes. The shot had come from behind the cover, and a cloud of black-powder smoke still hung in the afternoon air. Ryan stuck the SIG-Sauer around the edge of the door and put five spaced shots into the center of the cloud.

There was a shrill scream and a thrashing in the undergrowth. Ryan risked another look and saw the body of a young man roll out onto the path, blood streaking from two wounds, one in the groin, the other high in the chest. His Kentucky musket was still clutched in his right hand.

"Let's go," Ryan said.

The youth had obviously been placed there as a last-resort stopper to try to prevent the outlanders from making a break out the back. As Ryan darted out and sprinted to his right, away from the center of the ville, toward a narrow draw, there was no more shooting.

The massacre inside had taken away all enthusiasm for pursuit, and nobody came after them.

Ryan slithered down the rocky side of the draw, boots splashing into a narrow stream that ran along the bottom, flattening himself and looking back. The Armorer was only moments behind him, taking up a defensive position, staring behind them toward the squat shape of the Burgess gallery.

"Looks like we kicked the balls out of them," he said. "Stupes!"

Ryan nodded. "It was our blasters they wanted. Saw it in their greedy little dirt-poor eyes."

There was a single piercing scream from behind them, from one of the wounded men.

"Best get going," Ryan said. "No point staying around here. Head north."

They followed the ravine as it snaked in roughly the direction they wanted, toward the distant fortress of the Magus and Gert Wolfram.

The map showed that the blacktop ran parallel to the stream, but they figured that any possible pursuit from the ville would come along the road. After an hour's fast progress across the broken country, Ryan guessed that it was safe to assume they were away free, and he and the Armorer cut through some low, thorny scrub and picked up the highway again.

"MAP SHOWS WE'RE GETTING close to the section of the forest that they mined and laid traps," the Armorer said as they paused for a five-minute break in the middle of the afternoon.

The highway doglegged to the left, away west, leaving only a faint hunting trail to keep them heading in the direction they wanted.

There was a large camp site near a shallow, clear pool, and they sat there, lapping up the water to ease their thirst. Ryan scuffed his boot through a pile of ashes, turning up the rusted relic of an old Randall knife, bone hilt burned away, long blade still keen-edged.

"Wonder how long that's been there," he said, peering at it, rubbing the steel with his finger, revealing the initials G.C.

"Big fire," J.B. commented, head on one side. "Think it could be stickies?"

"Could be." He sat on a fallen log and stared at the calm pool, watching a foot-long dragonfly, colored a brilliant turquoise, darting back and forth. "Wonder how the others are getting on?"

J.B. pushed back the brim of his fedora, blinking at the shafts of bright sunlight that speared through the overhanging branches. "Got to hope they're fine."

Ryan glanced up at the sky, calculating time and distance and light. "Find a place for the night in about three more hours. Reckon that should put us something like halfway to their ville. All being well, we could recce late afternoon. Go in and try the rescue some time during the night."

"They'll be looking for us." J.B. yawned. "No way of walking around that."

Ryan grinned at his friend. "Like you said. Old times. Give it our best shot." He stood like a steel spring uncoiling. "Let's move it on."

Chapter Twenty-Six

Krysty lay out on the narrow bed, staring up at the ceiling, arms folded behind her head. Mildred dozed on one of the other beds, under the barred window of the hut.

In the next, identical shack along the row, she knew that Jak and Doc would also be resting. There was nothing else for them to do.

They'd been kept locked up ever since the powerful motorboat had delivered them to the landing on the east side of the Sippi the previous evening.

Krysty closed her bright emerald eyes, letting her thoughts go back to the time of their capture on board the *Golden Eagle*.

It had all been made so easy for their enemy, and she bit her lip in frustration at the memory of how they'd been slipped into the net.

"Triple-stupe," she muttered.

They had walked through the fog, along the glistening decks, not in the least suspicious of being led into a trap. Only when the half-dozen armed sec men had loomed from out of the mist, blasters aimed at point-blank range, did they realize what was happening.

Jak had been beaten unconscious when he went for his own Colt, and he was thrown into the bottom of the boat. Doc, Mildred and Krysty were disarmed and shepherded into the little vessel and whisked away into the gloom at high speed, bouncing and rocking over the river.

It was all done in professional silence, in a matter of a couple of minutes.

And the reasoning was all too obvious. Their capture gave Wolfram and the Magus a fistful of aces. Four aces. Laid on the table, solid and secure. Undeniably an unbeatable hand. While Ryan and J.B. sat helpless, without even a pair of deuces in their hands.

They'd been escorted to the center of the fortress, which was one of the most heavily defended places that Krysty had ever seen. By then Jak had recovered and he'd looked sharp-eyed around at the sec fences and moats and walls. The watchtowers and the power plants operated from water turbines from a wide stream that coursed through the site. He shook his head hopelessly at the overwhelming security he saw.

And the armed men.

Krysty had counted at least thirty before she and Mildred were separated from Doc and Jak and bolted into their own hut. There were eight beds in it, and it had obviously been used for guards rather than for the stickie slaves. It had its own shower room and toilet, with air-conditioning and a small kitchen unit, though the sec men told them that all meals would be brought to them in the hut. They wouldn't be allowed out even for any exercise until Ryan and J.B. turned up dutifully to carry out the work of setting up the mines and plantations again.

The plan had been explained to them all the following morning by Wolfram and the Magus, who had arrived at some point during the long night.

It was very friendly. The fat man sat back in his winged chair in his private quarters, hands folded across his capacious stomach. A balloon glass of good brandy was at his elbow, and a box of sugary, scented Turkish delight rested on a small table for him to pick at while he explained in his deep, bubbling voice what they wanted.

"And after this, you let us all go free? All of us?" Mildred asked.

"You have my word of honor upon it, my dear Dr. Wyeth. They bring back our ill-advised workers and set us up and running once more. And then you all are free as air."

"I fear that I would rather trust a rabid coyote," Doc said. "You and the monster with the metal eyes are notorious throughout the length and breadth of Deathlands for your cunning and evil. For your lies and your butchery. And you admit to this grudge against Ryan and John Dix."

The Magus was sitting cross-legged on a long sofa beneath a window. He pointed a metallic finger at the old man, his voice like an open razor. "Best way of stopping that bitching tongue from wandering and upsetting folks is to slice it out at the roots, Doc," he said quietly.

"Big talk, freak," Jak said.

The Magus looked for a moment as though he were going to attack the albino teenager, then he relaxed back on his seat, smiling mirthlessly. "Someone looking like you do should not toss around the name of a freak, you white-haired little mutant. A part of me hopes—hopes so much—that the Armorer and the one-eyed whore-son will fail in their task. I will so enjoy supping at the cold bowl of revenge."

"All you're fit for," Krysty said.

Wolfram lifted a pudgy, negligent hand. "Let us not have ill talking. This will be resolved, one way or the other, very shortly. We expect Ryan and John to have been landed last afternoon. They will have made some progress and camped for the night, not wishing to risk traveling through an alien and stickie-infested forest in the dead of darkness."

Doc was staring out of the window. "You truly make me wish to vomit, gentlemen. You take two women and a lad and an old man prisoner and use them as bait to try to destroy two of the bravest, finest men I have ever had the privilege of meeting. It is simply contemptible behavior."

The Magus rose at that and moved to stand by Doc. "You have no understanding, you old fool! This is not some game with rules and honor. They'd do it to us."

Doc turned and stared at the semiandroid. "You talk about honor? I don't believe you could begin to understand the word. Ryan and John have courage. Grace under pressure, someone once called it, years ago."

Wolfram sipped at his brandy. "Please, Dr. Tanner. This can be done without acrimony, without standing on ceremony. We believe that they will try a rescue, which will fail. If there is no loss of life, they will then submit to our wishes. We have faith in their ability, unless the passing years have taken the edge from their ruthless combat skills. They will defeat the recalcitrant stickies and drive them whimpering back to us. And all will be as well as well can be.''

Jak's hand was inching toward the small of his back, where Krysty knew he still had one of his throwing knives concealed, and she tensed herself, ready for violence. But the teenager changed his mind and relaxed.

Lying now on her bed, Krysty found herself slipping into an uneasy slumber. If Wolfram was right, then Ryan might be making his move with J.B. during the coming night.

And there was absolutely nothing that she could possibly do to help him.

Finally she slept, dreamlessly, tossing and turning from side to side, as the day wore on.

"THEY'LL LIKELY BE the three foremen that the fat man told us about."

Ryan and J.B. had been making good progress, tracking along the winding maze of narrow trails that cut in all directions through the coniferous forest. Each time the path forked, they simply took the route nearest to north, using the mossy sides of the trees to keep their bearings.

There had been no sign of two-legged life, though Ryan thought at one point that he caught the scent of a fire burning, but the wind shifted westerly and the smell disappeared.

There had been some signs of game in the soft patches of the trails, but both men agreed that to risk shooting at anything would be too dangerous.

At one point a fine stag suddenly appeared from the wilderness less than fifty yards ahead of them and stood and stared, unmoving. He was so close that Ryan could almost have hit it with his panga, and a single shot from the Steyr would have been a formality. But the threat from stickies in the neighborhood was too great, and he and J.B. watched helplessly as the magnificent animal finally tossed its head back, the antlers scraping at the low branches of a larch-pole pine, then vanished into the woods on the other side of the narrow path.

It was less than a quarter hour later that they came across the three corpses.

The shadowy clearing contained the lichen-covered remains of what might have been a hunting lodge. The roof was long caved in and gone, as were most of the walls, leaving only some of the thick, roughly carved, main upright beams and cross timbers that had divided the rooms.

It was these uprights and horizontals that the stickies had used as a frame for their sporting.

Some of the time the muties would indulge their extreme love for torture by fire in total immersion in flames, often spicing it with stolen blasting powder or even, if possible, plas-ex. But here they'd taken their time and used the fire in a slower, more subtle and delicate way.

"Been a hard passing," the Armorer said, studying the ravaged, mutilated bodies of the three men.

Two were tied upright, crucified, arms stretched out sideways, while the third of the victims had been hauled up to a cross beam and bound upside down, head toward the trampled earth. All three had been stripped naked. All of them were blackened, skin bloated as corruption worked its inexorable progress through their swollen tissues.

Ryan squatted on his heels, shaking dust from his jacket, laying the rifle on the ground. "Doesn't look like this happened all that long ago. Three, four days. Wolfram said they were taken longer than that. Stickies must have kept them alive since then, waiting for the right place for their funning."

There was still the faintest odor of gasoline hanging in the clearing.

Since the birds and predators of the forest had been at the soft parts, it wasn't that easy to see where their work ended and the labors of the muties began.

Eyes had been plucked from raw, crusted sockets, noses gone, the mouths peeled clear, lips vanished, showing the brown-smeared rows of teeth, exposed in the ripped jaws. There were clear burn marks all around the leathery, taut skin of the faces, where torches had been thrust against the living flesh. In every case all of the hair had been reduced to a blackened stubble.

The genitals showed similar horrific burning and gashing, and the bellies had been slit open so loops of dried intestines dangled in the ashes of the fires.

Hands had been cut off two of the men, and fingers were sliced away from the third victim. One of the bodies was missing both feet. It looked as though all of the major joints had been smashed with clubs: shoulders, knees, ankles, elbows and wrists.

Deep cuts had been inflicted across bellies and chests, which had then been flooded with gasoline before being ignited. Ryan sat in the stillness, almost able to hear the demonic whoops of delight from the hideous, capering stickies, drowning the moans and screams of their helpless, doomed victims.

As J.B. had said, it had been a long, hard passing for Wolfram's men.

"Least we know the muties are still around," he said, rising to his feet.

"Or they were a few days ago."

"Yeah. We going to cut them down?"

The Armorer turned away. "Won't do them no good, Ryan, will it? Might as well leave them. Any muties pass by and see the bodies've been disturbed might take it into their heads to follow our trail."

"Guess so. Northward, then."

"Watch out for the mines and traps that the map shows around this part. Between here and the fortress. Last thing that we need is to get ourselves blown up or caught in the steel jaws of the mantraps."

THE HUNTING TRAIL linked up once more with a good stretch of blacktop that showed signs of recent use by four-wheel wags. Ryan pulled out the map to refresh his memory. "Wolfram and the Magus's excavations are out that direction," he said, pointing east. "Not far."

"Think we should take a look?"

"Later, mebbe. If we get the others free, then there won't be any need."

"If they got wags, then we can use them to run," the Armorer said, wiping his sleeve across his forehead.

Ryan folded the map and put it in his pocket. "Not going to be easy. Those sec men looked tough. Bastards like Magus and the fat man have got them well trained. Good as they come. Still, talk gets us nowhere. Got to give it a shot. Come up with something when we've seen the setup."

THEY MOVED along the trail, still running northward, without any sign of traps or danger, though they kept clear of the verges, where they knew from experience that antipersonnel mines could do most harm.

"Light's starting to go," J.B. commented. "Time to find a place to hole up."

"Yeah. Feeling hungry. Don't see much sign of fresh game spoor."

"Stickies. Once you get a gang of those triple-rad-sick bastards sweeping through a part of the land, then it gets purged of life. What doesn't get chilled runs."

"Long as they keep away from us. Things go well, then we might not have to fight them."

J.B. looked across at him and grinned. "That'll be the day, pilgrim. That'll be the day."

Chapter Twenty-Seven

Once again Ryan and J.B. took to the trees for the night, finding a grove of splendid live oaks standing near a muddy pool, just off the trail, set among the mainly coniferous forest. It was the meeting point of a number of smaller, twisting tracks that snaked away in all directions.

On the map that Wolfram had given them, it looked as though they were less than ten miles from the fortress, plumb in the middle of the region that had been booby-trapped. In the failing light Ryan and the Armorer had peered carefully at the ground around the paths, looking for some signs of disturbed earth. But there was nothing to be seen.

The two friends once more used their belts to secure themselves in a fork, about thirty feet from the dangers of the ground, sitting together as the coppery sun sank to the west and the shadows deepened.

A half hour back they'd passed some bushes brimming with a rich crop that resembled large thimbleberries, tinted purple, but with an unusual scented sweetness. Both men had dark stains around their mouths from the fruit.

The alfresco meal had taken a little of the edge of

hunger away, but the talk turned to what they would have liked to have eaten for supper.

"Venison," J.B. said. "Roasted over apple wood and served with baked potatoes and fresh-picked peas. Topped off with a cherry cobbler."

Ryan nodded. "Could do worse. Breast of duck in a black-currant sauce with creamed potatoes, flavored with nutmeg, and lashings of gravy. Sliced beans on the side. And a steamed pudding with fresh cream and molasses."

The Armorer laughed and punched Ryan on the shoulder. "Enough. Dark night, but that's enough! I'll drown on my own spit if we keep going like this."

They were silent for a while as evening slithered toward full night.

RYAN WOKE WITH A START, aware of the familiar feeling of falling, a sensation that Doc had once told him was an atavistic response, dating back from primeval days when the hunter-gatherers would spend most nights in the trees to keep themselves from the ferocious beasts that roamed the primitive continents of the world. A slip and a fall would lead inevitably to a rending death.

He rubbed at his eye, glancing around, finding that a bright hunter's moon now shone serenely through the trees, turning the small lake into a silver mirror.

The only sound was a hunting owl, giving a soft hooting, warning of its presence, swooping wide-eyed between the trunks of the surrounding trees, weaving away toward the west as it caught the flicker of the human intruder's movement.

Ryan aimed his index finger after it, following its jinking flight, whispering to himself, "Bang."

Being awake, he realized that he needed to relieve the pressure on his bladder and he carefully unbuckled himself, trying not to disturb his companion. He looked all around before climbing down, feeling for the footholds on the slippery bole of the oak, the SIG-Sauer clumping against his right hip, the panga swinging on the other side.

He landed in the soft earth with a clumsy slide and a jolt, jarring his thigh that had been wounded so badly weeks back. "Fireblast!" He rubbed at it, bending and stretching to try to ease the sudden pain.

Walking a little way off from the tree to take a leak, he used the chance to exercise the stiffness from the leg, taking deep breaths of cool, damp air.

Something jumped in the dark water of the pool, leaving spreading circles.

Ryan stopped about fifty paces away from his sleeping partner, unbuttoning his pants and leaning with one hand against a stubby pine, catching the smell of pitch from a scar in the trunk, pissing steadily, the arc of liquid steaming as it splashed into the leaf mold.

He stopped, shook himself and buttoned up, standing still for a few moments, trying to clear his mind and think about the task that faced them. Their plan to reach the place and recce it around noon tomorrow with a view to a nighttime attack seemed feasible. But it wasn't yet much of a plan.

He opened his eye again, ready to rejoin J.B., snug in the live oak.

And saw the pallid, raggedy figure.

No, two of them.

Three.

They had the unmistakable, shambling demeanor of stickies, shoulders hunched, scrawny necks thrust out inquisitively, their heads thrown back, sniffing the night air, seeking their prey, closing in on the tree where J.B. was sleeping.

The moonlight was bright enough for Ryan to make out the brutish faces, with rudimentary noses like hogs, gaping, dribbling jaws, skin seamed with running sores, and the circles of voracious suckers that lined their hands and fingers, opening and closing, showing the tiny, razored teeth.

All three of the half-naked muties were holding crude daggers, with wooden hilts bound to rusting blades with knotted lengths of baling wire.

Ryan's first inclination was to draw the heavy automatic and blast the three creatures back to their own private hell. It would only take a handful of seconds at a range where he couldn't miss. Even with the silencer, the sound of the shots would carry through the silent woods, attracting the attention of any other muties within a quarter mile. And there was also a better-than-average chance that one of the stickies would scream out as he went down.

It was possible they were a single, small hunting party, but from everything he knew, it was likely the place was teeming with the runaway slaves.

Ryan slipped from cover, taking a few moments to look all around him, checking for the flicker of movement beneath the trees, watching beyond the pool for lean, solitary figures standing and waiting.

But it looked as if there were just the three.

They'd located J.B. Standing in a cluster, heads close together, they were whispering. Their backs were turned to Ryan.

The speed of their movement took him by surprise. Two of them cupped hands and hefted the third up the tree, allowing him to reach the first of the holds. Stickies were naturally clumsy, and Ryan had expected the climb to give them trouble.

Now the leader would be within reach of J.B. in a handful of seconds, his comrades already struggling to follow him up the gnarled trunk.

Ryan broke into a run, boots sliding silently through the packed pine needles and leaf mold. He drew the panga from its soft leather sheath as he ran, gripping the taped hilt tightly, starting to swing the heavy eighteen-inch blade, ready for the first lethal blow.

At the last moment the third of the stickies started to turn around, his feral senses catching some murmur of the attack. He was lowest on the tree, only a couple of feet off the ground.

The panga cut into the side of his neck, powered with all of Ryan's furious strength. The honed edge hacked clear through scabby skin, flesh, artery and muscle and the slight jar of the spine, through and out the other side. Blood jetted yards into the air, spinning black droplets in the harsh silver light of the moon.

There was a barely audible grunt from the dead creature as its sucking fingers relaxed their hold and it dropped at Ryan's feet. The misshapen head landed a frozen fraction of a second earlier, thudding heavily in the dirt and rolling a few steps toward the edge of the pool.

But by the time the skull thumped to the earth, Ryan was readying his second cut, twisting his wrists to present the blade on the backswing, cutting up between the spread thighs of the second, desperately scrambling stickie.

All hopes of silence vanished as the mutie threw back its head and screamed through broken teeth, loud and shrill, like a power saw slicing through granite. It was a raw sound of terror and agony, overlaid with the black knowledge of death.

The panga had thrust home deep under the stickie's genitals, severing them, ramming deep into the lower intestines, where a wrench of Ryan's wrist hacked the guts into threads of bloodied tissue.

Blood gushed over his arm and shoulder, flooding into the dirt. There was just time to remove the slick steel and step aside, avoiding the plummeting, dying creature, who landed on the corpse of its fellow.

But the last of the stickies was almost up at the fork of the tree, climbing with unusual agility, his leering face turning back toward Ryan. The mutie spit venom at him, his lidless eyes wide with triumph, knowing that he could no longer reach him, and J.B.'s sleeping figure was helpless in front of him.

Ryan dropped the panga and started to draw the blaster, his heart knowing that it was going to be too late. He was certain that he would be able to chill the third stickie, but only after the stickie had taken the life of his oldest friend.

He heard the thunderous boom of the scattergun, and the gibbering mutie was hurled backward as though he had been kicked from the live oak by an invisible mule. The body vanished in a cloud of acrid smoke, arms and legs flailing, landing four paces away, suckered fingers scrabbling in the leaf mold.

As the smoke cleared, Ryan could see the devastating effect of the M-4000 Smith & Wesson 12-gauge. Awakened from sleep by the scream of the castrated stickie, J.B.'s fighting reflexes had been swift enough to level and fire the shotgun, gripping it by the pistol butt, bracing it against his own chest. The shot exploded with twenty of the inch-long Remington fléchettes, the tiny, razored-steel darts that shredded anything in their path.

They had flayed the mutie's face, blinding, stripping away all the hideous features, pocking the raw bone of the angular skull, turning it into a ghastly, mocking ornament of violent death.

"Time to move," Ryan said.

J.B. quickly threw down the rifle, slinging the scattergun over his own shoulders, jamming on the fedora and sliding from the tree. "Hang on while I..." He pulled out his glasses and hooked them on the bridge of his bony nose.

"That shriek'll bring any bastard stickie within five miles," Ryan said, waiting anxiously.

"Ready. Yeah, and a bright moon like this is all we need. We going to hole up?"

Moving too fast was, as the Trader often remarked, sometimes worse than moving too slowly.

It seemed a high probability that there were more stickies in the surrounding forest, maybe a lot of them, which meant the risk of charging into them like headless chickens.

But the amount of cover was minimal.

They hadn't seen any buildings for some time. In any case they would be the first targets for any hunting muties seeking vengeance for their three slaughtered brothers.

"Don't forget those boobies and mines the map shows," Ryan cautioned.

They stood still, breath held, listening. The death screech of the second of the stickies had frozen the forest, silencing every living thing. Wherever they looked, Ryan and J.B. saw only stark silver light and deep, etched shadows.

"Can't hear anything." The Armorer bit his lip, shifting his feet as he noticed that the pool of blood from the three corpses was spreading near him.

Despite their clumsiness and general stupidity, some stickies were able to move quickly over short distances, and most of them had great stamina, being capable of holding on to a pursuit for hour after hour.

"Might as well carry on north." Ryan took a last look around. "Got a better idea, brother?"

J.B. shook his head. "North it is."

Chapter Twenty-Eight

Wolfram had insisted that his "guests," as he so ful-
somely called them, should join him and the Magus
for breakfast that morning.

They were all released from their locked and bolted
huts, and marched over to the quarters of the joint
leaders of the fortress. The sec men had their hand-
blasters drawn and cocked, circling the prisoners,
watching them warily. They were particularly suspicious of Jak's fiery spirit, keeping several paces away
from the albino teenager.

Doc had almost refused to join them, complaining
that he preferred to eat alone rather than with the
mongrel scum of Deathlands.

Mildred had taken his arm and gentled him like a
spooked horse, suggesting that there was no point at
all in antagonizing their captors.

"Costs us nothing to be nice to them," she urged.
"And it might help us in the long run."

Doc had grumbled and grumped. "Upon my soul,
Dr. Wyeth, but you are too much sweetness and light,
and I am cantankerous and evil livered."

"Yes, but we all love you, Doc," she replied,
squeezing his hand.

BREAKFAST WAS uncomfortable and stilted. Wolfram was the very model of easygoing good nature and surface charm. But it rang as false as a cougar's smile. The Magus was nothing but wormwood and gall.

Once they were seated, the fat man gestured for the meal to be brought in.

Sec men carried in dented silver chafing dishes, with polished covers, laying them at intervals around the long refectory table. Krysty watched with some interest, noticing that there seemed to be no women in the fortress at all, not even the sluts that might have been expected.

The food was basic, approaching adequate, leaning heavily on what the surrounding forest and river supplied: some long-boned fish with the heads left on, silver eyes boggling at the ceiling, jaws brimming with a triple row of serrated teeth; a leathery omelet, liquid at the center, larded with pieces of bacon and fat strips of pork. The best dish was some wafer-thin flakes of beef soaked in oil and served with chopped onions, sun-dried tomatoes and some olive bread.

"We had some scouts out in the wood last night," Wolfram said, once he'd helped himself, piling his blue-and-white plate high with food, scooping out several ladles of greasy fried potatoes and adding a half pint of ketchup.

"And what did they see?" Krysty asked.

"More what they heard," muttered the Magus, who was pulling a fish apart with his steel-tipped fingers.

"What?" Mildred asked, sipping at a mug of coffee sub.

Wolfram leaned back, making his deep-armed chair creak. "Couple of my best scouts were out, on my orders. Told them, dear fellows, to keep out of trouble. To watch and listen. Not become involved. That's what they did."

"Probably the shitters only went a hundred paces into the trees, then waited a few hours and came back out again," the Magus said.

"I think not. I trust them somewhat. Said they heard a gang of stickies moving south toward the ville that has the strange museum place. Tedious stuff. But I digress. My men say that they heard a scream."

"Just one scream?" Jak asked.

"Indeed, my white-haired youth, just the one. Nothing to build a reputation on, is it? A scream. It could have been a wild hog. Or a slaughtered stickie. Or even a one-eyed murderer who once rode with the arch slayer, the Trader, finally making his way aboard the final locomotive, westbound."

Krysty stopped eating, not sure whether the grossly fat man was playing a cruel joke on them all. Did he know more than he was saying? Was Ryan lying cold and dead somewhere out among the endless miles of pine trees?

"You look head-fucked," the Magus said, staring accusingly at her.

Krysty managed a bright smile at his cruel face. "No. I'm really fine. Could be you who gets head-fucked when Ryan and J.B. get here."

The Magus stared at her, and she felt a chill run down her spine, her sentient hair curling defensively around her nape. He lifted his hand and tapped his right eye with the steel nail, generating a metallic clicking sound. "I see what I see. I see what's going to happen. When debts are paid and accounts settled. You have the power of seeing, don't you?"

"Some."

"So, what does the future hold for you and for me? For all of us?"

Krysty rarely responded to that kind of challenge, having learned from her mother that the special talent of seeing that she possessed was Gaia-given and shouldn't be devalued, cheapened and peddled as though it had fallen off the back of a truck. But the snide probing of the Magus had gotten to her. She closed her eyes and sat back in her chair.

"You should not succumb to the fiend," whispered Doc, on her left.

"It's all right," she said. "Got everything in hand. It's all right."

It was impossible to describe to anyone else exactly how she felt when she probed inside her own mind. Ryan had asked her, and she'd made an effort to explain to him, aware of how vague and unsatisfactory it all sounded.

"It's not that I *see*. More a kind of a feeling, inside my mind. A kind of representation of what's happening or what might happen. Like watching a blurred vid that moves erratically through time and space. Shows me what *might* happen."

Ryan had shaken his head, unable to understand what she was trying to explain.

Now Krysty struggled to see something of the future for Wolfram and the Magus, for Ryan and for

J.B. Dix, for all of them over the next few dangerous days.

But it was clouded.

Shifting images gibbered at her from a gelid mist, dappled with daggers of red-purple chem lightning. The faces of all her friends—and the enemies—swam in and out of focus, smiling or snarling, in a silent mosaic of confusion.

But there was no sense of order, no glimpse of what the future might truly hold for any of them.

Krysty squeezed her eyes shut tighter, trying to close out the noise of the others eating. But the harder she concentrated, the less she could make out.

There were tiny flashes, like the visions seen during a vicious thunderstorm, crisp black-and-white images that froze for just a heartbeat and then disappeared: Ryan, water streaming down his face, running through the trees, a knife in his hand that wept blood; J.B. lying still, head thrown back, rain bouncing off his glasses; a picture that faded into the Magus in a similar position, steel eyes open wide, looking up into a darkening sky, snowflakes settling on the glittering, frosted lenses; Jak laughing, juggling with his knives in a tumbling array of whispering steel; Mildred shaking her head, the beads in her plaited hair bouncing and rattling, all in silence, while her mouth opened and closed as if she were trying to shout a warning; Wolfram naked in a bath of steaming water, smoking a large cigar while he picked at his crimson nails with a tiny golden stiletto; Doc leaning like an elegant dandy on his swordstick, sipping at a fluted glass of frothing white wine. His head was on one side, and he was staring intently at her, looking slightly puzzled, as if he'd been told something that he didn't quite understand, as though his world was slightly out of kilter with his senses.

A cold voice broke into her thoughts, as icy as the wind that blew between the worlds.

"You see nothing, do you?"

Krysty didn't reply to the Magus's sudden probing, seeking to keep herself wrapped warmly in the security blanket of her own visions.

But it wasn't possible.

The voice grated, like someone pushing a ragged thumbnail at the insides of her eyes.

"You hear me well enough in your fake trance. I know you do, Krysty Wroth."

Her eyes opened, and she swayed a little in her seat, looking down at her plate, scattered with the oily remains of her breakfast. She was aware that everyone was looking at her and felt Doc's hand on her sleeve.

"I'm all right," she said quietly.

"You saw my fate?" pressed the skinny man across the table form her.

"I saw a bleak and lonely passing for you," she replied. "The dogs licked your cooling blood, and not a living soul mourned for your death."

Krysty had been staring at the Magus and she saw, to her surprise, that the random, angry shaft had struck home. His jaw had sagged a little, and his eyes widened. He was holding a serving spoon in his right hand, and the metal bent and split as his fingers clenched on it.

Wolfram chuckled, the noise like gas bubbling through a tincture of warm honey. "My dear Magus, I believe that the green-eyed temptress has pierced your defenses."

"Shit she has! Just the usual kind of stupe lies you'd look for from the poxed slut of that cocksucking bastard Cawdor."

Doc tapped on his empty coffee mug with the handle of his butter knife. "He speaks well of you, too, Magus," he said very gently.

Jak laughed out loud, attracting the venomous stare of the metal-eyed freak. "Stare all want," he said to the Magus.

He turned to Wolfram. "What did the sec men find out in woods? Not dead Ryan. So, what?"

Wolfram shifted a little uncomfortably, sitting sideways, as if he were struggling to restrain a fart. "They came across the corpses of three stickies beneath a tree. Two had been hacked to death with some sort of cleaver. The third of them had his face stripped from his raw skull with a fléchette round from a Smith & Wesson scattergun."

"John's blaster!" Mildred exclaimed.

"Indeed. Cawdor and Dix had fled the scene long before my men got there."

"They see any sign of live stickies?" Krysty asked.

Wolfram nodded. "They were lucky not to be trapped themselves. It seemed that Cawdor and Dix had a lead, from their trail, of around forty-five minutes. But my sec people hid as they saw a group of nearly twenty stickies, hot in pursuit. They thought that it was likely that the muties would catch up with them around dawn.'' He paused. "Oh, they returned with all speed. But one said he thought that he heard an explosion, just as they got back to the camp here. Wondered if it might have been a mine. About the right time for the stickies to have caught up with the boys.''

He glanced at his ornate gold chron. "By now they should all have met up.''

WOLFRAM'S SCOUTS WERE good at their job, and their information had proved accurate.

Ryan became aware an hour or so before dawn that they were being pursued. It had started with the all-too-familiar feeling at the back of his neck.

"Hold on,'' he said.

"What? Feel something?'' J.B. looked behind them, taking his time, glancing all around. The moon was virtually gone, and the shadows under the forest were almost impenetrably deep. "Can't see a thing.''

"Nor me. But I'm sure there's something trailing us. Closing in.''

"Trail ends ahead. We could wait up and check.''

Ryan looked where the Armorer pointed. "Good one, bro. Hide around the corner and look back.'' He rubbed his chin. "Might be an animal of some kind.''

J.B. stared behind them again. "And then again, Ryan, it might not.''

"STICKIES!''

"Fireblast!'' Ryan shaded his eyes, trying to make out numbers in the pallid light of the early dawning. "Big gang.''

"Close on twenty," J.B. agreed. "Enough to scatter into the woods and give us a hard time if we screw up an ambush on them. They look strung-out, as well. Not a nice compact unit we could pour some chilling into."

"Best steps are long ones," Ryan said. "Go hard for a half hour or so and build up a lead. Then try and find a place to hole up, in the trees and brush. Hope they miss us."

The bend in the trail hid them from the pursuers, about six hundred yards behind them, moving steadily, snouts down, like hunting dogs.

The track snake-backed only fifty yards ahead, and as they reached it, Ryan skidded to a halt, diving into the shadows on the left, followed instantly by J.B.

On the next straight stretch, less than a quarter mile in front of them, was another large gang of stickies.

Coming their way.

Chapter Twenty-Nine

"Have to hide," Ryan said. "No choice. They'd see us any way we run."

"Be on top of us, from both directions, in less than two minutes." J.B. had the 9 mm Uzi unslung, ready in his hand, while Ryan had his index finger on the trigger of the Steyr SSG-70. There was already enough daylight for him not to need the Starlight nightscope, but the rifle wasn't much of a weapon for the close-range ambush of a numerically superior force.

His mind was racing. On every side was the featureless forest that had been surrounding them ever since they'd been dropped off the *Golden Eagle*. Apart from the narrow trails that occasionally meandered off to one side or the other, the forest was unbroken and largely impenetrable.

With the light increasing every moment, it would be far more difficult to simply lie still in the shadows and hope that the stickies went by. There was a long-standing body of strong rumor that the muties were able to scent out human prey with their snuffling noses.

"Get in deep, back to back. Mebbe they'll miss us. If not, then we fight."

J.B. straightened his fedora. "If I had a better plan, then I'd tell you. Let's do it."

But there was another development that neither man had reckoned on.

As they darted off the side of the track, Ryan's boots slipped in loose earth near the broken end of a fallen ponderosa pine, sending him flat on his face, hands outstretched, dropping the hunting rifle in front of him.

He lay there for a moment, shaken by the heavy fall, fingers brushing a bunch of thin, stiff twigs that protruded from the leaf mold—thin, stiff, *metallic* twigs.

"Fuck..." he breathed.

"You all right?" J.B. whispered, standing a yard away from him, taking a half step toward him to help him to his feet.

"Don't move, John," Ryan croaked.

"What?" He was more surprised at being called by his given name than anything.

"Mines. Got my hand on one."

"Where?" He stooped, his eyes narrowed behind the lenses, peering at Ryan's spread fingers and the tiny antennas that protruded between them. "Dark night!"

"Dirt's been dug over. Must be all around us. There's several trails going off here. Why they picked it to seed the mines. One wrong move..."

In the silence they could now hear the approaching stickies, chattering in their reedy, hoarse voices. In a few seconds they'd be around both corners, virtually on top of them.

J.B. acted fast, drawing his own long-bladed knife, cutting quickly beneath the antipersonnel mine that lay under Ryan's hand. "Keep your fingers still!" he hissed under his breath, loosening the earth, revealing the dark gray, circular metal shape. It was about eight inches across, with the delicate contact on the top, packed with hi-ex and lethal frags.

The stickies were closer.

As soon as the Armorer had it free, Ryan jumped to his feet, snatching the Uzi from the dirt, while J.B. picked up the mine in both hands, holding it out in front of him, like a mother with a newborn babe.

"What shall I . . . ?" he whispered.

"Throw it on the track," Ryan urged. "Quick."

It was a clumsy, heavy thing to dispose of easily. Ryan watched his companion as he swung it awkwardly around, like an amateur discus thrower, releasing it in a shallow arc toward the sharp bend in the path.

"Down!" Ryan yelled, diving for cover behind the nearest large pine.

As he hurled himself down, he glimpsed the first of the gang of stickies out of the corner of his eye, walking along the narrow track from the north.

They stopped as the metal disk landed among them, frozen in midstride.

Then the explosion concealed them.

It was flatter and more muffled than Ryan had expected, absorbed by the bodies of the muties and by the surrounding bank of trees. But it was still a frighteningly substantial noise, filled with smoke and the whistling ricochets of the jagged shards of the hot, splintered shrapnel, which hissed through the high branches above him.

Ryan didn't have time to cover his ears against the concussive effects of the land mine, so he closed his eye and opened his mouth to try to minimize the results.

The blast picked him up and rolled him over twice, covering him with loose dirt and leaves. He was vaguely aware of a sickening cracking sound as one of the large overhanging branches snapped through the middle and fell to earth, missing him by a couple of feet.

He knew that J.B. had been just behind him, but for the first few seconds he was so disorientated that he couldn't work out where his friend had landed.

After the sucking explosion, there was a heartbeat of uncanny stillness, like the motionless center at the frozen heart of a hurricane.

Then the screaming began.

And there was a strange burst of rain that pattered all around the immediate blast area, spotting on Ryan's clothes, hands and face, a soft, warm, sticky, crimson rain.

Ryan was partly deafened by the explosion, everything still sounding muffled and faraway. Even the piercing screams from the hideously torn and mutilated stickies seemed as if they were trickling in from another dimension. At his side Ryan was aware of J.B. struggling to his knees, glasses hanging crookedly from his blood-patched face, his hat lying in the dirt near his feet.

"Ace on the line!" the Armorer yelled. "Best finish them off now."

Now that the explosion had been and gone, Ryan realized that there had been a real danger of the concussion triggering off a chain reaction among any of the other land mines buried close by them. So far they'd been lucky.

So far.

He stood, able for the first time to appreciate the bloody scale of the carnage.

The mine had been pitched right at the feet of one of the gangs of advancing stickies. From the torn relics of mutated humanity, it seemed that there might have been close to a dozen of them. But it would take a careful computation of the amputated legs, hands and other assorted ragged limbs to try to match them to headless trunks and faceless skulls.

On one side, where the force of the explosion had been most powerful, it looked as though someone had taken the contents of a butcher's shop and heaved them into the splintered lower branches of the pines.

It didn't bear much resemblance to anything that had once been vaguely humanoid.

Just lengths of ragged cloth.

And raw meat.

The group of stickies that had been trailing Ryan and the Armorer had been just far enough back to be spared from the force of the land mine's blast. But they had come lumbering forward, standing and staring at the scene of the massacre with a brutish, grunting lack of comprehension, hands at their sides, rheumy eyes wide in curious dismay.

One or two of their wounded companions had managed to get to their feet and were staggering around in circles, mewing feebly, blood pouring from terminal gashes.

One was blinded, a great flap of skin hanging down from his forehead over the top part of his face, revealing the glistening expanse of smeared bone beneath. Another was clutching a jagged spike of resinous wood that had been driven clean through the lower stomach, spilling his guts into the trampled mud around his bare feet.

Ryan made himself a lightning summary of the initial butcher's bill.

Six or seven dead. Roughly the same number critically injured. One or two recovering from unconsciousness. And about ten in the second, hapless group.

Ryan left the Steyr in the dirt, drawing the SIG-Sauer from its holster, wincing as he rubbed away a gobbet of bloody flesh from the butt.

"Let them have it," he said. "And watch where you're putting your feet."

But before they could open fire, the blinded stickie had tottered across the path, hands groping at the sulfurous, smoky air, stumbling in among the torn trees on the far side of the narrow hunting trail.

In among the small piles of disturbed earth.

"Fireblast!" Ryan turned away and threw himself facedown in the dirt, immediately followed by J.B., who had only just picked up his fedora.

The second explosion seemed louder.

This time the two men were marginally better prepared for it, cupping their hands over their ears, closing eyes and keeping their mouths open to absorb the pressure from the land mine as the dying stickie detonated it.

Once again the white-hot shrapnel scythed out sideways and upward, ripping into the shell-shocked survivors of the first explosion.

This time, as Ryan rolled back onto his hands and knees, leveling the automatic, he realized that there were virtually no targets left standing.

The ground was a rolling mass of torn, bloodsodden flesh and smashed bones. The earlier screaming had almost stopped, replaced by a low chorus of moaning, dissonant and pathetic—utterly without hope.

In the middle of the carnage, a single stickie stood, miraculously unharmed. His clothing was even more torn than it had been before, and his body streamed with blood. But it was the blood of the others.

His hands were in front of his face, making feeble fluttering movements, as though he were trying to drive away an invisible cloud of tiny moths.

"Dark night," J.B. whispered, looking around and picking up his crumpled fedora, taking the greatest care where he set his combat boots.

"Best get out," Ryan said, having to clear his throat of the choking dust. "If there's any of the bastards still left alive in the woods, those explosions'll bring them running."

The Armorer nodded. "Sure will. Nothing attracts a stickie more than a big bang. Unless it's two big bangs."

The air was filled with the cloying, metallic stench of spilled blood.

Ryan leveled the automatic at the single unharmed mutie, hesitating with his finger taut on the trigger, shaking his head as the stunned creature slowly turned his face and stared blankly at him.

"Do it," J.B. urged. "One more or less doesn't make a difference."

"Does to me." Ryan sighed, easing down on the hammer and holstering the blaster again. "No, *compadre*. If the gods want this one to live, then we'll go with that."

J.B. coughed, slapping dust from his clothes with his fedora. "If that's the way you want it..."

Ryan turned and picked his way delicately among the raggled corpses, stepping past the dead and the dying and the critically wounded stickies, pausing to knock away a suckered hand that reached up toward him.

He brushed against the shocked, seminaked figure that stood motionless in the center of the carnage, wary as the lidless, watery pink eyes moved to follow him. But the mutie made no attempt to stop Ryan and the Armorer from leaving the blood-sodden, cratered patch of forest.

Ryan's ears were still ringing from the force of the twin explosions, and he pressed his hands against them. He was also dappled with mutie blood, the smell of it strong.

J.B. followed him, taking care not to walk anywhere near the edge of the trail. They headed north, almost side by side, Ryan slightly in the lead.

"Can't help wondering whether there's a bigger gang of muties roaming around the woods," Ryan said. "They have to be runners from the fortress of Wolfram and the Magus."

"Guess so. They'll—" J.B. stopped in midsentence, swinging around with the Uzi at his hip, opening up with a short burst of about a dozen rounds.

Ryan dropped into the gunfighter's crouch, sideways on, the SIG-Sauer springing into his hand, seeing immediately that it wasn't needed.

The last of the stickies had broken free from his trance and come after them, the faint padding sound of his bare, suckered feet in the damp earth drowned out by the moaning and crying from behind them.

He had run at them, hands held high, as though he were surrendering, but the voracious teeth glistened amid the circles of suckers. His mouth was wide open, baring the pointed, filed-down teeth.

He was so pale that he was like a living creature carved from a wind-washed bone, twisted and ugly, his scabbed face distorted with insensate rage at the two norms.

J.B. had spotted him from the corner of his eye and swung around, firing the burst of 9 mm full-metal-jacket rounds from the Uzi at his hip. The stream of lead cut the mutie almost in two, all the bullets hitting below the ribs, tumbling and rending through the soft intestines of the stomach, smashing the spine, exiting into the forest behind the creature.

He spun and fell, suckered hands pressed to torn flesh, going down and lying still in the trail.

"Nice," Ryan said.

They walked together north, toward the fortress of Wolfram and the Magus, leaving behind the place of massive death and still, bloody corpses.

KRYSTY AND THE OTHERS were escorted back to their cells after breakfast, with the bright dawn promising a fresh day, the sun climbing cheerfully from the eastern sky. The Magus accompanied them, leaving his fat companion to pick alone at the remains of the meal.

He watched as Jak and Doc were locked away first, standing a little distance from the sec men as Krysty and Mildred walked into their barred room.

"Enjoy your time," he said. "Soon Ryan and John Dix will be making their attempt to rescue you."

"Thought you reckoned the stickies might have gotten them," Mildred said, pausing in the doorway. "You changed your mind already?"

The slitted mouth opened in a parody of a smile. "Never underestimate your enemy."

"Specially when it's Ryan Cawdor and J. B. Dix, coming after you," Krysty added.

Doc's face appeared at the slatted window of his hut. "Getting a chill around the heart, Magus?"

"No. Not at all. They might come here soon. But they will fail. And we shall have our victory. And you might have your liberty."

Doc laughed. "Liberty. Scum like you would not know the meaning of the word."

The steel eyes stared incuriously at the old man. "And you would know?"

"Your kind of liberty? Surely. Count Mirabeau said, during the height of the Terror in the French Revolution, that liberty was a whore who fucked on a mattress of corpses. That's your kind of liberty, Magus."

"Think so?"

Doc nodded. "I know so. For men like you and Wolfram who live by the knout and the blade and the gun, there is no other kind of freedom."

"Cheap words, Dr. Tanner."

"You will not think so when Ryan spits in your open eyes, Magus."

The half android turned on his heel. "Lock them up," he snapped to the sec men. "Lock them well."

Chapter Thirty

"What's that?"

"Where?"

"Ahead, three o'clock. Just rising up above the tops of the trees."

J.B. stood on tiptoe, straining to see where Ryan had pointed. "Can't see anything."

Ryan grinned at his smaller partner. "You'll see it in a minute, bro. Climb higher."

"Oh, yeah. See it now. What is...? Looks like a hot-air balloon."

Ryan nodded. "It is. On a tethered cable, so it doesn't fly away. Twenty gets you one that it's coming from Wolfram's base. Using it as a floating ob platform. Looking out for us, I guess. Smart idea."

J.B. touched the butt of the Steyr rifle that dangled from its sling across Ryan's shoulders. "One round from that should do the job," he said.

"Might have some kind of walkie-talkie going. Time to send a warning before they go down. Don't want them to know where we are."

J.B. shaded his eyes against the bright sun that streamed in from the right side of the track. "What's glinting off the cover of the balloon?"

Ryan squinted, taking a few steps to bring himself under the shadow of the tall pines, having checked first that there was no sign of any more of the murderous land mines. "Think it's got some sort of armaproof cover on it. Fine titanium-steel mesh, mebbe. Sort of thing the Magus might've come up with."

"Think you're right." The Armorer had joined Ryan in the gloom. "Least they won't be able to make us out under here. Even with good glasses."

Ryan sniffed. "Trouble is, they'll be able to make us out if we move back along any of the trails. Have to stick to heart of the forest, and that'll really slow us down. Fireblast! All that we needed."

"Yeah, but we figured to go in some time after dark tonight. Should be able to cover the last few miles without too much difficulty. Can't be all that far now. Do it comfortably before night falls."

"Long as the stickies don't come gibbering out of the trees after us."

J.B. peeked up at the rising balloon. "Nothing but problems, *compadre.*"

"Come against swift and evil bastards like the Magus and Gert Wolfram, and you don't expect them to make it easy for you. Let's keep moving."

IT WAS HARDER GOING than the Armorer had guessed. The pines grew more densely together, making the friends push, bend and crawl through the soft carpet of needles. The balloon hung there, ahead of them every time they checked, riding about two hundred feet high on its cable.

They caught the glint of sunlight off binoculars, and were able to make out the dim shapes of at least three sec men in the reinforced basket.

Ryan twice unslung the Steyr and leveled it from the cover of the forest, peering through the laser image enhancer. He was tempted to open up on the spies in the sky and try to take them out, or even hope to bring down the balloon. But he was able to see the fine protective network of wires that covered the dark green fabric, so he held his fire.

IT WAS WELL PAST the middle of the afternoon when J.B. spotted the cable being wound in, taking the balloon back to earth. The occasional roaring of the gas-fired engine beneath it was muted, and finally turned off, indicating that the flying ob platform was done for the day.

"Makes life a tad easier," he said. They were now within a mile of where they figured the fortress had to be, and it would have been hard to get closer without one of the sec men spotting them, even among the pines.

They waited until the balloon had vanished below the tops of the trees, which took an unconscionable time. Ryan sat down, his back against a slender ponderosa, closing his eye, snatching a few minutes of needed sleep.

J.B. joined him on the floor of the forest, keeping awake. He pushed back the fedora, taking off his glasses and giving them a good polish, constantly checking the woods around them to make sure there was nothing and nobody moving along the trail.

But everywhere was still.

They'd seen precious little wildlife during the entire day, which could mean that there were stickies in the area, frightening off all the game with their distinctive, raw, foul smell. There had been a family of pygmy wild boars, scuttling along and crossing the trail, the hunchbacked sow turning and staring venomously at the two intruders into their domain, eyes glowing like smoldering embers in the semidarkness. But Ryan and J.B. had stood still and waited, watching the animals finally turn away and go about their own business.

There had been a strange silver-backed snake, like nothing either of them had ever seen. The reptile had been close to twenty feet in length, with half a dozen pairs of residual stumpy legs that helped to move it at a fast-walking speed. There was also a row of silvery horns along its back, six inches or more in length, tipped with an oozing crimson ichor.

Both Ryan and J.B. were glad to see the mutie snake barely falter, turning its spade-shaped head for a quick glance, before heading westward.

There was also a chattering flock of birds, their orange wings barred with emerald stripes, with unusually long beaks. They had darted out of the trees, circling the two men, diving close enough for them to feel the fluttering of their wings against their heads.

But they, too, had swiftly lost interest and headed away, vanishing toward the fortress.

Now, with the light going fast, the surrounding forest had become quite still and silent.

"I can hear men calling," J.B. finally said, making Ryan blink awake. "Very faint. Ahead of us. Could be sec men tethering the balloon at the fortress. Close enough."

Ryan yawned and stretched. He stood, muscles creaking in his back and shoulders. "Could do with a couple of hours' decent rest," he said. "Might as well get back on the trail…see what kind of a recce we can carry out before full dark. Then snatch some sleep before we make our move."

"They'll be expecting us," J.B. said, easing the scattergun on its sling.

"Course they will. We know that they know. They know that we know that they know."

"Trader used to say that expectation is a sword that can cut both ways."

Ryan stepped carefully back onto the track, seeing more of the marks from the wide tires of four-by-four wags. "Be good to take one of their vehicles," he said.

J.B. grinned wolfishly. "I'd rather taken a shine to escaping in the balloon. That'd be real traveling in style, wouldn't it? Up, up and away."

THEY WERE LESS than a mile away, and it took them about a quarter of an hour at a brisk walk before they saw the perimeter sec lights glowing brightly ahead of them. The lights were set on tall watchtowers, and each tower held at least one pair of armed sec men, with light machine guns and gren launchers. Linking the towers was a high double fence of razor wire, dotted with white porcelain terminals every few yards, showing that it was charged.

The two men crouched under cover and took in the defenses of the fortress.

J.B. whistled under his breath. "Dark night! what wouldn't I give for a war wag or two and a well-trained crew? Pop the place like a hammer on a ripe melon."

"But we don't have a wag. So that seems to leave just you and me, bro."

THEY WENT ALL the way around, stopping on every flank to study the fortress in more detail. The dazzling lights made it brighter than midday, allowing Ryan and J.B. to see every detail of the place, inside and out.

By the time they got back to their starting point, they'd been there nearly two hours, and they were both feeling pessimistic.

"We agree that they're probably in those two adjacent huts," Ryan said.

"With the barred windows and the sec men patrolling? Must be there."

There was a long silence, broken by Ryan. "Not going to be easy."

"No."

"Best move back out of the fringe of the lights and do some combat thinking."

J.B. was staring at the pair of buildings where they figured Mildred and the others were being held prisoner. "Yeah."

THE MOON HAD DULY put in an appearance, pouring down irregular silver pools in among the patches of deep, black shadow under the trees.

Ryan took out his panga as they sat together in one of the small, bright clearings, using the point to sketch a detailed plan of everything they'd seen of the fortified camp: the outer fence and the towers, the sec men's barracks and the block of concrete buildings that they had guessed was where Wolfram and the Magus had their headquarters.

"How many men?" Ryan asked.

"Counting those in the towers, the walking dudes and those who are probably off shift at the moment, it has to be something like forty or fifty. Shit-lot of men, and they had a good mix of blasters. Revolvers and shotguns."

"Remingtons, Colts and Smith & Wessons," Ryan said thoughtfully. "And they all looked like they knew how to use them."

"One of the best-trained sets of sec men I can remember. Did Wolfram have such good people back in the old days?"

Ryan grinned, his teeth white in the faint glare of the towered lights. "Funny thing, memory. Times I can't hardly recall what I had for breakfast a couple of days ago. Yet I can remember that expression on the face of a gut-shot woman up in the Shens, from…twenty-five years ago. Clear as a bell. Yet you ask me about the fat man's sec forces when we rode with Trader, and it all seems lost in a fog. I reckon he must have been good, even all the way back then. How do you recall them?"

The Armorer sniffed. "Tough. Not as many men as he's got now. And he and the Magus weren't kind of officially together. Not going to be that easy, amigo."

They decided to make a further circuit of the fortress camp, keeping well back in the screen of low bushes, ducking under the branches of the dense wall of spruce that ringed much of the forest ville.

They watched while the guards changed over, presumably ready for the night shift, and saw supper being taken on trays to the couple of barred huts where they were almost certain that Krysty and the others were being held captive.

"Don't look too strong," Ryan said. "Blow away the bars or go in through the doors."

"Sec men everywhere." J.B. borrowed Ryan's rifle, using the Starlight nightscope to make out better what was going down. "Mebbe try and set up some sort of diversion."

"Magus and Wolfram'll be expecting us to try something like that," Ryan replied.

"Then it'll have to be good, won't it?"

THE CAMP HAD a rear entrance, and the evening patrol that came out through the high gates took Ryan and J.B. by surprise. There were a dozen sec men, all in camouflage gear, faces darkened, moving out at a sudden, fast trot. They headed along a snaking trail that would lead them almost directly to the point where the two friends had been skulking.

"Fireblast!" Ryan hissed, tugging at J.B.'s sleeve, jerking him away from the track, heaving him deeper into the shadows of the endless pines.

It was almost pitch-dark, and they stumbled along by instinct, trying for silence, hearing the steady padding of the patrol, seeming to be closing in on them.

The Armorer had taken the lead as Ryan stopped a moment to glance behind them, peering through the undergrowth toward the lights, seeing that the sec men were barely fifty yards away, moving almost parallel to himself and J.B.

There was a sudden dull thud, like a powerful spring being released, and a vicious crack. Just in front of him Ryan saw a sharp movement in the leaf mould, as if some living creature had sprung from cover and snapped at J.B.'s ankle. The diminutive figure gave a shocked gasp of pain and went down like a poleaxed steer, clutching at his lower leg.

Where the massive mantrap had clamped shut on him.

Chapter Thirty-One

Ryan flung himself down on top of his oldest friend, holding onto the slim, writhing figure, his right hand fumbling for J.B.'s open mouth. He clamped his fingers over the stretched lips, squeezing tight.

"Hang on, hang on..." he whispered in J.B.'s ear, aware of the Armorer's harsh, agonized breathing. "Get it off you, soon as the patrol's gone by."

He felt J.B.'s head nodding, the movement stilling, with only the faint metallic chinking of the thick chain that tethered the trap deep into the ground.

Ryan risked a glance up, aware of the risk of the filtered lights from the fortress camp picking out the pallor of his face among the trees.

The patrol was moving at a slow walk, covering both sides of the narrow trail to the south, blasters at the hip. As the men moved through the dappled moonlight, their skillfully camouflaged clothing made them occasionally invisible. They were fully on the alert, their heads turning from side to side, seeking the fugitives, Ryan and J.B., not knowing that they were lying within twenty feet of them.

Ryan pressed his face into the dirt, straining his hearing, catching the faint padding sound of combat boots moving away and past.

Beneath him he was aware of J.B.'s pounding heart and the faint sound of his fingers scratching in the pine needles as he fought against the crushing pain of the serrated teeth of the mantrap.

Finally Ryan risked another glance.

The trail was deserted, and the forest of spruce was silent. From the nearby camp he heard the sudden crash of broken crockery and a bellow of laughter, sounding as if it came from the small kitchen block.

"They gone?" the Armorer whispered, his breath slicing between Ryan's fingers.

"Think so. Gotta be quick. Could be back here any time. How is it?"

J.B., half sitting up, groaned. The chain clinked again. "Bad."

"Broken?"

"Can't tell. Numb. Caught me just above the ankle. Top of my boot might have saved the worst of it." He was breathing hard, his tense voice suggesting that he was on the ragged edge of shock.

"Best take a look at it."

"Help me sit straight."

Ryan slid an arm around his friend, feeling him trembling. J.B. reached for his right hand and gripped it tightly, so tightly that Ryan winced in pain, feeling his sinews creaking under the pressure.

"Pains me," J.B. breathed, clasping Ryan to him. "Knew that . . . if I cried out, we were lost."

"Be fine. Sit still now. Can you let go of my hand so I can take a good look at the problem?"

"Sure, sure." The grip relaxed, the Armorer giving a shuddering sigh. "Be all right. Going to take some work to ease open that spring."

Ryan moved sideways so that his own shadow no longer fell on the mantrap. He peered at the damage, weighing up what should be done. What could be done. Then he glanced back over his shoulder to check that the sec patrol wasn't making an unexpected return toward its base.

The trap was nearly five feet long, with a double row of sharp teeth. But the intention of the device was to catch and hold, rather than to snap or amputate. The points were covered in a coating of what looked like thick rubber, which muted the effect of the powerful spring that the Armorer had triggered. If it hadn't been for that protection, Ryan had little doubt that J.B.'s lower leg would have been splintered like a dry branch. Arteries could have been severed, turning the thing into a cold killer.

He reached out and touched it tentatively. J.B. pulled away and winced, gasping in pain. "Careful, amigo," he breathed. "Kind of touchy."

"Sure. Like Mildred says, we're going to have to break some eggs to make this omelet."

"Long as you don't break my leg in doing it. Best try and use your panga."

Ryan nodded. "My guess, too."

He laid the rifle out of the way, unsheathing the eighteen-inch steel blade, sliding it inside the double row of teeth, trying to find some way of bracing it so that he could exert the considerable pressure it would need to free the Armorer's trapped limb.

J.B. was sitting up straight, leg out in front of him, watching Ryan's efforts.

"Looks like the spring's got some kind of a lock pin," he whispered. "Set and braced with a hair-trigger release. Need to open it far enough to be able to set it again."

"I can see that. Can't see how to do it. Nothing to set the blade against."

They rested in silence for several long beats of the heart. J.B. finally patted Ryan on the shoulder. "Got an idea. Use the butt of the scattergun. Put it in and then slide it along until it fits snug. Then I'll try to hold it still while you push in the panga. Bit at a time. Gain us an inch and then another. And then another."

Ryan saw what his old companion meant. "Could work. Risk of it slipping and then clamping tighter."

"Have to take that risk. If I can just hold the M-4000 steady, it should work. And if I fuck up, then it's all down to me, isn't it?"

Ryan nodded, his dark curly hair tumbling over his forehead. "Might as well get it started, then."

"I'm cold," J.B. said, hunching his shoulders. "Guess that must be shock creeping in on me."

"Let's do it." Ryan took the proffered scattergun and jammed the pistol grip between the teeth of the mantrap, working it carefully in until it jammed in the narrowing gap. J.B. sat frozen and still. There was enough light for Ryan to see his friend's clenched teeth.

"Now the blade," the Armorer said. "If I tell you to stop, then do it. Means I'm about to yelp out, and that would likely put us both on the last train west."

Ryan had carried the long panga for many years now and knew to a hair's breadth precisely how strong the tempered steel was.

He levered it gently in, while J.B braced himself in the opposite direction, using his free leg, digging it into the damp earth, hanging on to the barrel of the shotgun.

"Don't think it'd be better... try dig out trap?" he asked. "Be easier?"

Ryan paused. "No. Earth gives us pressure. Otherwise have it floating around. Here we go."

The chain clattered as J.B. suddenly kicked out and gasped. "Rad-blasted painful, Ryan."

"Have to be done. Unless you want your leg cut off. I could do that."

"Don't think Mildred would love me so much if I turned up as a gimp to rescue her. Keep going."

Ryan decided to go for it in one big push. Not warning his partner, he simply threw all of his weight and strength against the taped hilt of the panga. There was a shudder of movement, and the sound of the teeth grating against the scattergun. Then more movement and a loud click as the safety catch caught once more, holding the powerful trap open.

J.B. gave a muffled half scream and toppled sideways, dropping the blaster, bringing his knees up into the prenatal position and moaning. He reached down to touch the place above the ankle where he'd been trapped.

"Hurts like a bastard," he breathed. "Would appreciate holding your hand again for a few seconds, old friend."

Ryan gripped his fingers, feeling the shaking. "Hurts while the blood flows back. Give it a while, then we'll take a look and see what the harm is."

They sat together in the cool stillness.

IT TOOK SEVERAL painful minutes to unlace the combat boot and slide it off the swollen ankle. Ryan probed as gently as he could, making J.B. move the injured leg, rotating the foot in both directions.

"How's it feel?"

The Armorer was leaning back against the bole of a half-grown pine, studiously polishing his glasses, his fedora pushed back on his forehead.

"Not broken. Stiff. Slow me down some. Hinder any tightrope walking I might be thinking of. And it's going to take the edge off my famous, gold-medal-winning tango."

"Want to try standing?"

"No."

Ryan grinned. "Need a hand up?"

"No. Yeah." He reached for Ryan and heaved himself erect with a single movement, spitting out a muffled curse and hopping around, keeping his bad foot off the ground.

"Best try and get that boot back on before the swelling gets too bad and you can't manage it."

"You'd have done well as the grand inquisitor of the Spanish Inquisition, Ryan. Torture's your trade. Help me sit down again, and I'll get the bastard thing on."

It took several more minutes of painful wrestling before the boot was on and laced. It was halfway through the process that Ryan caught the sound of movement, behind them, along the southbound trail.

"Patrol's coming back," he whispered.

"Didn't go far."

"Just checking a wide perimeter, I guess. Get down flat and keep still."

The sec men moved past, keeping silent, in an impressively well-ordered patrol, vanishing through the open main gate of the forest camp.

"Think that's it for the night?" J.B. asked, finishing tying his boot.

"Who can tell? Wolfram's a wily rodent. And the Magus plays games nobody else knows."

IT BECAME OBVIOUS very quickly that the leg injury was going to be too serious for them to do anything combatwise for several hours. Ryan left J.B. resting among the undergrowth, while he scouted deeper into the trees, finding a narrow, fast-flowing, icy-cold stream. With support the Armorer was able to limp the quarter mile to reach it, peeling off the boot again and bathing the injured limb.

"Feels good," he said, stretching it out and examining it by the light of the moon.

There were several deep indentations around the top of the ankle, black-purple in the silvery glow, all of them badly swollen. There had been very little blood, but the bruising seemed to have gone through to the bone.

J.B. kept moving the foot, wincing and muttering under his breath, trying now and again to take some weight on it.

"Easier?" Ryan asked anxiously.

Time was passing, though he didn't want to put any undue pressure on his friend. They hadn't eaten properly for some time, though the chilly stream water was reviving. It was vital that they got their attack under way as soon as possible, taking the best advantage that they could of the remaining few hours of darkness. It was already past midnight.

"Little bit better. I can walk, but I still can't run. When we finally make our plan, we'd best take that into account. Put me somewhere to stand and shoot, and you do the chasing around."

"Yeah. Guess we best come up with a finished plan and do it soon."

They both stared at each other and grinned at the absurdity of it all.

Chapter Thirty-Two

The wag rumbled up the trail from the south, bucking and heaving over the old quake ripples in the surface. It was the rebuilt cab of a predark semi, dappled with old strips of wasted chrome, and hooked up on the back was an armored flatbed piled high with crates.

The moon was almost hidden behind some ragged clouds, and Ryan angled his wrist chron toward it to try to make out the time. "Ten minutes after three," he whispered to J.B. "Night's passing on by."

The Armorer had been dozing at his side, waking every now and again, wincing in pain, biting his lip and massaging his badly bruised leg, trying to restore something close to full movement in it.

"Wonder where they've been."

Ryan peered through the screen of trees, uncomfortably aware of the number of alert sec men who patrolled inside the wire, as well as those watching through night glasses from the range of tall towers around the perimeter of the fortress.

"Looks like they're stopping. Guards coming out and checking it. Don't think they were carrying anything of great . . . Wait a minute."

"What?"

Ryan flattened himself in the short grass, staring intently. "Refueling it."

J.B. wriggled over alongside his companion, sighing as he dragged his injured foot across the rough ground. "Fuel! Now, that could be—"

"Could be really something," Ryan agreed. "Never noticed that they got gasoline here."

"In that small building without windows. Backing onto the kitchens."

Ryan nodded. "Yeah. Door's open to it. I can just make out a couple of real big tanks. Could be a thousand gallons each. Could be."

"Full or empty?"

"If they're full and we can get inside the camp and at them, then we got us the biggest and best diversion you could ever think of."

J.B. grinned, his teeth white in the darkness. "Bring every stickie running for fifty miles around."

"Surely would."

The two friends watched as the wag was refueled, with a half-circle of sec men standing around it, arms ready, looking out through the brightly-lit wire into the forest beyond.

"Those lights could be a mistake," Ryan said thoughtfully. "Makes it almost impossible for them to spot us out here. Because of the downward glare. But we can see them easy as turds in a bowl of vanilla ice cream."

"Only problem is how to get in through the gates. Once we manage that, we can likely take out all the lights. You blow the gas. I'll whack the sec guards and release the others. And away we all go."

"Sounds about as easy as falling off a log." Ryan grinned and punched J.B. lightly on the shoulder.

"Trader used to say that most plans sounded terrific when you made them. And most plans looked terrible after you'd tried to carry them out."

"Can't argue with what Trader said." Ryan stood and wiped his hands on his pants. "Fact is, most of his plans seemed to work out all right. In the end."

"Yeah. But there was that time way up in the high plains country, with the cesspool filled with dead horses when—" The Armorer stopped talking and put his head on one side, listening. "You hear what . . . ?"

"Another wag?"

"Think so."

"Coming this way. Could be the chance we want to get inside. Got to work this out real fast. Soon as the wag stops in front of the gates . . ."

THE SENIOR SEC MAN in charge of the entrance gates to the camp was Balliol Davichaux, a tall, skinny cajun with most of his left hand missing, the result of a tangle in the bayous with a mutie gator.

Both the fat man and Steel Eyes the Warlock had drilled into every man in the fortress what would happen to anyone who captured either of the men who were out in the woods, trying to spring the redhead and the other three outlanders.

And what would happen to anyone who neglected his duty and got lazy or careless.

Balliol Davichaux had worked long enough for Wolfram to be certain he didn't want the second choice. Gert Wolfram and the Magus were both capable of taking punishment and torture to unimaginable deeps.

There was enough light spilling from the towers to reach about fifty yards down the narrow track. The wag was now in sight, about two hundred paces away. Like its predecessor, it carried replacement parts for some of the mining equipment wrecked by the rampaging stickies before they'd upped and abandoned the camp, leaving a dozen corpses behind them.

"Ready the gates!" he called, walking out, his M-16 under his right arm, eyes darting around the fence and into the darkness beyond.

Six men were with him, each knowing his duty, each someone that Davichaux knew that he could depend on if the chips went down.

"Eyes triple-open!"

The wag was less than fifty yards away, slowing, grinding through the gears. The lights reflected off the shield, making it impossible to see who was driving. Davichaux expected it to be the taciturn Kentuckian, Nate Ruell, behind the wheel, with a couple of sec men riding shotgun.

Since the trouble blew up with the stickies, the route through the woods in the armored wags had become a great deal more dangerous. Three vehicles had been terminally taken out in the past four weeks.

Just as the wag stopped and the gates swung open, there was a burst of shooting from among the trees.

Davichaux spun, leveling the carbine at where he thought the shots had originated. Two men were down, yelping and clutching at bullet wounds in the lower legs. It looked as if whoever had done the firing wasn't all that good a shot and had aimed too low.

"Drag them out of the way!" the sec boss called, backing off, his eyes focused on the shadows beyond the circle of light.

There was no more shooting.

Both wounded men were hustled away by their colleagues, and Davichaux walked alongside the wag, gesturing to Nate Ruell to roll down his window. "Sons of bitches out yonder shooting in at us."

"Sure it's not stickies readying a big attack? Saw a dozen or more of them out on the track. One tried to jump us, but he fell under the fuckin' wheels. They're out there, all right. Only a mile or so off."

Davichaux shook his head. "Stickies don't use automatic blasters. Not that I heard."

Ruell sniffed and spit in the dirt. "Mebbe. Want her fueling now?"

Before Davichaux could reply, another couple of shots clattered out, the bullets ricocheting off the metal roof of one of the huts, whining away into the high branches of the trees beyond.

"Best get under cover," the sec boss said. "One of you go tell Wolfram we got us some company out there."

All the sec men disappeared behind walls and huts, leaving the camp surveillance to their colleagues in the high towers, though all of them had their attention directed beyond the fence, into the darkness. They waited and watched for more shooting.

On the flatbed, between the wooden crates, Ryan Cawdor lay still and waited.

PEERING OUT FROM COVER, it was possible to take in most of the layout of the camp, including the tethered balloon that swayed gently against the trees on the far side of the fortress. The titanium-steel security mesh that protected the delicate membrane glittered coldly in the spotlights that ringed the entire camp.

Ryan waited, hearing the voices of the guards close by, unable to see any of them because of the rough wooden crates that surrounded him. His right hand held the patterned grip of the SIG-Sauer, which was cocked and ready to fire.

These were the crucial few minutes of their hastily reworked plan.

The engine of the wag was ticking over as it waited, just beyond the camp entrance. J.B. hadn't fired again for a couple of minutes, with his badly aimed shots designed to keep the sec men jumpy and under cover, rather than trying to chill them. It was a fine balance.

A man's voice rang out, harsh, with a pronounced Deep South accent, as if he'd just crossed over Pontchartrain with his breath reeking of gumbo and jambalaya.

"Git that fuckin' wag all the way inside and close the damned gates. Don't want none of them stickies slippin' in on us. If that's who it is."

The engine revved and they jolted forward. Ryan's guess put the driver crouching down below the sides of his cab, jabbing at the pedals, trying to keep out of sight of the invisible marksman in the trees.

He flattened himself, squinting out of the corner of his eye, glimpsing the tall gates closing behind them and a group of uniformed men, cowering behind a low stone wall, their leader waving an M-16 at the driver of the wag, pointing for him to bring the vehicle out of the line of fire.

The engine cut out with a throaty cough, the wag jerking forward. The driver had obviously stopped it in gear, opening his door and hurling himself out onto the ground, his feet pattering as he darted for cover.

Ryan wriggled forward, peering through the gaps between the cases, and saw that they were close to the refueling hut. The group of sec guards were all on the right side of the rig, huddled together. As far as he could see, there was nobody waiting on the other side.

He eased his way across, taking a last quick look around, finding that the coast was definitely clear to the left. Ryan rolled silently off the back of the armawag and moved along the side toward the cab. He stared around the front of the wag, then quickly cat-footed out behind the fuel hut, where he crouched and waited in a pool of deep shadow.

He heard a door crash open and the unmistakable voice of Gert Wolfram.

"Davichaux!"

"Yes, sir?"

"You got your brains sleeping up your ass?"

"No."

"Let them leak from your dick?"

"No."

"Then where the devil are they? Because I don't believe you're using them."

"How's that, Boss Wolfram? We got the wag in safe. Want us to go out in the woods after the shoot-ist? Could mean us taking some losses."

"Not the way that person's shooting. It has to be either J. B. Dix or Ryan Cawdor doing the shooting, with what sounded to me like an Uzi. Anything occur to you about that, Davichaux? About the poor shooting?"

"No."

"Cawdor or Dix can put a 9 mm full-metal-jacket round through the eye of a gnat at fifty yards. How come they're doing so badly here?"

"We got two wounded." The sec boss's voice began to sound both aggrieved and puzzled.

"In the legs. Rest of the shots missed sitting targets, Davichaux. Made you run for cover. Didn't see you or anyone else checking on the back of the wag when you let it in through the gates."

"Why?"

Now Wolfram was losing his calm, urbane edge. "Ever heard the expression 'a diversion,' man?"

"Oh, yeah. Get it. Want me to go see?"

The Magus was also up and around, his voice as cold as liquid nitrogen, hissing across the open space of the camp. "Do it, Davichaux. Quickly."

"Sure thing."

"And do it slow and careful. I have a nasty feeling that the dice have just rolled against us."

Ryan knelt in the darkness, waiting.

Ready.

DAVICHAUX FELT COOL and relaxed, muttering florid curses under his breath as he stepped around to the back of the wag, conscious that the Magus's order had laid him out in the open, under bright lights, a sitting

target for anyone in the woods. The carbine rested on
the remains of his left hand, right index finger steady
on the trigger.

He peered in among the cases, making sure that he
could see the whole back of the flatbed.

"Climb up, that's right," Wolfram bellowed. "Only
way to see."

"Hope the chiggers swim up your cock and eat out
your balls, you tub of fuckin' lard," Davichaux whispered, swinging onto the truck, checking it out.
"Nothing here, sir!" he called. "Nobody but us
chickens."

Ryan could see the sec boss's angular shadow,
stretched out along the trampled earth, creeping
within inches of where he crouched.

For a moment he wished that he'd taken up the
Armorer's offer of the Uzi. He could have sprayed the
nearby group of sec men at point-blank range and
chilled them all in a single burst on full-auto.

One of the Trader's most-repeated sayings related
to time and regrets: "Worry about what you haven't
done, and you find yourself flat on your back with the
rain beating in your open eyes."

Ryan tensed, watching the shadow of the sec man,
hopping from the wag, hearing the icy voice of the
Magus urging him on.

Boots scraped in the dirt, the shadow moving.

Now.

Chapter Thirty-Three

Davichaux had been born alongside the big Sippi and once worked a shrimp boat close to Norleans with a fat, elderly man called Baptiste. Then there'd been a big blow in from the Gulf, around ten years earlier, and the boat had foundered. What remained of Baptiste had been found thirty feet up in a pollarded live oak, draped in Spanish moss, swinging in the warm wind.

Davichaux's wife and two children had also been drowned in the flooding and he'd moved on, running all over Deathlands. He finally finished way north, up the river, working for Wolfram and for the Magus.

Now his running was done. He was thirty-one and he wasn't going to see thirty-two.

As he stepped around the back of the parked wag, he was able to see beyond the open door of the squat fuel bowser, into the pool of stark shadow.

He blinked for a half second, starting to swing the carbine to the firing position, staring, paralyzed, at the crouching figure. He had a momentary impression of a big man in a ragged coat, something white around the throat; broad shoulders and a deep chest; a mat of tangled black hair; an eye missing; narrow, cruel lips peeled back off glittering teeth in a snarling, feral, murderous grin; and a huge knife that looked close to two feet long, the blade like a mirror in the spilled light.

"Shit..." the cajun whispered.

Ryan powered up from his shadowy hiding place, using the panga like a sword, needle-point first, lunging past the stock of the M-16, thrusting it into the sec man's belly with all of his strength.

He twisted his wrist as he felt the steel slice through soft tissues, cutting open the wall of hard muscle, grating on the bones of the lower spine. The wide blade tore open Davichaux's guts, spilling a gout of blood over Ryan's hand and arm, pattering in the damp earth beneath his boots.

The sec boss's nerveless fingers opened, allowing the blaster to fall. Ryan neatly plucked it from the air with his left hand while simultaneously wrenching out the panga with his bloodied right hand.

Davichaux took a couple of staggering steps backward, out of sight of his colleagues and Wolfram and the Magus. The lines were down, his spinal cord severed, his life gushing from him as the coils of bluish intestines tumbled around his feet.

"God's plenty," Ryan breathed, not even sure where the thought came from.

The man slumped down, hands pressed to the gaping wound in his guts, as though he were trying to reassemble himself. He fell from his knees flat on his face, nose breaking with a pulping sound like a crushed apple, booted feet moving for several seconds before he was still.

Ryan took a slow breath, keeping his self-control, aware of the section of sec men less than ten yards away from him. There was no sign that they, or anyone else, had seen the sec boss go down. But it would be only seconds.

"Lights!" he yelled, using the carbine to open fire on the powerful lamps that were strung around the fence and the main guard towers.

He heard an instant response from the Armorer, the sharp crack from the Steyr SSG-70 he'd left behind with some spare ammo. Ten fast, measured rounds were fired from the hunting rifle, from a range of less than sixty yards, maximum, with the aid of the laser image enhancer and the Starlight nightscope. It was like shooting carp in a barrel with a 16-gauge scattergun.

The carbine he'd taken from the hands of the dying man was sighted-in a touch high, but Ryan was able to put out a big sec light with every round.

At the first shot he heard the Magus's lightning response. The steel-eyed freak had instantly worked out what had happened, calling out to the slower-witted sec men.

"Cawdor's inside, by the wag. Warn Davichaux that—" He stopped as his rapier-sharp brain made the necessary leap, guessing that the sec boss was already down and done for. "Move in on the wag. Stop Cawdor getting at the gas!"

Ryan smiled grimly as he heard the metallic voice rising up the scale, cracking with the strain.

Meanwhile he dropped the empty carbine, hearing J.B. still shooting steadily, with a remorseless accuracy, at the lights. Already two-thirds of them were shattered, and the whole compound was much more dim and gloomy.

He glimpsed a face peering from the barred windows of the hut where he believed Krysty was being held. But Ryan was way too busy to think about that step, further down the line.

"GOT TO BE."

Mildred was at Krysty's shoulder, staring into the open space, able to see the parked wag by the fuel container. From their side the women could also see the huddle of cowering sec men, none of them wanting to follow their boss. Krysty had spotted Davichaux as he jumped off the bed of the truck and disappeared behind it.

"I'm sure it's Ryan inside and J.B. shooting the lights from outside the fence," she said. "Can't see the corpse of the cajun sec man."

"The gates were bolted." Mildred shook the locked shutters across the windows. "If only we could get out there and give some help."

"Best just wait and keep our heads down."

Mildred pointed. "There's the fat man and iron eyes, by their quarters."

"Could be they'll try and use us as hostages," Krysty said. "Be ready to do what we can."

"Getting real dark out there."

"Yeah," Krysty whispered, closing her emerald eyes tight, lips moving in a silent prayer. "Gaia, help him!"

RYAN HAD LEFT two spare clips for the Steyr with the Armorer, as well as the full ten rounds in the mag. J.B. squinted through the sight, aiming at the cluster of lamps on the farthest guard tower, close to where the gas-filled balloon swayed and curtsied at its mooring.

His combat-honed brain had been keeping a careful count on what he'd fired. There were three rounds left. After that he'd be down to the Uzi, which wasn't ideal for closing down the lights, and the powerful scattergun, which was totally useless for that.

But once he got inside, the Smith & Wesson M-4000 12-gauge would come into its own.

All Ryan had to do now was to break open the gates for him, using the darkness as cover, and, hopefully, set the gas off in what would be a gigantic explosion of fire and noise.

"One left," he breathed to himself, steadying the stock against his shoulder, his finger steady on the trigger. Only a handful of the searchlights remained lit, dappling the forest fortress with deep lakes of darkness and occasional puddles of brightness, ideal for a killing ground.

At the back of his mind J.B. had the itching worry that the bands of stickies they knew were around might be creeping up soundlessly behind him, that the first warning would be when the toothed suckers stripped circles of skin and bloody flesh from his face or throat.

He and Ryan had discussed timing, aware that if the plan worked, with its fireball of crudely refined gasoline, it would quickly bring in every stickie for miles.

J.B. fired the last round, feeling the kick of the recoil, just catching the sound of splintering glass and torn metal. He quickly slung the warm blaster across his shoulder, crouching, ready to move.

WOLFRAM WAS JIGGING from foot to foot, like a child desperate to go to the john. Sweat beaded his pallid face, and his tiny eyes flicked nervously from side to side, settling on the skeletal figure of the Magus standing motionless a few paces from him.

"Well?"

"What?"

"Stop them."

"You got a magic wand, Gert?"

"You're the Warlock. The fuckin' Magus! Do something to stop them."

"Dix is stuck in the woods. Cawdor is pinned down by the wag. Time's running for us, Gert."

"You say?"

The long, goatlike skull nodded slowly, the eyes with their sheen of cold pewter turning blankly toward him. "Right. That's just what I do say."

"Then we're going to win?"

The Magus considered that, pausing as the shooting from the darkness among the trees finally ceased. "I would think . . . probably. Yes, probably."

AS SOON AS the shooting stopped, Ryan took a deep breath, wiping his right hand down his pants. He drew the SIG-Sauer, readying himself for the next phase of the plan.

"Where is the driver of the wag?" The voice of the Magus rang out, unable to conceal a note of concern.

"Here."

"Name?"

"Nate Ruell."

"You got the keys?"

There was a long pause, and Ryan tensed himself. The driver was hiding with the half-dozen sec men only a few yards off, around the other side of the small building that held the gasoline, on the opposite flank of the silent wag.

"Asked where the keys are."

"In the wag." The three words dragged out like a fishhook that went clear down into the belly.

Time to move.

"Then go and..." the Magus began in a shriek that sounded like a power saw going through a sheet of plate glass. But Ryan was already in motion.

To the cowering sec men, the sudden appearance of Ryan Cawdor, out of the flickering semidarkness, was like an ultimate demon from the fiery heart of the worst of nightmares.

Three of them pissed themselves and two, including Ruell, lost control of their bowels.

Within eight seconds, they were all dead.

Ryan stood, legs slightly parted, holding the automatic in both hands in front of him at chest height. He sighted along the barrel at point-blank range, firing into the mass of helpless bodies, planting the bullets in the upper chest, the full-metal-jacket rounds ripping into lungs, hearts, throats and spines. Arms and

legs flailed, voices screamed and choked, blood splattering, hanging in the air, shadowed black.

The spent cartridges tinkled against the stone wall
of the hut, rattling at the bottom of the open door, a
couple of them hitting the iron gas tanks.

Eight seconds.

Ryan had been holding his breath, wincing slightly
against the racketing cacophony of the powerful
handblaster. Now he relaxed, knowing that he still had
four rounds left in the weapon, knowing that all the
sec men, and the unlucky driver, were dead or dying,
fingers scrabbling in the pools of bloodied mud, limbs
moving under and over each other.

The one-eyed man spun on his heel, stooping inside the little hut, reaching with his left hand and
opening up the faucet on the bottom of the tank.
Gasoline gushed, the noxious fumes making him blink
as he backed away.

"So far so good," he whispered to himself. "Yeah,
so fucking far, so fucking good!"

Chapter Thirty-Four

Jak was kneeling by the door to the prison hut that he shared with Doc. He was working intently on the lock, using the blade of one of his throwing knives to try to pick it. Though he'd been searched three separate times, the sec men had failed to find all of his concealed blades.

"Any good luck at all, my cunning locksmith?" asked the old man, who was standing by the shuttered, barred windows. "I feel that time is somewhat of the essence in this matter. Our fat friend, Wolfram, keeps looking over in our direction and calling some orders to the Magus, which, I fear, might relate to some plans involving us."

"Probably," the teenager grunted, levering harder at the lock, worried that he might snap off the point of the beautifully balanced blade.

"Should we essay the windows?"

"'Essay.' What's that mean?"

"Attempt."

Jak hissed in frustrated anger. "Bitch won't move. What's happening outside?"

Doc turned his watery blue eyes back to the gap in the heavy shutters. "Dark has come down upon us. I believe that it might mean that our trusty colleagues have finally op'ed the seventh seal and loosed all of the apocalyptic forces of perdition, pestilence and might.''

''Shooting stopped,'' Jak said, sheathing the steel. ''Rifle. Then burst from Ryan's handblaster. What now?''

THE GASOLINE SPLASHED all around the steel tips of Ryan's combat boots, filling the night air with dense fumes. The faucet on the second tank had been stiff, difficult to turn, but he had finally levered it open. Knocking on the metal sides, he could tell that both of the tanks were full, each holding what had to be close to a thousand gallons of gas.

The last of the dying sec men gave a sepulchral groan and lay still. Away near the main buildings, Ryan glimpsed the contrasting silhouettes of the Magus and Wolfram, scurrying out of sight into their own quarters.

With the gas flooding all around him, it was time to move on.

The one-eyed man crouched low and ducked into the cab of the parked wag, seeing the keys swinging gently back and forth in the ignition. At last the sec men in the towers decided it was time for them to get into the game. The shooting from the woods that had kept their heads down had stopped.

There was a sharp crack of rifles. Ryan heard no hint of a second echo that would have meant the blasters were being aimed away from him and the truck. Bullets began to howl off the armored roof of the cab, and the shield erupted inward, showering Ryan with shards of glass.

The warm engine coughed into instant life, and Ryan, crouched under the dashboard, kicked the gearshift into reverse. The cab door was open on his side, and he was easily able to correct the steering, aiming directly for the locked gates of the big fortress camp.

The powerful vehicle rumbled backward, more shots pinging off the sides and roof. The compound was nearly dark, and the chances of anyone actually hitting Ryan were remote.

The sec gates folded up like wet paper, the chain snapping, locks breaking.

In the sideview mirror, Ryan spotted a slightly built figure, loaded with blasters, come sprinting from the forest and throw itself flat on the bed of the wag. He immediately pressed down the brake and shifted into the lowest forward gear.

J.B.'s voice soared above the bedlam of shooting. "Let her go, bro!"

THE MAGUS HAD STOPPED on the porch of his long hut, staring silently back at what was happening by the gates. He saw the wag destroy them, leaving a tangled heap of sec metal, and then stop, watching as the Armorer joined Ryan. Despite the semidarkness, his metal-sheathed eyes saw perfectly, making out the patch of the spreading lake of gas, almost black against the dirt, his computer mind clicking over. He knew what was going to happen.

Wolfram was close by, in the doorway, jamming a polished, long-barreled revolver down the front of his pants. The Magus's sensitive nostrils were filled with the acrid stench of his companion's sweat of fear.

"Why don't they shoot him?" the fat man moaned, fingers fumbling with a spare mag, spilling it on the wooden planking. "Stop him?"

"Can't see him," the Magus said softly. "By all the gods and demons, but they're good."

"But we'll still win?" Wolfram asked desperately.

The Magus laughed gently. "I don't believe we will, friend. No, I am beginning to think that, despite all, you and I are about to lose."

"Lose! How can we fucking lose, you fool?"

The tall, skinny man turned slowly on his heel, the silvery light from the last few lamps bouncing off the dull surface of his metal lenses. "Take care, Gert," he whispered. "Do take care with what you say."

"I didn't... What are we going to do now?" He wiped perspiration from his cheeks and forehead. "Should we get away into the forest and run for it?"

"Waddle for it," the Magus replied contemptuously. "No, we will not run." He paused. "Not yet. We shall go and reacquaint ourselves with our prisoners and find some way to make them useful. And if they can't be made useful, then they can always be made dead."

"GATES ARE DOWN," Mildred shouted.

Krysty was at the rear of the hut, trying to tear away at the shutters at that side of the building. She turned and rejoined her friend.

"Did J.B. get aboard?"

Mildred nodded. "Yeah. It only stopped a second and then came forward again."

The wag had grated to a halt again, close to the tangled bodies of the slaughtered sec men, at the side of the small block-built hut that held the gasoline.

"What are they doing now?" Krysty asked.

THOUGH HIS PALE PINK EYES, part of the distinctive albino coloration, meant that his sight in the bright noonday sunlight was weak, Jak's vision in poor light was remarkably good. He shaded his eyes and peered from the shuttered window.

"Ryan's in the cab, and J.B.'s on back. Gasoline all over place."

Doc sat on one of the narrow beds, holding his head in his hands. "Upon my soul, but I confess to being a deal less than well. What I believe was once called 'feeling blah' back in the olden times."

The teenager turned. "Might have to move fast, Doc. Guess could try and use us as hostages. Sort of trick Magus would think about."

Doc stood, shaking his head, his shoulders slumped. "Before God, but I am exceeding weary," he pronounced. "Went the day well, my brothers?"

"Don't slip away now, Doc," Jak said, kneeling by the old man and shaking him firmly.

"Slipping and sliding away... A good day is one without pain, and a bad one..." He rubbed his forehead. "I disremember what a bad one was."

"Doc," Jak said, shaking him harder. He glanced over his shoulder, seeing that Wolfram and the Magus were standing in the doorway of their own quarters, looking toward the huts that held their prisoners.

"But we that are left will grow old," Doc muttered, his eyes staring at the blank wall.

Wolfram and the Magus, accompanied by a half dozen of their well trained and heavily armed sec men, started to move across the open space of the main compound.

"Doc!" Jak yelled desperately.

"'Dr. Tanner' to you, my dear little crossing sweeper, ragamuffin, urchin."

Jak slapped him hard across the face, leaving the print of his fingers on the pale skin. Doc nearly fell over, standing, fists clenching, a trickle of blood worming from the corner of his mouth.

"What...? Set the welkin of my teeth a-ringing with that sturdy buffet." He touched his mouth, examining the smear of crimson. "And tapped my claret into the bargain." He grinned lopsidedly at the teenager. "Wandering, was I?"

"Yeah. Sorry about that but didn't have choice. You all right now?"

Doc nodded. "I am in the very best of health." He looked out the window. "And ready for anything."

"READY, J.B.?" Ryan called, lifting his voice above the cascade of lead that rattled against the armored cab.

"For anything."

"You got a self-light handy?"

"Sure." A moment later the Armorer was crouched by the open door of the cab, the last few lights reflected off the lenses of his glasses. "Can you take the rifle?"

"Any ammo left for it?"

"Nope."

It took only a couple of seconds for Ryan to reload the Steyr from one of the capacious pockets of his coat. He struggled in the confined space to sling it back across his shoulders, making sure it wasn't snagging on anything that might slow him when he had to move.

"SIG-Sauer reloaded?" J.B. asked anxiously.

"Egg-suckin' time, Granny," Ryan mocked. "Get that self-light ready."

"Go like a bomb when it blows," the diminutive figure warned, ducking as a bullet gouged into the dirt under the wag, splattering him with a mixture of mud and gasoline.

"Best blow it now. Won't be long before we get us some unwanted company. Not to mention a spark that could put us on the last train west."

"You ready?"

Ryan braced himself. "Ready."

"On three."

J.B. counted it down, the self-light gripped firmly in his right hand, ready for ignition.

"One and two..."

Ryan, every muscle tensed, began to move, powering out on the blind side of the cab.

"Three!" the Armorer yelled, flicking at the device with his thumb, producing a tiny, weak flame. He lobbed it into the center of the spreading lake of gas.

Chapter Thirty-Five

Ryan's feet slipped in the wet, clogging dirt as he leapt out of the cab, following close behind J.B., who had a slight start on him.

He had holstered the automatic, feeling it bounce on his hip as he stumbled and nearly went facedown on the edge of the gasoline pool.

With a desperate effort he fought for his balance, recovering with a sideways stagger, running hard, not even bothering to try to jink.

Bullets might chill him.

Might.

The imminent explosion definitely *would* if he wasn't far enough away from it when the flames ignited the cloud of vapor and the whole two tanks went up.

One factor that he'd taken into account with the sketchy and amended combat plan was the theory that the solid bulk of the armored wag should give them a vital measure of protection from the devastating blast.

The Trader often said that theories weren't worth piss-holes in the snow.

The force of the explosion was crushingly terrible, with a blazing power that surpassed in a quantum leap anything that Ryan had imagined.

Fire and heat and shattering light . . . and Christ receive thy soul.

KRYSTY HAD SPOTTED the feeble flicker of fire thrown down by J.B. and instantly saw what would happen. She had a flashing inner vision of the sweeping power of the blast to come and grabbed at Mildred, pulling her to her knees.

There was just time to whisper an urgent warning and cover her own ears against the explosion.

The building rocked under the shock wave, and every shuttered window blew in, covering the two women, and the whole floor, with tiny shards of razor-sharp sec glass.

The front door was kicked off its heavy hinges, leaving it lying across one of the beds at a drunken angle. After the single deafening boom, the whole compound was flooded with silence.

Krysty shook her head, splinters of glass tinkling from her tightly curled hair. "Time to move," she said, finding that her voice sounded harsh and thin, as though all the air had been sucked from her lungs.

Mildred turned and looked out through the open door, coughing in the whirlwind of dust. "Got us some company coming," she said.

The Magus was running through the whirling dust and flames with an odd, insectlike gait, half flowing and half scuttling, his feet seeming to barely touch the ground. It was a bizarre and frightening image of clumsy grace. The massive Wolfram, waving a blaster, was lumbering behind him, bellowing out for some of the sec men to join them.

"Time to move," Mildred said, pointing to the broken windows at the rear of their prison hut.

IT WAS ONLY AFTERWARD that Ryan realized he and the Armorer had made a serious miscalculation on the quantity of gasoline in the tanks. Neither of them had suspected that the containers were much larger than they appeared, with most of their bulk buried beneath the earth, meaning that the explosion was infinitely more devastating than they'd expected.

The massive armored wag was lifted off the ground and blown through the air, crashing and rolling over and over, pursuing Ryan and J.B. across the compound like some vengeful behemoth, windows smashing, paint igniting, lights splintering, tires bursting into smoky flames.

Ryan was stunned by the maelstrom of noise and heat, smelling his own hair smolder, his clothes scorching, the giant fist of the shock wave hurling him violently away from ground zero of the fireball. He was tossed helplessly toward the razor wire of the sec fence.

It seemed to last for an eternity, though it was probably less than five seconds before he lay still, shocked and bruised, staring back at the gigantic globe of orange, yellow and crimson flames, streaked with flashes of silver, threaded with a web of spreading smoke that was soaring high into the night sky.

"That'll bring all the stickies for miles," he croaked, but he couldn't hear himself speaking over the thunderous roar of the gas eruption.

He tried to sit up, but he felt sick and dizzy, so he remained motionless for a moment, fingers fumbling for his weapons, making sure nothing had gone missing. Out of the corner of his good eye he could see J.B.'s crumpled figure feebly trying to struggle onto his hands and knees.

The booming was fading away, echoing and swallowed in among the trees. The blazing gas was still making a loud crackling, roaring sound, but compared to the rumble of the explosion, it almost seemed like silence.

Ryan swallowed hard and managed to sit, drawing the SIG-Sauer, looking across at his old friend. "All right?" he yelled, the words just audible to his own fractured hearing.

The Armorer nodded, turning his head blindly. "Living. Seen my glasses?"

His eyes were oddly bare and vulnerable, like a helpless, blinking rabbit, his hands scraping over the blackened, steaming earth around him.

Ryan made it to his feet, stumbling slightly, gasping for breath in the stinking, baking air. He caught the glint of glass a few paces beyond where J.B. was searching.

"There." He pointed with the muzzle of the automatic.

"Oh, yeah. Thanks." J.B. wiped crusted dirt and smeared gasoline off the lenses and adjusted them on the narrow bridge of his nose.

Ryan's hearing was returning to something like normal, and he could hear screaming and yelling.

The destruction of the two huge tanks had sprayed the entire area of the camp with burning gasoline, and the place was a mass of small fires. All of the huts had shattered doors and windows, and most had roofs that were already ablaze. Several of the gun towers had also been knocked sideways by the sheer force of the blast, tipping sec men twenty and thirty feet to the ground.

Several of them were also on fire.

Men whirled like flaming dervishes, arms flailing, pillars of smoking fire billowing around them. Hair had been burned from their flayed skulls, skin peeling and blistering. Mouths were open, screaming for help, lidless eyes rolling blindly as they staggered around, bumping into one another.

There was a sudden, startling explosion as the gas tank of the burning armawag went up.

Ryan and J.B. were both up on their feet, standing close together, looking around at the scene of desolation and flaming slaughter.

Smoke blew around them, thick, hot and choking, making it difficult to see what was happening over on the far side of the fortress camp.

"Get the others out!" the Armorer croaked, brandishing the Uzi in his right hand.

"Watch out for Wolfram and the Magus. They'll guess we're in after Krysty and the rest."

A stumbling figure loomed from the murk, holding a blaster. Smoke seeped from the sec man's pants and shirt, and strips of blackened skin dangled from his chest. Barely breaking stride, hesitating as his brow furrowed, he hardly seemed to see Ryan and J.B. The barrel of the small automatic started to lift, and Ryan shot him carefully through the middle of the face. The 9 mm full-metal-jacket round blew away a fist-sized chunk of the back of his skull.

DOC HAD TAKEN a glancing blow across the side of the head from a falling roof beam. The hut was directly in line with the full force of the explosion, and one end wall had caved in completely, opening it up to the night. Burning gasoline had been dashed all over the entire building, in through shattered windows, setting the splintered walls alight, inside and out.

Jak knelt beside the old man, arm around his shoulders, quickly beating away a few small flames that flickered on the stained frock coat.

"Wake up, Doc!" he yelled, his voice cracking with the excitement.

The pale eyes blinked open, and a gnarled hand brushed a curl of hair away from the forehead. Doc grinned vaguely. "By the Three Kennedys! The whole place smells as though someone has spilled some gasoline and then... Ah, now my memory begins to function a little better. Ryan and dear John Dix have—"

Jak shook him exasperatedly. "Fuck it, Doc! Whole place burning. Time got out. Sec men be here any second now. Magus and fat man."

Doc nodded, reason and sanity seeping back into his face. "I am with you, dear snow-topped child. But we are a little devoid of weaponry, are we not?"

"Lotta chills out there. Get us some blasters. Check out Krysty and Mildred. Look for Ryan and J.B. and run. Get out here like goose shit off a shovel."

Doc allowed himself to be stood up and brushed down. He looked around through the smoke and flames that were rapidly destroying the hut. *"En avant, mes camarades,"* he said, coughing hoarsely. "One for all and all for one. Upon my soul, but this is both the best of times and the worst of times."

Jak began to drag him toward where the doorway gaped wide open. "Move it, Doc," he snapped.

GERT WOLFRAM'S PROUD forest ville was in ruins.

The high sec fence had been felled in a dozen places, and more than half the gun towers were either down or were well ablaze. The explosion of the two gas tanks had been so hugely devastating that scarcely a single building was undamaged. Only the main dormitories and the quarters of Wolfram himself, and the Magus, were far enough away to have avoided the initial blazing spray.

Barely thirty seconds had passed since the moment of ignition, and at least a quarter of the sec force was either dead or badly wounded. And all of the rest were deeply shocked and utterly disorganized.

Even Wolfram himself, for all of his deep-rooted cunning and evil wit, was barely running along on automatic, following the only man in the camp who seemed to have some semblance of combat sense left.

"Let's run in those huts and chill some of the sons of bitches, Magus," he panted, stumbling through the swirling, stinking fumes, waving a pudgy hand to try to clear his sight. He breathed noisily through his open, blubbery mouth, his tiny eyes flickering from side to side.

The lean figure just ahead of him paused and turned, the steel-trap mouth clicking into a grim smile. "Why not walk on over and chill them all, friend?" He laughed loudly, the voice rasping like a hacksaw blade down a windowpane. "Best chance of getting out of this, Gert, is to take some hostages."

The fat man nodded. "Yes, yes. I see that, Magus. I like that idea, indeed I do."

"Then let us get on with it."

BEFORE STARTING the last phase of the rescue attempt, Ryan and J.B. stood together, checking out the compound. The sky was beginning to lighten a little with the first promise of the false dawn, just visible through the wreathing clouds of stinking smoke that smeared their way above the pines.

"Wonder when the stickies are going to get themselves interested in the explosion and the fire and the smoke?" Ryan said. "Reckon we want to be away from here before they come running for some of their fun."

J.B. nodded. "Sure." He pointed. "Look. Fat bastard and a metal-eyed, skinny bastard heading for the hut where they got Krysty and Mildred."

But the smoke thickened and obscured the two figures, hiding them from sight.

Chapter Thirty-Six

Krysty lifted her right foot and kicked out at the back door of their prison hut, the heel of her blue Western boot smashing into the smoldering wood, just below the lock. The whole structure shivered but didn't yield.

"Again," Mildred gritted, glancing over her shoulder through the thickening smoke. "Wolfram and the Magus are nearly here."

Krysty balanced herself and struck again, whispering a hasty prayer to the Earth Mother, Gaia, to give her extra strength to break out. This time the lock splintered away, and the door swung open onto the compound, close by the kitchen block, which was already well on fire.

The two women were in such a hurry to get out that they bumped into each other in the doorway, nearly stumbling down the stairs at the rear.

But there was no time for apologies.

Krysty grabbed Mildred by the arm. "We can double around the side and make for their rooms."

"Get our blasters?"

"Sure."

At that moment a young unarmed sec man, his eyes streaming from the gas fumes, came around the corner of the building and ran straight into Mildred. He threw a clumsy punch, dealing her a glancing blow on the shoulder.

"Bastard!" she snapped, bracing her wrist and smashing the heel of her hand into his face. Using all her strength, she struck him at the base of the nose, splintering the cartilage and septum, driving razored shards of bone upward through the back of his skull. The power of the blow sent them through the soft tissue, into the forepart of the brain, chilling him instantly.

The woman pushed the slumping corpse out of her way. "So much for my healing hands," she said quietly.

"Keep low and move around the front," Krysty warned. "Need to get our blasters."

JAK HAD MANAGED to get Doc out of the burning building and into the semidarkness of the open space by the kitchen block. A handful of sec men had gathered near the rear entrance of the fortress, looking as though they were deep in clinical shock. They were huddled in a tight little group, paying little attention to their escaping prisoners. Beyond them, waving gently in the breeze, Jak could see the great globe of the balloon, tethered among the trees, its steel-coated surface reflecting the ruddy glow from the fires.

For a moment the teenager took stock of their situation. Wolfram's domain was ruined forever. That was certain, with flames gathering strength, leaping from hut to hut, the tarred roofs blazing with a bright orange ferocity, the smoke thickening above the surrounding pines.

Jak squinted through the murk, looking beyond the ruined wag, seeing a couple of familiar figures. "There's Ryan and J.B.," he said.

"Where?"

"There." He pointed with one of his throwing knives. "And there's Krysty and Mildred, hiding by building where were locked in."

"Are those dear fellows, Master Wolfram and Brother Magus, anywhere to be seen?"

Jak shook his head. "No. Mebbe done runner."

THE INSIDE OF THE HUT was burning fiercely. The Magus led the way, the barrel of his blaster probing at the flaming walls like the tongue of a rattler. Wolfram, hand over his face, a kerchief pressed across his mouth, was coughing at his heels.

"They're gone...." he spluttered.

"Not far. Still a chance to retrieve them and tuck them up our sleeve."

"I'm worried about..." He stopped in the middle of the sentence, letting the words trickle away into the crackling inferno all around them.

"About what, my moist partner?" the Magus asked. "Nothing to do with stickies being attracted by the noise and fury and fire? Could it be that, Gert?"

"Yes. Yes, fuck their mutie souls! We know they're out in the woods." His swollen tongue stumbled over the words in his growing terror. "Hundreds of the sick bastards. They'll come. The gates are down. The fence destroyed. Men dead. Everything lost to the flames. We must get away, Magus, before they come running and find us helpless."

Behind them one of the main roof timbers collapsed in a shower of bright golden sparks. The Magus wiped a glowing splinter of wood from the steel lens over his right eye. "The back way out seems best," he said quietly. "Now."

RYAN SAW the drama unfolding, catching the glint of Krysty's bright red hair against the dark wall of the hut, Mildred following her out and the brief, savage scuffle with one of the young guards. He also saw the fat and thin figures entering the front of the same building, the flash of blasters drawn in fists, and Jak and Doc making their own escape from the second hut.

"Sec men seem to have given up," J.B. commented. "Blown the heart from them."

"Look like they're ready to break and run."

"Before the stickies arrive," the Armorer grinned. "Figure they got the right idea, bro."

"Krysty's going for Wolfram's HQ, after the blasters. Best go help them."

RYAN'S INTUITION WAS right about the survivors among the sec men. They'd been enlisted by Wolfram and the Magus over a period of several years and had come to totally depend on their evil, talented masters. Whatever they were told seemed to come to pass, and life was tough but rewarding. There'd been trouble over the stickies, but the fortress still functioned and Wolfram had promised them that the good days would swiftly return.

Then there'd been the expedition on the riverboat and the taking of the four prisoners, none of which looked capable of causing any serious trouble. The four had been locked up safe and secure.

All they had to do was watch out for the two men, Ryan Cawdor and John Dix. Word connected them with the legendary Trader, over the years. But he was long dead, and the ancient myth gathered dust in dark corners.

Now these two strangers had come from the forest darkness, bringing fire and unbelievable destruction and death for so many of their colleagues. It was obvious that the camp was finished, that the unbeatable Wolfram and his sinister sidekick were staring into the bleak abyss of defeat.

And it had all happened in less than fifteen minutes, fifteen minutes from safety and comfort to total chaos.

And then someone mentioned the stickies.

"Out there. Know that. Hundreds of them. Fence kept them out. Fire draws them. The explosion must've carried for fuckin' miles at night. They want revenge for what we done. Hundreds of them. Suckers with those razor teeth to strip a man to the bare bone. The flames'll bring them. Hundreds of the fuckers."

Even as Ryan and J.B. began to make their cautious way across the compound, the withdrawal began. Leaving their dead and their wounded, the sec force simply melted away into the night, breaking the locks off the rear gate to the ville and moving off in small groups into the waiting woods.

Altogether about forty or so left the camp, most of them heading for the Sippi.

No more than three of them eventually reached safety and civilization. The rest perished beneath the dark pines.

THE WOODS FOR MILES around were moving.

As the dawn gathered power, the shadows became visible. Slumped, stooping figures shuffled with surprising speed through the narrow paths and trails, dull eyes fixed on their bare feet. Suckered hands grasped at the air, and mouths sagged open, thick threads of blood-flecked yellow-green phlegm dribbling over scarred chests.

They followed the omnipotent lure of the distant explosion that had stirred the land all about, woken the creatures from their crimson dreams of torture and agony and fire. The smell and flavor of flames, deep in the heart of the forest, stirred their twisted souls.

There was a destination for them, all coming together from every quarter of the compass, heading for the place of dying and heat, where their dull minds knew their bitter enemies lived.

It was a time of coming together.

Very soon.

KRYSTY RAN into the open door of the largest of the buildings in the compound. A small fire burned brightly in one corner of the pitched roof, but the rest was relatively untouched. She was ready to encounter sec men, but the whole place was deserted.

The smell of sweat and stale food and liquor lingered in the air, still riding over the stench of gasoline that permeated the whole ville.

It was dark, the main generator of the camp having ceased to function in the past four or five minutes, but enough light was filtering in from the coming morning for them to see their way inside.

"Wolfram's room," Mildred said, pushing open a side door, shaking her head in disgust at the 3-D pornographic posters that covered the walls. There were heavy floral draperies over the shuttered windows and soft scatter cushions in pallid shades of silk and satin. By the bed lay a plaited whip, with matted thongs. A ceramic Buddha held several sticks of highly scented incense that still smoldered. "More like a whore's boudoir," she commented before moving down the corridor.

"The Magus." Krysty paused in an open doorway to a totally bare room, painted in various shades of gray, panels of steel drilled to the walls. It contained a single iron-framed bed, covered by one white blanket. A black chest of drawers seemed to hold all of the Magus's possessions. The only ornamentation was a length of coiled chrome chain, dangling from a corner of the ceiling.

Krysty shuddered at the bleak chill.

"Where are . . . ?"

"There." Mildred had gone ahead into the open space that had been used as a dining room. On a side table were all of their weapons.

Krysty snatched up her own Smith & Wesson double-action 640, checking automatically that it was fully charged. Mildred kissed her Czech ZKR 551 target pistol, weighing it in her hand, knowing immediately from the balance that it held all six of the big Smith & Wesson .38 rounds.

"Now let's do some business," she said.

Had they looked around, they would have glimpsed a tall, elongated silhouette of a man standing stock-still, behind them, in the entrance to the building. He was less than a dozen paces from them, his goatlike head to one side, a bitter half smile on his twisted mouth.

The Magus turned to Wolfram, who was about to push past him, checking him with a hand on the arm.

"No," he whispered. "The race is lost. They have their blasters and the others are coming."

"We can get men—"

"No, Gert. A wise man knows when to fold his hand and quietly leave. The rats have deserted the ship, and we are sinking. I feel company coming through the woods toward us. They will not be merciful." He touched Wolfram lightly on the cheek with a steel-tipped index finger. "Farewell."

Next moment the hall was empty, and Gert Wolfram was standing alone.

THE FRIENDS MET UP in the shadowy hallway of the main building.

"No time for talk," Ryan said. "Reckon stickies'll be on their way from every damned direction. Sec men have done a runner. Get your blasters and we'll head out."

"Seen Wolfram or Magus?" Jak asked, strapping on his satin-finish Colt Python, the blaster banging against his skinny thigh.

Krysty nodded. "They were both after us, but they've vanished."

"Keep a watch out for them," J.B. warned, snatching the moment to give Mildred a quick hug and kiss. "Still time for them to do some back-shooting."

Doc flourished his rapier, half drawing it from the ebony sheath. "Sooner we get away from this jungle hellhole, the happier I shall be."

J.B. looked at Ryan. "We can stand and fight the muties when they get here. And I reckon that won't be long."

"Can't we hide in the forest?" Krysty asked.

Ryan sniffed, looking around the deserted compound. "Guess not, lover. Wolfram said they had a shit-lot of stickies. Could be a hundred or more. They come in from out there with the way they got of scenting norms..." His eye was caught by the first dawn light on the canopy of the bobbing balloon. "No," he said. "There's our way."

Chapter Thirty-Seven

The only pause came as they reached the rear gates of the fortress, which swung open on their broken hinges. A sec man was lying by them, hideously burned, resembling a charred log with jagged branches. One bloody eye blinked open from the blackened skin of his face, and his tongueless mouth opened and closed.

Ryan barely broke stride, unsheathing the panga in a whisper of steel and kneeling to slit the dying man's throat, dodging the flood of arterial blood.

"Getting soft in old age, Ryan," Jak mocked.

"Nothing's forever," he replied, heading through the fringe of the trees, along the beaten track to the balloon.

A metal-runged ladder dangled from it, and a mooring line with a large grapnel dug deep into the soft ground.

"Will that fragile basket carry us all in safety?" Doc asked doubtfully.

"Sure. And the wind's from the west. Take us roughly in the right direction to get back to the redoubt." Ryan tugged at the line. "Let's all get aboard, friends. I'll get ready to let her free. J.B., set light to the burner."

There was a flicker of flame and then a deep roar as the large gas jet caught fire. Ryan guessed that the balloon probably operated on a dual system. It was something he'd come across a couple of times before in other parts of Deathlands. There would be two layered skins, one of which would contain a quantity of some light gas, like helium. Rare and expensive. The second would be a more conventional backup of heated gas, and this was what would give the main lifting power to the balloon.

Everyone except Ryan and Jak climbed quickly up the swaying ladder, with Doc needing help from both above and below. Jak pushed at his skinny thighs and ass while Mildred and Krysty heaved at his wrists to topple him up and over, safe and snug into the large wicker basket.

"Up you go," Ryan urged, patting Jak on the shoulder. "Be right there."

The teenager scampered up with the agility of the true acrobat, his shock of white hair appearing over the rim of the basket, grinning down. "Ready to set sail," he called.

The wind was rising, whipping up clouds of stinking smoke from the burning buildings, wrapping it around Ryan in a coughing shroud as he stood by the taut tethering line, blinding him for a crucial moment.

Krysty's warning scream cut through the darkness like a straight razor.

He spun, blinking, reaching for the blaster, realizing in that instant he was too late.

Wolfram was on top of him, flailing at him with an enormous bowie knife, the blade cutting a narrow gash across the material of the right sleeve of Ryan's coat.

"Fuck bastard," the fat man panted, trying to close with him, using the sixteen inches of steel with strength and skill, creating a weaving arc of hissing steel that drove Ryan back beneath the balloon.

"Back off the bastard and I'll chill him," J.B. yelled from above.

But Wolfram kept in close, making Ryan dodge and weave, unable to snatch a moment to draw his own blaster. The fat man was licking his lips, sweat frosting his forehead, grinning crazily at his one-eyed enemy.

"Have you, bastard, have you," he gasped.

Krysty warned him again, her voice amazingly calm and gentle, carrying a whole new layer of fear. "Stickies, lover. The stickies are here."

Ryan risked a glance from the corner of his eye, his mind almost losing concentration at what he saw. There they were, the muties from the woods, dozens of them in a long, straggling line, emerging from the forest.

They made their way along the damaged fence, toward where the broken gates beckoned them into the fire-dappled fortress, shuffling onward, unstoppable.

Their rheum-rimmed eyes turning toward the two fighting men, drilling directly into the unmistakable capering figure of Gert Wolfram. The movement stopped, and they began to mutter and murmur, a name, two syllables.

"Wolfram ... Wolfram ... Wolfram ..." It became louder and louder, faster and faster.

Ryan took a half step away, his eye locked to the streaming face of the fat man, seeing the doubt and fear creeping across the swaying jowls, the sudden hesitation in the movements.

"Come for you, Wolfram," Ryan whispered. "And they're going to get you."

"No, they ..."

"Wolfram ... Wolfram ... Wolfram."

Now they were moving again, toward the open gates, fingers opening and closing, the suckered teeth visible in the dawn's early light.

"Come up, lover," Krysty whispered.

There was a fraction of frozen time when Ryan could have drawn the SIG-Sauer and put a 9 mm bullet through Wolfram's face. But he let it pass, choosing not to chill the fat, evil man himself.

Instead, he leaped for the ladder and swarmed up it effortlessly, climbing over into the swinging basket. "Cut it," he said to Jak, who slashed through the ropes with his drawn knife, allowing it to tumble to the earth below.

"Let me come in with—"

"Full up, Wolfram. Have to take your chance with your ex-slaves," Ryan called.

The balloon was now ready to go, tugging at the single tethering line that held it to the ground. Wolfram dropped his large knife and gripped the plaited rope in his pudgy fingers, making a desperate effort to climb it. His huge weight and the pressure of the heated canopy was now pulling hard, and the buried, hooked grapnel suddenly popped free from the dirt, releasing the balloon.

The stickies were within fifty paces as the basket started to rise majestically into the air, and they began to yell out in sudden, crazed rage, seeing that it was carrying Gert Wolfram away with it. They broke into a stumbling, clumsy run, attempting to follow.

"Cut it," Krysty said. "Cut him free, lover. Or the muties'll grab hold and pull us back down. Butcher us."

They were lifting with agonizing slowness, the grapnel trailing only a yard from the ground. Wolfram was screaming as he fought to climb the rope, his feet kicking for purchase. The scream had become an endless, high, thin sound, stretching on and on. His head was strained back, blood-filled eyes popping as he stared directly up into Ryan's face.

The stickies were thirty paces away from him, all reaching up toward the dangling man as though they were worshiping a god from the sky.

"Goodbye," Ryan said, reaching over and slicing the rope through with the honed edge of his panga.

Wolfram dropped like a vast sack of sand, hitting the ground, both ankles snapping with an audible crack, his knees popping a moment later.

Freed from his dragging weight, the balloon shot upward, rising quickly above the level of the highest surrounding branches. The basket was fifty feet up, the way clear of any threat from the stickies.

But they no longer had any sort of interest in Ryan and the others.

All of their attention was centered on the weeping, crawling creature that lay in the dirt, surrounded by them. As Ryan and the others watched in fascinated horror, the circle of stickies closed in over Wolfram.

The wind carried the balloon gently away toward the east, rising higher in the stillness.

Oddly the screaming didn't stop until they were several miles away.

THE TORTURING AND KILLING of Gert Wolfram and the total destruction of the camp with the skillful use of fire took most of the rest of the day, and it was evening before the stickies, sated with their funning, finally drifted away in small groups into the surrounding woods.

It wasn't until the next dawn that some dried bracken stirred across a tumbled bear's den, about a bow shot from the main gates of the devastated fortress, and a pair of steel-sheathed eyes peered out from the shadows at the morning, judging that it was probably safe to move on once again.

To move away into the rest of Deathlands.

Chapter Thirty-Eight

The trip was uneventful.

The wind was light and brisk, and the hunting birds flew by with their beaks sheathed. Only once was there any threat, and that came around noon, from a raggedy man with a Kentucky musket who fired a single shot at the soaring balloon.

He was a fair shot at extreme range, and the spent ball pinged off the protective steel sec netting that covered the entire canopy. Nobody bothered to return the fire.

"COULDN'T BE BETTER," the Armorer said, checking his tiny sextant and wrist compass. "Carrying us on a true reckoning toward the redoubt. This rate we should be there some time in late afternoon."

THE LANDING WAS SOFT and gentle on a patch of verdant meadow, scaring away a herd of browsing deer.

Half an hour later they were all gathered in the control room, ready to go into the gateway chamber.

"Think the Magus got away?" Jak asked.

J.B. nodded. "Man like that, you'd have to see his corpse staring up at the sky before you believe he's chilled. And even then . . ."

Krysty linked her arm through Ryan's, smiling up at him. "We came through again. Won. Wonder where we'll all end up next."

Ryan opened the door of the gateway, catching the smell of stale air. "Who knows, lover? I've been wondering about how Dean's getting on. Mebbe we should go visit the Rockies, down the line, some time in the next few months."

Mildred was first into the chamber, sitting on the floor, her back against the wall. "What I'd like next is to find someplace where we can all have a real long rest. Somewhere with no shooting or killing."

One by one they joined her, Ryan pausing at the door, ready to pull it shut and trigger the jump mechanism. "Everyone comfortable? Then let's go, friends."

Doc was staring blankly across the chamber. Krysty touched him on the arm as Ryan closed the door and sat next to her. "Jack for your thoughts, Doc."

The disks in the floor and ceiling began to glow, and there was a faint humming sound. Mist began to gather near the ceiling. Ryan sat quickly, seeing that J.B. had already taken off his glasses and folded them safely into a pocket. He felt the familiar darkness closing over his mind.

"I was thinking of those that we shall never meet again, Krysty, my dear," Doc replied, his voice sounding a little blurred around the edges. "So many good, good companions that we have lost forever to the grim reaper."

"Might see them again, somewhere on down the line," Ryan muttered.

"I think not, Ryan." Now the old man's voice was echoing around the armaglass walls, becoming fainter. "They will grow not old, as we that are left grow old. Age will not weary them, nor the years condemn." Ryan felt his hold on consciousness slipping away, and he was barely able to hear Doc's last words. "At the going down of the sun, and in the morning, we will remember them."

Remember them.

Ryan closed his eye.

Don't miss out on the action in these titles featuring THE EXECUTIONER®, and STONY MAN™!

The Red Dragon Trilogy

#64210	FIRE LASH	$3.75 U.S. $4.25 CAN.	☐ ☐
#64211	STEEL CLAWS	$3.75 U.S. $4.25 CAN.	☐ ☐
#64212	RIDE THE BEAST	$3.75 U.S. $4.25 CAN.	☐ ☐

The Executioner®

#64204	RESCUE RUN	$3.50 U.S. $3.99 CAN.	☐ ☐
#64205	HELL ROAD	$3.50 U.S. $3.99 CAN.	☐ ☐
#64206	HUNTING CRY	$3.75 U.S. $4.25 CAN.	☐ ☐
#64207	FREEDOM STRIKE	$3.75 U.S. $4.25 CAN.	☐ ☐
#64208	DEATH WHISPER	$3.75 U.S. $4.25 CAN.	☐ ☐
#64209	ASIAN CRUCIBLE	$3.75 U.S. $4.25 CAN.	☐ ☐

(limited quantities available on certain titles)

TOTAL AMOUNT	$
POSTAGE & HANDLING	$
($1.00 for one book, 50¢ for each additional)	
APPLICABLE TAXES*	$_____
TOTAL PAYABLE	$_____

(check or money order—please do not send cash)

To order, complete this form and send it, along with a check or money order for the total above, payable to Gold Eagle Books, to: **In the U.S.:** 3010 Walden Avenue, P.O. Box 9077, Buffalo, NY 14269-9077; **In Canada:** P.O. Box 636, Fort Erie, Ontario, L2A 5X3.

Name:_____

Address:_____ City:_____

State/Prov.:_____ Zip/Postal Code: _____

*New York residents remit applicable sales taxes.
  Canadian residents remit applicable GST and provincial taxes.

GEBACK15

**Blazing a perilous trail through
the heart of darkness**

JAMES AXLER

DEATHLANDS®

Eclipse at Noon

The nuclear exchange that ripped apart the world destroyed a way
of life thousands of years in the making. Now, generations after the
nuclear blight, Ryan Cawdor and his band of warrior survivalists
try to reclaim the hostile land, led by an undimmed vision of a
better future.

It's winner take all in the Deathlands.

The postal system branches out...from
first-class to *first-class* terror

THE Destroyer

#104 Angry White Mailmen

Created by
WARREN MURPHY
and RICHARD SAPIR

Hell is being hand-delivered in a rash of federal bombings
and random massacres by postal employees across the
nation. And CURE's Dr. Harold Smith sends Remo and
Chiun to root out the cause.

Look for it in October, wherever Gold Eagle books are sold.

Don't miss out on the action in these titles featuring
THE EXECUTIONER®, and STONY MAN™!

SuperBolan

#61445	SHOWDOWN	$4.99 U.S. $5.50 CAN.	☐ ☐
#61446	PRECISION KILL	$4.99 U.S. $5.50 CAN.	☐ ☐
#61447	JUNGLE LAW	$4.99 U.S. $5.50 CAN.	☐ ☐
#61448	DEAD CENTER	$5.50 U.S. $6.50 CAN.	☐ ☐

Stony Man™

#61904	TERMS OF SURVIVAL	$4.99 U.S. $5.50 CAN.	☐ ☐
#61905	SATAN'S THRUST	$4.99 U.S. $5.50 CAN.	☐ ☐
#61906	SUNFLASH	$5.50 U.S. $6.50 CAN.	☐ ☐
#61907	THE PERISHING GAME	$5.50 U.S. $6.50 CAN.	☐ ☐

(limited quantities available on certain titles)

TOTAL AMOUNT	$
POSTAGE & HANDLING	$
($1.00 for one book, 50¢ for each additional)	
APPLICABLE TAXES*	$_____
TOTAL PAYABLE	$_____
(check or money order—please do not send cash)	

To order, complete this form and send it, along with a check or money order for the total above, payable to Gold Eagle Books, to: **In the U.S.:** 3010 Walden Avenue, P.O. Box 9077, Buffalo, NY 14269-9077; **In Canada:** P.O. Box 636, Fort Erie, Ontario, L2A 5X3.

Name:_____

Address:_____ City:_____

State/Prov.:_____ Zip/Postal Code: _____

*New York residents remit applicable sales taxes.
Canadian residents remit applicable GST and provincial taxes.

GEBACK15A